THE
GOLDEN
CASTLE

DAVID TANNER LAUKA

To Jill, for giving me the strength to face my past. –

David Tanner Lauka

PROLOGUE

"Ok, gather round everyone. I think it's time for a story."

Margaret and her family had moved to the area only a few weeks before and throwing a Halloween party was her way of getting to know the neighbors. The past several years had been fraught with difficulties for Margaret, moving from one place to another, men coming in and out of her life and the constant struggle to give her children a roof over their head and food on the table. But finally, her patience had paid off. She had found a suitable man who was all too eager to insert himself into the fabric of her family's messy lives. They were from completely different worlds: She was from a poor and fragmented family. She was poorly educated and naïve to the world around her, and she welcomed almost anyone who would show her love, affection, and support. He, on his part, was a man of well-means. Just a few years ago he'd come from a steady two-parent household from the suburbs of Detroit. His parents loved little children and were so grateful to hear he had met a nice young woman with four young boys whom they could call grandchildren. Margaret was yet to discover he was intolerant, violent, pathetic, and relentlessly looking for someone who would finally recognize and appreciate his brilliance.

It was a collision of worlds, between the two of them, and the impact of their union rippled through the hearts and minds of Margaret's young children, still impressionable and eager to understand what the world had to offer them and what the world wanted from them. Their union was the planting of a dark seed that would strike terror into the hearts of their children and consume their thoughts into adulthood, and so it was only fitting that Margaret christen the home by throwing a Halloween party for all the neighborhood children to attend.

"Come around, children, I have a story for you."

They stopped bobbing for apples and chattering to one another and gathered round to listen. She most certainly had a story, one which none of the children were quite prepared for:

"When I was a little girl my mother loved to play the tarot cards and understand what the spirits had in store for her and our family. She taught me at a young age how to cast the cards and interpret the signs and invite friendly spirits into our home to watch over us and make sense of the world. This had been going on for quite some time and I enjoyed it quite a bit. One day, my mother brought home a Ouija board. Do you children know what that is? It's a board with every letter of the alphabet on it and on either side of the board, it also has the words Yes and No. The point of the game is to summon spirits and ask them questions about the future, or the past, or about dead loved ones.

"Anyway, my sister and I were very curious about the game and one night we went down into the basement and decided to use the board and see if it actually worked. There was a piece of glass that we were both supposed to put our hands on. We had to ask a question and the spirit would guide our hands to the answer on the board. So, my sister and I decided to ask a few questions. Our great aunt had passed away earlier that year and we wanted to talk to her and ask her what heaven was like. So, we began asking questions. 'Is anyone there?' we asked as we both held the glass and waited in anticipation to see if anything would happen. It didn't take long before we both felt our hands moving. I was stunned and I told my sister to stop playing games, and she looked at me and told *me* to stop playing games, and we were both in disbelief that this piece of glass seemed to be moving on its own and guiding our hands to the inevitable answer: 'Yes.' Someone was with us in the room and answered our question.

"We were both so excited that we had made contact with someone, whom we were hoping would be our great aunt, so we asked a series of questions about our lives, our past, and our family to see if the spirit understood. 'How many siblings do we have?' to which the board responded, 'three.' 'How old am I?' I asked and the board responded, 'Thirteen.' One after another the board answered each and every one of our questions, things about our lives, things we never told anyone. It knew all our secrets, all our desires, and all our hopes and dreams. Naturally, we thought this must be the spirit of our great aunt Debra. So, we finally gathered the courage to ask the identity of this spirit and asked, 'Are you our great aunt Debra?' I could feel the glass begin to move, moving towards our answer, but it wasn't the answer we were looking for. Slowly we felt the glass slide over the word 'No.' And we both began to panic and tremble, wondering what we had gotten ourselves into.

"We thought maybe it was an even more remote ancestor, maybe my great grandfather. So, we asked again, 'Are you our great grandfather George?' and again the glass glided over the word 'No.' By that time we began to freak out, wondering who this could be, hoping this was a friendly spirit, so we asked, 'Are you one of our relatives?' and, again, the glass glided over 'No.' Now our hands were beginning to tremble in fear; we didn't know what was going on. Who could we possibly be talking to that knew so much about our family? This really scared us but we felt that we should prod deeper and hopefully find out that this spirit was a kind-hearted spirit who could help us in life. So, we finally asked, 'Are you kind?' My teeth began to chatter as I waited patiently for the spirit to respond, and slowly the glass made its way over the word 'No'. By now we were freaking out and my sister said we should be done with the game and throw it away, but I wanted to find out who this was, hoping that might help. So, I told my sister we would ask another question to help figure out who it was we were talking to. We agreed we would ask for the identity of the spirit and so slowly and with much fear I finally asked, 'What is your name?' And slowly the glass began to move. First, it was over the letter L, and after the L came U. After the U it hovered over the C. By now our arms were shaking and we both regretted we had ever started using the board in the first place. But we continued to watch the glass move, watch the spirit guide our hands towards the answer we thought we wanted.

"After the C it slowly hovered over the letter I and that was enough for me. I threw the glass at the wall and ran upstairs to tell my mother what had happened. She didn't seem very concerned about it and told me that nothing was the matter and all was fine. I tried telling her that this was serious, that there was something in the basement that we had awoken, something that responded to our call and we weren't sure what to do about it now. My mother just laughed it off, saying it was likely just our imagination running wild, and that even if it were a spirit it certainly meant no harm. Perhaps spirits have a sense of humor and they are just joking with you, she told me. But this didn't feel like a joke, I was absolutely terrified. My mother was finally able to calm me down and get me ready for bed. So I brushed my teeth and put on my pajamas and decided to put the experience behind me and finally fell asleep.

"So, I was sleeping, and it was the middle of the night, and I was under the covers when I felt the room get hot. I was beginning to sweat, and I could smell something strange in the room, like sulfur, or maybe something burning. It was very strange and overwhelming, and I tried to fall back asleep, but it just kept getting hotter and hotter, and the smell got so bad that I couldn't take it anymore. I finally decided to lift my head from under the covers to see if maybe someone had turned up the thermostat, but the thermostat wasn't broken, and there wasn't a fire. Instead, I was surprised to see someone in my room, maybe not some*one* but some*thing* is a better way to describe it. It was some half-man half-beast creature staring directly at me. This creature had the head of a goat with two horns on its head, and in between the horns was a strange symbol. He had dark, shaggy hair as black as night, darker even if that was possible. And I was staring right at him and paralyzed in fear and couldn't yell for help. My whole body went numb from this creature in my room.

"I couldn't believe what was happening and thought it must have been a dream, but children it wasn't a dream, for I had just woken up from the heat and the smell of something burning. This was the spirit that my sister and I had summoned earlier with the Ouija board, and it had come to pay me a visit and let me know that it was real and had intentions of his own, that it wasn't kind and it didn't like me, not at all. It had bloodred eyes and had this look on its face that it was so mad at me, that for some reason it hated me and wanted nothing more than to kill me. I didn't know what to do. I was so scared. I felt my jaw open wide in surprise to see this creature gliding towards my bed. I was so scared, children, and felt completely helpless so stop this creature, whom I believe was the devil. It finally crawled onto my bed and its shaggy knees hit my covers and the stench of sulfur and burning hit my face. It was so potent and powerful I thought I might pass out. But, I didn't pass out and I watched as the creature continued to creep onto my bed and into my personal space until it was finally a mere inch from my face.

"This was probably the scariest moment of my life, and I wasn't sure what the devil wanted with me. It just stared at me as if it were so mad at me. And although the devil didn't say anything to me I almost felt like it crept into my mind for I could hear someone say, 'I hate you, forever and all time.' This was too much for me, to think the devil could actually get inside my head, and I passed out. I woke up in the morning and ran straight to my sister's room to ask her if she had a visit from the devil, but she said she didn't. I told her what happened to me during the night but she thought I was making the whole thing up, that I was trying to scare her. She thought I'd been moving the glass of the Ouija board too and that now I was trying to scare her with this story of meeting the devil. But this was no story, children. This was real and it has taken me a long time to move on from the devil and what happened that night.

The devil followed me around for some time, and when I finally left home, I lived in a few houses that I know had evil spirits living in them. The furniture would move around at night and I would hear voices in the walls. My boys would get so scared at night saying that there were faces in the walls trying to talk to them. It was very scary stuff, children, and I really regretted ever playing around with the Ouija board. Fortunately, I met a good man from a good family who was able to scoop me and my boys up and give us a good life where the devil had no power. But let that be a lesson to you, children, be very careful with these things, and be very careful who you trust and what you open yourself up to. Do you hear me? Especially you, Aaron. Are you listening, Aaron?"

Aaron sat in front of his mother, mouth completely agape at this horrible story. He couldn't believe it was real and was terrified at the thought of such evil existing in the world. His body was completely numb from the description of the devil, the heat in the bedroom, and the smell of the sulfur burning. He was only four years old. He wasn't prepared to hear how evil the world could be. But the truth had been made known and Aaron would never look at the world the same again. His eyes were now open. There could be some spirit in the world that hated him and wanted to do horrible things to him.

"Did you hear me, Aaron? You have to be very careful who you spend time with because evil is lurking around every corner, honey. It's all around you," she told him. Aaron sat amidst the other children and slowly nodded his head. Yes, he understood what his mother was telling him. Aaron continued to nod his head mindlessly when the doorbell rang. "Hold on, children, I'll be right back."

Margaret headed up the stairs leaving the children alone in the basement to absorb the story. It was eerily quiet in the basement while Margaret was upstairs. She seemed to be greeting someone she was familiar with. After a short conversation, Margaret headed back down.

"Good news, Aaron. Your Grandfather is here to take you trick-or-treating. Isn't that nice of him?" This was Aaron's adoptive grandfather, the father of Margaret's new husband who had adopted Aaron as his own son. Aaron barely knew his adoptive grandfather and wasn't quite sure what to make of him. He seemed friendly in ways that made Aaron quite uncomfortable, but maybe that's what men were like. He was part of the family now, since his own father had gone.

Margaret grabbed Aaron by the hand and led him upstairs. Aaron felt as if he were gliding up the stairs and almost felt his spirit leave his body. Aaron felt the room get hotter, much hotter, and he could smell something burning. He wasn't sure but the pungent smell of burning hit his nostrils as he made his way upstairs and caught the gaze of his adoptive grandfather who was eagerly waiting at the door to take Aaron away. Aaron's senses were on overload, feeling as if his whole body were on fire and that someone or something must be burning, and he felt like his mother must be tugging him towards the doorway. Aaron's adoptive grandfather, for his part, had a slight smile on his face, and he held a burning pipe in his hand and was blowing the pipe smoke into the air.

"Are you ready to go, son?" the man asked. Aaron didn't respond. He was still envisioning the devil invading his mother's space, as this stranger was invading Aaron's own space.

"Don't be scared, Aaron, he's your grandpa and he's going to take you to get some candy. It will be fun!" his mother chided him.

"Yes, Aaron. We're going to have a lot of fun. You'll see," the man said. But Aaron didn't know how to not be scared, knowing that evil was everywhere, at every corner, waiting to bare its ugly head. *Be very careful of who you let into your life, Aaron, because evil is lurking around every corner.* His mother's warning rang in his head as the man grabbed him by the hand and led him towards the car. Aaron found himself in the backseat of his adoptive grandfather's car and could feel the car pull away from the driveway. It was pitch black outside and Aaron felt as if he were surrounded by darkness and the darkness were encroaching in upon him, and he felt as if he were being enveloped by the darkness. The only light Aaron could see was the glow of his houselights which were slowly fading away.

CHILDHOOD
DREAMS

CHAPTER 1

The boy's heart began to explode with excitement and joy, for he found himself in that rare moment of gazing upon a shooting star, or perhaps the fleeting appearance of a rainbow after a storm. It was the glimmer of hope that he was able to experience in this brief moment of ecstasy. He wasn't sure if he was awake or dreaming, but as he drifted further and further into the stratosphere, he was so grateful for the enchantment on the horizon.

These were rare but beautiful moments and Aaron wished he could make time stand still and soak up the peaceful ambiance forever. The further he floated the wider his smile grew as he knew the wondrous sights and smells that awaited him. His feet finally touched down and he felt as if he must be in heaven, for as far as the eye could see was the invisible beauty of creation made known, and the ground beneath his feet was so gentle, so kind, that he felt he must be walking on a cloud.

Everything around him was so lovely that it was hard to describe, but at the same time, it was all eerily familiar, as if someone had gathered all his favorite stories and thrown them into a world that embodied love and where he was a prince. He looked down and the streets seemed as if they were a soft, clear crystal, with the most beautiful stars underneath. To his left was an enchanted forest filled with magical trees and beyond the enchanted forest was the great mountain where the dwarfs were feverishly digging for more gold, diamonds, and other precious metals. To his right was the sea of tranquility and he could see the heads of mermaids and mermen alike popping out of the water to welcome Aaron back into their world. Behind him he could see the brave adventurers in their ships who had returned from their travels to new and exotic lands, filled with wonder and excitement.

"Hello, Aaron! Good to see you again my dear boy! Don't forget to explore the ruins of the ancient city just past Vulture Island; it's a treat!"

He looked behind him and he could see his brothers in a distant meadow enjoying the warm breeze of a late summer day.

They waved at him, "Hello, Aaron! Isn't this amazing?"

"It most certainly is, Thomas and Ruben!" he yelled back. "It most certainly is."

He looked above him, and the various planets, galaxies, and solar systems seemed so close to him that he could almost reach out, grab a star, and put it in his pocket. And in the sky were great dragons, winged creatures, and all fantastical and wondrous things a boy could imagine. Aaron's heart was exploding with ecstasy as the world cast a spell on him.

Aaron found himself in the most incredible world surrounded by the people and creatures he loved most. He often daydreamed of such things, but this was no dream, this was real in a way he could hardly describe. He could taste the dew in the air, smell the lilies from the valley, and feel the wind blowing between his fingertips. Perhaps his soul had left his body and he was in heaven, and Aaron desperately wished to stay forever.

But the greatest spectacle was what lay ahead: the golden castle. It was always his destination, and yet always out of reach. In the distance, he could see the sun reflecting off the golden walls as if it were a glaring fireball, and just above the walls, the tips of the castle could be seen in which he knew his father, the king, resided, and was desperately waiting for his return. So far it had been an impossible task, but Aaron was determined to reach the kingdom walls and embrace his father who loved him more than words could ever express. And his father would bestow upon him the keys to the kingdom and together they would rule over paradise for all eternity.

Aaron wasted no more time and took off in a mad dash down the clear crystal path towards the castle walls. He knew time was running out and the shooting star of the moment was about to burn out so he picked up speed, violently pounding his feet on the ground. Aaron could feel hope building in his chest as the distant castle was a mere fifty yards away. Tears filled his eyes from gratefulness and spilled down his cheeks.

Aaron both laughed and cried at the same time at the thought of finally meeting his father, the king. If he could just reach the walls, he knew he would enter paradise for all eternity.

He was fast approaching the walls when to his great surprise a large celestial being glided out of the city gates towards him. He had four wings: two wings to fly with and another two that were covering his eyes, and he was wearing the whitest of robes held up by a golden belt, and in that belt was a long sword bedazzled with a giant emerald in the hilt. Aaron began sobbing tears of joy, for he knew his father had sent out an angel to carry him into the castle, and Aaron could see the angel stretch out his arms and so Aaron did the same. But instead of scooping him up in his arms, the angel was signaling him to stop his pursuit. He opened his mouth and began speaking.

The angel was repeating some short phrase Aaron could barely understand, but as he drew closer the words became vaguely familiar.

It was a garbled whisper at first: "Food for fodder, food for fodder, food for fodder."

But that couldn't be right, it made no sense. Aaron must have misheard the celestial being. The angel, who seemed to have a concerned expression on what could be seen of his covered face, advanced further towards Aaron and the language became clearer, and a little louder: "Zeus no farther, Zeus no farther, Zeus no farther."

Aaron wasn't sure what to make of this message, but he was beginning to lose hope that he would be able to make it through the castle walls, as the angel was now blocking the entrance to the castle. The angel was a mere ten feet away and continued speaking to Aaron and Aaron felt he could hear the angel even more clearly.

"Zeus is no farther, Zeus is no farther, Zeus is no farther." Aaron's father, the king, must not be home, and it appeared the angel was sent to accompany him back from whence he came.

Aaron was heartbroken, for all he wanted was to belong in a world that loved him, and he knew he would soon be ushered back into a reality that was quite stark from the ecstasy he had just experienced. The angel grabbed Aaron by his hand and guided him back through the stratosphere and into his planet's own atmosphere. Aaron's heart sunk as he knew what was on the horizon, the pain that was in his immediate future. And at first, it was just a speck on a map, but after a few more seconds it came into full picture: Aaron's adoptive grandparent's house. He was desperately trying to backpedal, feverishly kicking at the air in hopes of redirecting his course.

"No, no, no! Not Again!" he shouted. But, alas, it was to no avail.

And for some reason, he could still hear the angel's voice, but this time he was shouting in Aaron's ear, "Zeus is no farther, Zeus is no farther, Zeus is no farther!"

The tears of joy that had adorned his face quickly became tears of sadness, pain, and hopelessness. He was now hovering just above the roof of the house and he could feel his heart beating through his chest to the strange tune of the angel shouting, "Zeus is no farther, Zeus is no farther, Zeus is no farther!" As their bodies began to glide through the roof and into the attic Aaron began kicking the air and clawing at the roof as if he were possessed, as if anything was better than what lay ahead.

"Please, no! Don't take me back! Don't take me back! I'll do anything! I'll do anything, just tell me what to do!" he cried. But the angel continued to guide him further down into the house. "I'll do anything! Just tell me what to do! Just tell me what to do!" he kept pleading until they were hovering at the far corner of the bathroom connected to his adoptive grandparent's bedroom.

This was familiar territory, and he suspected that by now he should be used to what lay before him, and yet the sting of what he saw, what Aaron knew he was soon to experience, was overwhelming. He closed his eyes, desperately wishing not to see what was happening below; the tears streamed past his cheeks and down his naked body.

"Zeus is no farther! Zeus is no farther! Zeus is no farther!"

The confusion was all too much for Aaron, and he knew that there was no use in wishing the moment away. So, he slowly opened his eyes to discover the horror that lay ahead; the disgusting reality that was his life. There they were, two naked adults hovering over a bath full of water, and they were holding someone's head down, a child's head down, whose arms and legs were frantically kicking in panic.

Aaron no longer wept but accepted his fate as he glided towards his destination. And Aaron was instantly jolted by the frigid water that he was being dunked in, under the pressure and weight of his adoptive grandmother's hands. Aaron's lungs were on fire and on the verge of exploding, he knew that death was imminent. He feverishly kicked his arms and legs, but his strength was no match for his oppressor; there was no way out.

And just as he felt he was about to pass out he could feel his head being yanked up by his hair and out of the icy tub to the shouting of, "Who is your father?! Who is your father?! Who is your father?!" But Aaron was so confused with the question and was so terribly startled by the simultaneous taste of both heaven and hell.

He was gasping for air and trying to focus on the question at the same time.

"Who is your father?! Who is your father?! Who is your father?!"

Aaron knew the clock was ticking and that the time was almost up to come up with the right answer. He could feel her hands pull even tighter on his hair and he desperately tried to contemplate the answer while also inhaling as much oxygen as he could. But they were sick of waiting, sick of putting up with their wretched, no good, worthless adoptive grandson.

And with great disgust, he heard his adoptive grandfather instruct his adoptive grandmother, "Put him back in the water." And with that Aaron could feel his head descend back down into the icy abyss as the vision of the golden castle and the king that resided within all but erased from his memory.

CHAPTER 2

aron sat squished in the backseat of his parent's van sitting shoulder to shoulder with his four siblings heading out for a beach getaway.

There were his older brothers Thomas and Rueben who were twins, and then there was Adam the oldest brother. Sally was the youngest in the family. All five of them squeezed into their parents' van for their small adventure. Aaron could feel his brother Thomas squishing him towards the window and he felt like a sardine in a can and so to pass the time he looked outside the window and watched the clouds pass by, dancing as they went.

"What are you looking at, Aaron?" Thomas asked, shoving his elbow into Aaron's side.

"Don't you see it?" Aaron responded with his own question. "In the clouds. Can't you see its tail whipping around?"

"No, I don't see anything," Thomas replied, squinting his eyes.

"Well," Aaron replied with a dreamy sigh, "He's there, and he's smiling at me. I think I'll call him Wolfy because of his big, sharp teeth."

"Ok, Aaron," Thomas replied, rolling his eyes and returning to playing with his action figure.

"I think Darold would've liked Wolfy," Aaron whispered to himself. As soon as the words left his mouth he heard the tires screech, and the seatbelt dug into his belly as the car came to an abrupt stop.

"I'm not going to say it again," Aaron's adoptive father told him, glaring at him from the driver's seat, "I'm your father, not Darold." The adoption papers had been signed five years ago when Aaron was three. "Do you hear that? There is no Darold. All of you, there is no Darold, so stop talking about him!"

"Ok, Dad," all the boys responded glumly.

"Hey! Daddy! You're not their daddy, you're my daddy! My daddy, you silly poof ball!" Sally responded, giggling, commenting on the man's large gut.

"Well, I am your daddy, sweety," he responded, trying to explain it to Sally. "But remember, now that I adopted them they're my kids, too, whether they like it or not," he replied, glaring at his sons through the rearview mirror. "You got that boys?"

"Yes," they all replied, even more glum than before.

"Good. Now everyone shut up so I can hear my own thoughts for a change," Aaron's adoptive father said as he merged back onto the highway. Aaron didn't respond, he just looked up and watched

Wolfy winking at him, eager to swallow the poof ball whole and take Aaron away.

"Hey, Aaron," Sally called out from the middle row of the van. "Aaron. Aaron! Do you hear me?!" She called out, turning around to get his attention. "Aaron!" She finally screamed, snapping Aaron out of his trance.

"Huh?" Aaron responded.

"Aaron, why did the dog eat his teeth?" Sally asked, only four years old. "Aaron, why did the dog eat his teeth?"

Aaron continued to stare out the window, shaking his head as he replied, "I don't know, Sally. Why?"

Sally began to giggle as she erupted into laughter, "Because he's stupid! Isn't that funny, Aaron?!"

Aaron continued to shake his head, trying to ignore her.

"Keep it down, Sally, would ya?" Adam called out.

"I told you to shut up, Adam! What don't you understand? Shut up or I'll make you shut up when we get to the cottage. Got it?!" roared the man. Adam folded his arms over his lap and showed the scowl on his face in rebellion. It was a quiet ride the rest of the trip.

When they finally touched down at the cottage Aaron and his brothers wasted no time and sprinted immediately towards the beach, leaving their things in the van.

"Hey! Where do you think you're going? Get back here and unpack!" the man yelled as he chased after his sons.

"Oh, for Pete's sake, let the boys have some fun. This is supposed to be a vacation!" Aaron's mother called out, chasing Aaron's adoptive father who tripped over and fell to the ground. Aaron's mother grabbed him by the arm and helped him back up. "Just let them play, they can unpack later."

They were finally out of sight from their parents and the boys erupted in excitement as the beach came into view.

Aaron lagged behind and his brother Ruben quipped, "Hey, Aaron! Why are you running like you shoved a stick up your butt?" Ruben laughed and Thomas joined in.

"Whatever," Aaron responded, as he waddled towards the beach.

"Did you stick it up your butt when you were at grandma and grandpa's house?" Ruben quipped again, laughing at his own joke.

Aaron stared out into the water, distancing himself from his brother's words and whispered to himself, "Whatever."

"Oh, come on! Don't be like that, Aaron," Ruben said as he trotted over to Aaron and grabbed him by the hand. "We're finally free from that big turd!"

"Yeah! Ted the turd! Ted the turd!" laughed Thomas. "We're free from Ted the big turd, so let's make the most of it."

Aaron smiled and let out a slight chuckle as he imagined the big turd tripping over himself chasing after them. He stood ankle deep in the cold water and peered into the blue horizon from the shore, watching the sun melt into the lake and casting a golden shadow over the shoreline. "Do you see it?" Aaron asked with a smile.

Thomas rolled his eyes. "What is it now, Aaron?"

"The castle, in the sky. Over there," Aaron pointed towards the golden shadow. "Don't you see it?"

All three of his brothers chuckled together, chiding Aaron, "Yeah, Aaron! Look at that."

"Isn't it the most magical thing you've ever seen?" Aaron asked, mouth open wide in complete awe and wonder.

Ruben put his arm around Aaron. "Yes, Aaron. It's the most magical thing I've ever seen. And this weekend we are no longer children. We're pirates on the hunt for treasure! The four adventurers setting sail into a new world!"

Aaron's imagination came to life as the world melted away and they splashed along the shore, in the shadow of the golden castle. He looked out over the horizon and pointed at the setting sun. "If we can just make it to the other side, we can get to the castle! We could live with the king and we'd become princes and we'd never have to come home. Wouldn't that be amazing guys?"

Adam looked at Aaron with a big smile, "Well, what are we waiting for?" And the four boys exploded with joy and feverishly looked for sticks, fallen logs, and anything to tie them together as fast as they could.

Adam quickly took charge of the operation and put his brothers to work. "Thomas, you look for vines, rope, or seaweed. Anything to keep the ship together. Ruben, you gather the steadiest pieces of wood you can find. We'll need at least ten." Both Thomas and Ruben took off on the beach in search of their supplies and Adam walked over to Aaron with a smile and put his arm around him. "And you, Aaron, I need you to chart the course to the castle. It sounds like you can see it the clearest. Do you think you can handle that?" Adam asked. He was twelve years old, four years older than Aaron.

"I think so."

"Ok good," Adam said. "We're counting on you!" He ruffled Aaron's hair, messing it all up.

Thomas and Ruben finally came back with their supplies and Adam began construction of their ship for their great voyage to the golden castle. And as Adam began assembling, the branches became planks, the seaweed rope, and slowly they built a ship worthy of the highest adventure.

"What should we call ourselves?" Adam asked.

"How about the Adventure Boys?" Aaron responded.

"Ok, Aaron, Adventure Boys it is," he said with a smile. "Ok, Adventure Boys, are you ready to set sail for the castle?"

"Yes!" they all screamed in unison. The sun was now setting, so they grabbed the ship ever so carefully but with great spirit and readied themselves for the adventure ahead.

"That big turd won't stop us now!" Ruben said as he helped carry the ship into the water.

They were closing in on the lake and their ship was ready to set sail, but before they could set it in the water, they heard the big turd yelling in the distance. The boys tried to stay focused and ignored him, and dropped the ship into the water.

"We've got to hurry up guys, he's almost here!" Ruben shouted.

"He's going to get us!" Aaron cried.

"No!" Thomas rebutted, "No, we're going to make it!" he said as the four boys crammed together on the ship and began paddling with their hands.

"Let's go! Adventure Boys, prepare for the adventure of a —" Adam was interrupted as their adoptive father tipped the ship over, causing the four boys to tumble into the water.

"Give me that," their adoptive father said as he took their ship and shoved it further into the lake. "Play time's over. Get your asses back to the cottage and unpack. Now!"

CHAPTER 3

It was an uneventful ride home from the cottage as the children did their best not to provoke their adoptive father further. The van finally arrived back home and the boys kept their heads down as they entered the house with armfuls of things. Ruben was carrying a box of used dishes.

Just as he walked towards the porch Ruben felt a searing pain in his toe. "Ow!" he cried. He'd stubbed it on the cement porch.

"Keep moving, Ruben!" his adoptive father said.

"Oh, leave him alone! Can't you see he's hurt?" his mother responded.

"It's ok, Mom," Ruben told his mother as he felt the nail pull away from his toe. Squirts of blood hit the porch. Ruben half hopped into the house doing his best to not smear his blood into the carpet.

"Ok, kids, come and get it!" Aaron's mother called out a few minutes later. Ruben limped into the kitchen to find his mom had placed a big pot of spaghetti on the kitchen counter. They all lined up to fill their plates and then sat at the kitchen table. Eventually their adoptive father joined them and grabbed his own plate of spaghetti. He sat down and glared at them from across the table, casting a silent tension into the air.

"You boys think you can keep disrespecting me. You keep testing me. Well, one of you will find out soon enough what happens when you test me long enough," the man said as he scanned the table, looking at his sons. "So, who will it be? Which one of you is tough enough? Anyone?"

The boys ate their dinner quietly as the man scanned the room, daring his adoptive children to make a sound. Ruben's foot was really starting to pound now. Next to him Aaron twirled his spaghetti around his fork and the rest of his siblings sucked down their meal as quietly as possible while his mother busied herself with cleaning up. The throbbing in his toe was making his head swim. He couldn't help letting out a small moan. Aaron nudged him to be quiet. Ruben looked down and saw the blood seeping onto the linoleum. His eyes became agitated, and tears began to spill onto his dinner plate as he tried to take another bite of spaghetti. But his whimpers were too loud and it was now too late.

"What do we have here?" asked Aaron's adoptive father. "Poor, fat, pathetic Ruben hurt his little toe?" Ruben's lips were quivering but he did his best to ignore the man and attempted to take another bite of the salty spaghetti.

"Daddy! Daddy! Why are you so mean?" Sally asked.

"Just stay out of this sweetheart, ok?"

"But Daddy! I want nachos! Can I get nachos? And ice cream! Ice cream nachos! Can I have that, Daddy?"

"Yeah, sure. Whatever, sweety, just eat your dinner."

Ruben was grateful for Sally's distraction and did his best to ignore the comment, but his foot throbbed even more, and the salt from his tears had spoiled the sauce so he spat out the spaghetti, which spilled off his plate and onto the dinner table.

"God damnit, Ruben! Can't I eat in peace without you eating like a pig and crying like a damn baby?!" The attention was getting to Ruben, who, like Thomas, was only nine years old and didn't know what to do.

"But daddy! When can we get the ice cream nachos? When?" Sally asked again.

"Just, not now. Just give me a minute, ok sweety?"

Ruben tried to hold his composure now that the attention was off him again, but his whimper turned into a sob and he sucked in air with slight moans between the sobs. He shoveled the spaghetti back into his mouth quickly and the sauce smeared into his face and chin in the process. He began to hyperventilate, and the food came spilling back out between sobs, so he buried his head into his plate in defeat. He could hear his adoptive father's hands slam on the table and feet stammer across the floor.

Ruben felt a warm sweaty hand squeeze the back of his neck and force him into the bathroom. "Look at yourself!" Aaron's adoptive father pressed Ruben's face close to bathroom mirror. "Ruben, the fat slob, ruining my meal again! If you can't control yourself then dinner is over! Clean your fat ass up and get to bed! And stop crying!"

"Ice cream nachos! Now! Daddy?" Sally called out again.

Aaron, Thomas, and Adam finished their dinner quietly, ignoring Sally's demand for ice cream nachos and listening to Ruben sobbing in the bathroom as he cleaned off his face and limped upstairs to his bedroom.

"Don't be so hard on him, he's just a boy!" Aaron's mother lamented.

"Margaret, this is my house and I'll be damned if I let your children run wild in my house."

"But Daddy! The ice cream nachos! Please! Please! Please!" Sally goaded further and jumped on her father's back who was still seated at the dinner table.

"Ok, sweetheart, just give me a minute, ok? Adam, go run to the convenient store and get a tub of ice cream and nacho chips," the man demanded as he handed Adam a five dollar bill.

"And while you're there can you get me a Diet Coke? And a bag of butter scotches while you're at it," his mother asked as she headed to the back porch and lit a cigarette.

~ ~ ~

Aaron finished his spaghetti and put his dishes in the sink. He was going upstairs when he heard his name called.

"Aaron." It was his adoptive father. "Don't forget, grandma will be here tomorrow afternoon to take you to gymnastics class and then you're going to stay the night over there."

He'd been staying over his adoptive grandparent's house since he was around Sally's age.

"Ok," Aaron replied as he went up the stairs to his bedroom. He quietly put on his pajamas and curled into the bottom bunk in his bedroom and watched as his brother Thomas climbed into the top bunk. There they both silently wished they were somewhere else.

Someone, please help me, he prayed silently, staring at the flies smacking into the outside of the windowsill. *Please, someone take me from this place. Take me anywhere but here*, he pleaded with a yawn. He rubbed his eyes again and watched as the moonlight hit the oak tree in the back yard and cast a large shadow on his bedroom floor. And as the flies continued to buzz and smack into his window, he slowly drifted off to sleep.

~ ~ ~

Thomas could hear the chirping of crickets and the buzzing of flies outside his bedroom windowsill, desperate for shade from the warm late summer night. He could see the crow's nest resting on the tree branch outside and the beady red eyes staring at him. He lay back on his upper bunkbed thinking about the world he found himself in and wondering if his birth father, Darold, would ever return. And he wondered if he would ever have to spend another night at his adoptive grandparents' house again. The thought made him cringe, and so he too said a simple prayer: *Please, someone protect me and keep me safe. Someone, anyone, please watch over me.*

Thomas finished his prayer and listened to the flies smack outside the windowsill seemingly growing in number and felt as if he and his siblings were all sitting ducks, and it was just a matter of time before their adoptive father did something real horrible to one of them. He could feel the man closing in on them and there was nothing he could do about it. But, for now, he was safe in his bedroom and would rest soundly in the safety of his own bed. As the flies picked up their intensity and ferocity to enter his room, he slowly closed his eyes and lulled himself into a deep sleep.

Thomas slept soundly, for a moment, but then he felt a whipping against his face and his eyes and nose. And he heard a loud buzzing in his room that jolted him out of his slumber. He opened his eyes and saw the flies swirling all around his room. They had somehow managed to make their way in, and not just a few but a lot, and they were all swirling around looking for something to devour.

The scene confused Thomas, but it was the whispers that set him on edge. He was used to Aaron talking in his sleep and sometimes speaking unintelligible words, but these whispers were from a much deeper voice and certainly didn't belong to Aaron. These were whispers from a stranger who'd somehow infiltrated their room along with the horde of flies. Now he was whispering unintelligible words beneath his bunk. Thomas thought it must be a dream, some strange idea he'd conjured up from a troubled mind, but he could feel the flies whipping across his face, so he had to find out for sure. He slowly turned his shoulder and head and peeked over the rail of his bunk and was horrified to discover they weren't alone. There was a man leaning over onto Aaron's bed and whispering to Aaron in unintelligible words. He had a long, black cloak that draped across the bedroom floor and looked like it was weathered from the sun from incessant wandering.

Thomas carefully and quickly turned his head and shoulder back onto his pillow and out of sight of the intruder who brought a horde of flies with him into their room. The man spoke in a deep baritone voice and gave the impression that he was casting a spell over Aaron or perhaps giving Aaron a very specific set of instructions. Thomas was terrified. There was no place he was safe; powers could infiltrate his bedroom at will. His heart began to beat louder, and louder, and louder and the symphony of swarming flies mixed with the pounding of his own heart created an orchestra of despair that Thomas couldn't stop. Thomas covered his ears and closed his eyes, imagining he was somewhere else, but a fly darted into his nostril, causing him to sneeze and alerting the intruder that he was being watched.

Thomas covered his mouth wishing he could somehow stuff his sneeze back inside his body. But the damage had been done and Thomas could hear the shuffling of feet and the creaking of floorboards and could sense the stirring directly beneath him. Thomas felt like crying, knowing he had nowhere to go and there was no one to help him. The orchestra of despair burrowed into his ears as he saw the two clawed hands grab the rail. The hands slowly pulled until the intruder's head came into full view and they locked eyes. Thomas was paralyzed in fear and saw the man with brown hair and blood-red eyes glaring at him for interfering with his work. He had a symbol on his forehead and his head was in the midst of a tornado of flies swarming all around him.

The man clutched the rail with such anger and ferocity that the wood began to wilt, and Thomas knew that his claws were meant to tear flesh and cut bone. He was expecting the man to kill him where he lay but he opened his mouth and with a deep echo in his voice asked Thomas, "What do you see, boy?" Thomas didn't understand the question because he didn't know what he saw. He was confused with what he was looking at, so he didn't answer.

The man asked him again, "What do you see, boy?"

Again, Thomas was unsure how to answer and hoped his soul would soon leave his body. But he remained in his bed staring at the man swarmed by flies who had grown impatient with Thomas and glared at him and screamed, "What do you see, boy?!"

Thomas finally responded, "I see five dead flies."

The man looked at Thomas with a devious smile and told Thomas to say it again.

"I see five dead flies."

"Louder!" the man cried.

Thomas' whole body was shaking, and he was on the verge of urinating but he mustered the strength to say it again. "Five dead flies."

The man's eyes began to radiate the deepest reds, oranges, and yellows and with a look of complete dominance he asked again, "What do you see, boy?"

Thomas was terrified and the moment was all too much, so he stood up and screamed at the top of his lungs, "Five dead flies! Five dead flies! Five dead flies!"

The man smiled at Thomas's answer and replied, "Yes, Thomas. They will all be dead soon enough."

After the man made the proclamation, he opened his mouth and released an army of flies that completely engulfed Thomas, causing him to scream in fear at the top of his lungs.

Thomas felt the man's hands shaking his head mercilessly until he felt the lights turn on and was embraced by his mother.

"Thomas! Honey, are you ok?" his mother asked, caressing his head.

Thomas looked around the room and noticed there were no flies, "It must have been a dream."

"Honey, why did you scream five dead flies? What happened? I just came from Adam's room who was also screaming about five dead flies. Did you two watch a scary movie together about dead flies?"

And then Thomas remembered what the man said, how the five flies would die soon enough, and his blood ran cold.

CHAPTER 4

"Go on, now, Aaron. Drink it up." Aaron's adoptive grandfather forced the cup up to Aaron's lips, causing some of the syrupy concoction to spill down his pajamas. But Aaron did as he was told and swallowed hard on the drink that made his throat burn and his stomach hurt. "That's a good boy, Aaron," his adoptive grandfather told him as he funneled every last drop last drop of the drink down Aaron's throat. Aaron felt warm all over and stood still as the walls began to spin around him. He took a step towards his fold-out bed in the living room, but he tripped and stumbled to the ground.

Aaron chuckled to himself. He was feeling very silly and couldn't help but laugh as the walls continued to spin. His whole body felt warm, and he could feel his hands and feet go numb and he chuckled even more when his adoptive grandfather grabbed him and carried him to his bed. He thought of the silly movie he'd watched earlier where all the grown ups were rubbing and tickling each other and he chuckled even harder. He stared up at the ceiling and began laughing when the ceiling smiled at him and began changing colors in sync with the beating of his heart.

"This is so silly!" he said aloud as he watched the colors change, but it was the eyes that formed behind the smile that excited Aaron. Next came the arms and legs and feet as it slowly pushed itself towards Aaron. "Here he comes!" Aaron said to himself, watching the man push himself out of the ceiling, arms outstretched wide. Aaron welcomed the man who was changing colors from green to blue to orange to red until they all swirled together.

"Hello!" Aaron greeted the man with a sloppy smile with drool spilling down his chin. The man smiled back at Aaron with a wide smile and wide eyes and grabbed him by the hand and led him down a hallway. Aaron's eyes were droopy but he had a smile as he watched the walls warp inwards and change colors as the man led Aaron further down the hallway. Aaron's heart started beating faster and faster and he watched as the walls changed colors faster and the walls warped closer until he finally made it to the end of the hall.

"Hi, everyone!" Aaron called out with a big smile. He stepped into the room that was swirling all the colors of the rainbow and the man shut the door behind him and Aaron couldn't help but laugh at all the people in the room who were changing colors and smiling at him. He felt someone grab him and throw him into the air and he landed on a big, soft, fluffy pillow and chuckled as he landed. All the smiling people in the room drew closer to Aaron and began tickling him and he watched the walls swirl and he laughed to himself as the tickling turned to grabbing. His body began to shake but he didn't mind. Aaron just laughed and listened to the projector spinning and watched the film begin to roll on the ceiling as he stepped into his favorite movie.

"Wow!" Aaron said aloud, as the golden castle came into full view. "That's amazing!"

Aaron burst into laughter, filled with awe and wonder as the grabbing turned to biting and scratching and the brightness of the golden bricks blinded him completely.

"Wake up, Aaron. Wake up son, it's time to get up." Aaron felt his adoptive grandfather's hand gently nudging his bare shoulder and he awoke from his slumber. He slowly opened his eyes and found himself at the edge of his adoptive grandparent's bed curled up into a ball. "Come on now, Aaron," he said with a smile. Aaron, however, was feeling groggy and he could tell his hair was a mess and he was feeling a bit sticky. He rubbed his eyes and stretched his arms to the ceiling while yawning, doing his best to listen to his adoptive grandfather.

Aaron eventually found himself standing on his feet and made his way to the bathroom where his pajamas were strewn across the floor. He stumbled as he put his clothes back on but finally found himself dressed and walked into the kitchen where he poured himself a bowl of sugar puffs at the kitchen table. The radio was on in the background and his adoptive grandfather was reading the paper and smoking his pipe. His adoptive grandmother was sewing a karate outfit for Aaron. He'd recently watched a movie about a young boy learning karate and had begged her for his own karate outfit.

He spooned in another heap of sugary cereal into his mouth trying to remember what had happened last night and why he was so sore.

"Now did you want the sword or the bonsai tree on the back?" she asked Aaron as she continued sewing his outfit.

Aaron scratched his head, struggling to put a thought together. He finally mumbled, "The tree."

"Alright then," his adoptive grandmother smiled at him, putting down her needle and swatting at a fly on the windowsill. "Also, don't forget to put away your video games. And please remember to rewind the video from last night."

"Ok, ok," he said, feeling exhausted and overwhelmed.

"Hey, now!" his adoptive grandfather chimed in. "I don't think we ask too much, just clean up every once in a while, and try not to eat too much ice cream for Pete's sake!" he chided with a chuckle and wink in his eye.

Aaron chuckled as he slurped down the remaining milk in his cereal, "Ok, Grandpa, I'll try not to."

"That's my boy! Now, speaking of favors, we do have a friend coming over who we'd like you to say hi to."

Aaron swallowed down the cereal and ignored the pounding in his head. Then he heard someone knocking on the door and got up to put his cereal bowl in the sink, trying to focus on the suds in the bowl.

"Aaron, honey, please go down to the basement for now. We'll call you when it's time to come back up to say hello."

Aaron headed towards the basement and saw a man enter the house from the corner of his eye, setting him completely on edge. He walked quickly towards the basement, looking straight ahead and hoped he didn't notice him. He scurried quickly down the steps and found some toys to play with, praying the man didn't see him. He did his best to pretend he wasn't upstairs, but his voice carried into the basement from the air vents, and he couldn't help but listen in on the conversation.

"He'll cooperate. I promise," he could hear his adoptive grandfather say.

"Are you sure? There are very specific instructions. He must lie completely still and not cry out in pain." The words hit Aaron like a ton of bricks, and he instinctually covered his mouth with both hands to keep from screaming. The air vent continued to carry the conversation into the basement and Aaron collapsed to the ground in fear of what they had planned for him. The sound of buzzing static hit his ears and his fingers tingled as he slipped in and out of consciousness. His eyes grew wide, and he began blinking uncontrollably, and the buzzing grew louder as the lights flashed on and off. He was panicking, and he looked across the room to see something in the wall smiling at him and the entire wall warped towards his direction. It began changing colors again, and its smile grew wider and attempted to free itself, lunging violently towards Aaron. He covered his eyes and ears and curled into a tight ball pleading quietly, "Please go away. Please go away. Please go away."

The static finally died down and when his fingers stopped tingling he opened his eyes to find everything back to normal, but Aaron could hear the visitors speaking again. He was talking with his adoptive grandfather about a ritual that would take place at the end of October, something about sacred meals or summoning spirits and the shedding of blood. Aaron wasn't sure what they were talking about but his ears pricked when he heard his name mentioned again.

"Well, you're right. Aaron is just the right age. He seems to possess all the right qualities, and he is very well-trained. He could be perfect for the ceremony, but this is a substantial amount of money and we need assurance he'll cooperate."

Aaron heard his adoptive grandfather chuckle. "Trust me, for that amount of money I guarantee he'll cooperate every step of the way."

Aaron swallowed hard, trying to make sense of what he heard. They were talking about some important ceremony. And he was perfect for it. Perhaps he was a very special boy after all and that he really was a prince being prepared to meet a great king. He forced himself to believe it as he heard the basement door creak open and the voice of his adoptive grandfather summon him upstairs. He felt as if he were floating upwards as he ascended into the living room. He barely noticed the visitors as his adoptive grandfather grabbed him by the hand and sat him down on the couch.

"Ok, Aaron, I've got some good news. You've been invited to a party!" Aaron's grandfather said with a loud exclamation.

Aaron shuffled his eyes between his adoptive grandfather and the visitor. "What kind of party, Grandpa?"

"Well, you see Aaron, it's uhm, hmm, it's uh, it's a surprise party! Yes! That's it! My friend is throwing a surprise party for someone very special, someone very special indeed, and he has invited you to the party! Isn't that nice of him?" he asked Aaron, shaking his head yes suggestively.

"If it's a surprise then how will he know to come to the party?" Aaron asked in a confused tone.

"That's a great question, Aaron. A very great question. And the answer is, the answer is, is that he wants to meet you! Yes, that's it! I told him what a wonderful grandson you are, what a very special boy you are, and he said he just had to meet you."

"Is that true Grandpa?" Aaron couldn't help smiling. Someone thought he was worth meeting.

"Oh, it's true, Aaron. And you are a very, very special boy indeed. The man you are meeting is a very special man who would only meet with you. No other child would do, Aaron."

"Really, Grandpa?" Aaron asked, feeling completely giddy.

"Well, of course, Aaron! But, you see, Aaron, we can only have the party if you agree to meet him. Otherwise, he won't show up, and we want him to show up because that's when the real fun begins! And there will be other children there, Aaron. You'll play games and there'll be punch and dancing and costumes. Why, I think it could be the best night of your life!"

Aaron stared off into the distance and imagined what a wonderful time he was going to have. "Grandpa, will the party be in a castle?"

His adoptive grandfather's eyes lit up and responded, "Why, yes! Yes, it is, Aaron! You are a very clever boy, aren't you? How did you know?"

Aaron smiled at his adoptive grandfather, feeling very proud of himself, "I just had a feeling Grandpa."

"What do you say? Can I count on you to come with me?"

"Ok Grandpa," Aaron responded with a smile. "I'll go."

"That's a good boy, Aaron! That's a very good boy! Now my friend here has a game he'd like to play with you, and I told him how much you enjoy playing games and how good you are at them. Will you please wait for him while he gets ready to play?"

CHAPTER 5

"Aaron, are you listening?"

"Huh, what?" he asked as his adoptive grandfather snapped him out of his spell.

"I asked if you were listening, about my friend who would like to play a game with you."

"What? A game?"

"It's alright, just go ahead and get ready," Aaron's adoptive grandfather told the man and directed him towards the bathroom. He was holding a paper grocery bag and stared at Aaron as he walked down the hallway and into the bathroom. "Aaron, ok then. I just need you to play with my friend for just a few minutes, ok?"

"Uhm, what games does he like to play?" Aaron asked.

"Well, I think we are playing hide and seek today. Yes, that's it," his adoptive grandfather responded. Something was up. Aaron began whimpering and rubbing his eyes to hide his tears, and his adoptive grandfather ran over to him, "Hey, hey now, Aaron. Everything is going to be alright. It's just a quick game of hide and seek, that's it. It will be fun! And you know what?" Aaron tilted his head slightly towards his grandfather in acknowledgement of his question. "I bet we can find you a new video game to play later today. We can go to the store and pick something out together!" Aaron formed a slight smile on his face. "And after that we'll eat some ice cream and then we can watch a movie together!" Aaron thought about the new video game and wiped his eyes. "That's the spirit, Aaron! This will be fun, I promise!"

"Ok, Grandpa," Aaron finally relented.

"Great! Now just wait here for a few more minutes and he'll come out to play. I'll be down in the basement and will be back soon," his adoptive grandfather said before scuddling down the basement steps.

Aaron waited in the living room, twiddling his thumbs and trying to think of what gave he could choose in the shop later. After some time, the man finally came out of the bathroom wearing a clown suit and wearing white face paint dotted with red specks. There was a long moment of silence and Aaron watched as the man's eyes grew wider and wider in sweet anticipation and the largest smile adorned his face.

"Hello Aaron, my name is Bobo," the man said as he slowly glided towards Aaron. Bobo's smile slowly faded and he began licking his lips and staring at Aaron with a confused look on his face, as if he were unsure of what he was about to do and what would happen next. "I think you'd better run."

Bobo lunged towards Aaron who sprinted out of the living room and into the family room, but Bobo overtook Aaron and immediately began groping him and punching, slapping, kicking him, and licking him. Bobo completely overwhelmed Aaron, but Aaron's adrenaline kicked in and he pushed Bobo's head away from him. Bobo was caught off guard and bit Aaron's index finger, and Aaron screamed and poked Bobo's eye and ran towards the bathroom. He could hear Bobo's footsteps behind him in hot pursuit, feel the heat of his breath down his neck and it sent chills down his spine. But Aaron finally made it to the bathroom and shut it on Bobo's face who immediately began sobbing.

Aaron could hear the man crying outside the door, pouting over his predicament. The man finally stopped crying and began banging on the door, trying to pry it open. And there Aaron was, locked inside the bathroom with nowhere to go, praying to God that this lunatic wasn't real, just a figment of his imagination. But the banging only intensified as Bobo continued screaming like a wounded animal. "Open the door! Open the door! Aaron! Aaron! Open the goddamn door!" And then Bobo began sobbing again. "I promise I won't hurt you, Aaron. I just want to play, I just want to feel your smooth, supple skin on my face, that's all. Please, Aaron!" Aaron held himself and curled tightly into the corner of the bathroom waiting for Bobo to go away.

Several minutes passed and Aaron felt confident the lock would hold so he took a deep breath. He heard footsteps coming up the basement steps and his heart sank. Then Bobo's crying turned into a whimper and he could hear his adoptive grandfather consoling him. It was at that moment that Aaron knew Bobo would find him after all. He could hear his adoptive grandfather calm Bobo down and reassure him everything would be ok, and that's when he heard the key enter the doorknob. Aaron turned around and to his horror could see the doorknob slowly beginning to turn. *Oh no*, Aaron thought, dreading what was to come, but as the door slowly began to open Aaron could feel himself become faint and was on the verge of passing out. A blinding light poured through the crack in the door and it overwhelmed the senses and as Bobo's head began to peak through the doorway Aaron completely collapsed.

When he finally came to Aaron found himself in an entirely different world, and Bobo was nowhere to be found. He was now in a beautiful meadow filled with flowers and gentle grass. He saw the sun beaming through the sky and could feel its warmth on his face. The fear evaporated from him and a smile formed on his lips as the gentle breeze blew away all the cares in the world. He closed his eyes and soaked in the rare and fleeting beauty of the moment. He spread his hands out wide and walked amongst the wildflowers, feeling the flowers bush up against his palms. The aroma of the flowers mixed with the gentle cool breeze created an environment of ecstasy for Aaron, and as he looked into the sky and saw the great giant stars, planets, and the flying dragon, he knew he was home.

He continued walking through the meadow which he noticed was spotted with large oak trees. Fifty feet tall, one hundred feet tall, the trees seemed to reach right into the sky and created a bridge between men and God, and it was in one of those wonderful oak trees that he saw his brothers Thomas and Ruben playing. Aaron's smile broke into a laugh as the ecstasy of the moment began filling his lungs. This couldn't get any better.

Aaron immediately began running towards his brothers. "Aaron! Aaron! I'm so glad you made it! We've been waiting for you all day!" Aaron was so grateful they were here and was so grateful that they were sharing in the joy of the moment.

"Thank God you're both here! Now everything is perfect." Aaron told them.

"So, are you ready to play?" Ruben asked.

"Of course! What do you want to play?" And with that the boys began a spirited game of tag, followed by hide and seek which was immediately followed by tickle fights and wrestling matches. They chased after each other and tackled each other to the ground and laughed in each other's arms. It was a beautiful moment for Aaron, one he hoped would never end. After they were exhausted from all the games they sat in the tree and told stories of monsters and brave men. They talked about all the wonderful things they wanted to do together and all the cute girls in school. It was all the things Aaron would have liked to have done with his brothers at home. At least here he was safe to tell them his ideas and dreams.

The sun began to set, and Aaron could feel things were winding down, and in the distance, the majestic tips of a golden tower sprouted from the ground: *the golden castle*. He and his brothers locked their eyes on this majestic castle, wondering what mysteries and adventures resided within its walls, what sort of king was responsible for such a kingdom.

"I'm sorry this has to end, Aaron," Thomas told him. "I'm sorry this beautiful world has to end, and I'm even sorrier for the world that awaits." Aaron let the apology linger in the air as he fixed his eyes on the golden castle and determined to pay whatever price it was to enter its walls and meet the king inside. He knew down in his heart the king would embrace him like a son, the son he always wanted. He would tear him away from this wretched existence that was forced upon him. If he could last long enough, and endure the pain, he would be rewarded generously with the gifts of the king. Perhaps he would be allowed to stay here forever, him and his brothers, and experience the unending love of the king.

Aaron knew something horrible awaited him in the other world, something horrible always waited for him.

"Can we just stay here a little longer?" Aaron pleaded with his brothers. "The sun is just beginning to set and it looks so beautiful. I just don't want this to end."

"Don't worry Aaron," Ruben assured him. "You'll be back again, and sooner than you think. You'll meet the king and it will be everything you've ever dreamed of. And soon enough you'll meet a new friend, and he'll be by your side and tell you everything about the king and his kingdom. This friend is as old as the stars and has known the king from the beginning. He can tell you everything he likes and how you can please him, so be sure to listen to him and do everything he asks of you. But for now, you'll have to go back and accept what is happening. Please, do your best to imagine you are wrestling a large wildebeest and it will all be over before you know it. And then you will see us again, someday soon. I promise you."

Ruben hugged his brother and patted the top of his head and slowly pushed him into the ground, out of paradise, and back to the underworld. Aaron could feel his body being pushed deep into the dirt and he felt almost as if he were being rebirthed into another world. He could feel the dirt all around his face and body and he kept falling deeper into the ground. Deeper, deeper, deeper until he finally hit solid earth. Aaron kept his eyes closed and could feel Bobo caressing him and licking his face, smearing his face paint on Aaron's body. They were both on the bathroom floor, naked, and Aaron could feel Bobo's tears soak into his skin. Bobo grabbed Aaron by the hair and chin, pressing his lips on Aaron's ear.

"That's all I wanted, Aaron, that's all. Why couldn't you just give it to me?" the man whimpered, as if he were deeply frustrated with Aaron. All Aaron could think of was the majestic towers of the beautiful golden castle and the king within its walls who would soon tear Aaron away from his miserable existence.

CHAPTER 6

Where was he? And more importantly, how did he get here? Everything seemed too incredible to be true and Aaron was struggling to grasp the beauty of his surroundings. The clearest blue sky filled with big, bright stars that seemed dangerously close. For some reason, he felt as if he had been hit by a truck. He felt like a newborn child finally opening his eyes and acclimating to a brave new world. It was through some painful struggle, some jarring and terrifying circumstances he was being birthed into another realm.

He adjusted his eyes further to soak in his surroundings. Light was beaming from beautiful golden walls, which held an even more beautiful golden castle behind it. This brought an enormous smile to Aaron's face as he realized where he was, the place he always wanted to be: in the land of the king. Everything was so perfect. He wasn't quite sure what brought him here but he was beyond giddy for whatever adventures awaited him.

He sat up, feeling dazed, and decided to bask in the heat of the day and let the warm breeze wash over his face. He was no longer in a rush to enter the castle and find the king. The time would come if the king felt he was deserving, but until that time he would merely soak up the warmth that radiated from the castle, imagining what mysteries, treasures, and adventures lay within its walls. He closed his eyes and took a deep breath to suck in all of his greatest fantasies that were coming to life before his very eyes. He sat up, lungs filled with pure joy, and allowed a giant smile to unfold.

He could hear the sound of animal hooves pounding on the soft, clear crystal path heading towards his direction, so he opened his eyes to see who or what was coming his way. It was a creature Aaron was unfamiliar with, half-animal and half-human and it was prancing in Aaron's direction as if it were the most jovial and delightful of creatures that ever existed. This creature continued to frolic towards Aaron singing some unknown friendly tune which warmed Aaron's heart and he knew immediately he liked this creature and hoped they could become friends.

"Well, hello, Aaron! I'm so glad to see you again!" the creature said to Aaron as if they had known each other for years. The creature walked on animal hooves but had the arms and torso of a man. Its head was some type of animal that Aaron wasn't familiar with, and it had a tattoo on each of its biceps written in a language he didn't understand. Aaron remembered hearing about such a creature before in a storybook, a faun, he believed it was, and as he recalled fauns were the friendliest of creatures which gave Aaron all the reason to embrace this warm soul.

"I'm sorry, do we know each other?" Aaron asked the creature, who just chuckled at the question.

"Stop playing games with me, Aaron. It's me, Lucian, and I've been waiting for you!"

Aaron was confused. "You have been?"

"But of course! Don't you recall our adventures? Oh, but of course you don't. I take many forms and maybe you haven't seen me in this form yet. You see, this is a special land, a very magical land where anything is possible and all your dreams come true. The last time you were here I may have been a frog, or a leopard, or perhaps a dwarf. However, this is my truest form," Lucian told him.

"Oh, ok. So, are you a faun then? I think I read about fauns in one of my grandpa's books."

"You're very clever, aren't you, Aaron?" Lucian asked with a chuckle as he danced over to Aaron's side. "As a matter of fact I am, my dear boy! And you know what they say about fauns, don't you, Aaron?"

"Well, I think they're friendly and helpful, right?" Aaron asked.

"You're very smart, Aaron. Very smart, indeed! And I've been sent by the king to help you find him."

"Oh, really? Do you mean it, Lucian?"

"Of course, my sweet boy!" Lucian responded with a sparkle in his eye.

"Well, I've had pretty crummy luck so far trying to meet him. I don't think he wants to see me, and I think I just need to stop talking about him." Aaron admitted.

"Oh, don't say that, Aaron. That's not true, not true at all! He's seen your exploits and has marveled over your courage in the face of peril."

"I don't remember ever being brave. Are you sure it was me?" Aaron asked.

"Of course! Remember when you almost drowned as you fetched the sacred sword at the bottom of the sea?"

Aaron thought about it for a moment. "Well, yes! Yes, I do remember that!"

"And how about the time you saved the small boy from the wildebeest and plucked the stone of desire from its mouth? Don't you remember how you wrestled until it fell to the ground exhausted?" Lucian asked.

Aaron wore a bright smile as he replied, "Yes, Lucian. Yes, I do!"

"Good! All the royal guard have heard of your exploits and their bravest knights can't wait to meet you. You see, Aaron, you've been trying to take the straight path down the crystal road to enter the castle. And that's no way to go, Aaron; no way to go at all. There is a special path, Aaron, a secret path that's the best way to reach the castle. You see, this is a very special place, a very magical place and it's easy to get lost. But I won't let that happen to you, I promise. But you must trust me and let me guide you to the castle. Can you do that, Aaron?" Lucian asked with a smile.

"Yes, Lucian, I will! But I was wondering, do all fauns have that symbol?" Aaron pointed at Lucian's forehead.

"Oh, well that's a great question, Aaron. No, that's a very special symbol because I am a very special faun. It's a marker for children to know I am their guide to reach the castle, and that I can take many forms and have special powers that other fauns don't have. And I will use my special powers, Aaron, to make sure you find your father, the king!"

"Thanks Lucian," Aaron responded, only half believing him. "That all makes sense now! Oh, and I really like your horns!"

"Why thank you, Aaron! I know they are large with pointy tips, but they aren't meant to hurt anyone. I don't know if I am even capable of hurting someone!" Lucian laughed sheepishly.

"Oh, ok, so what should we do?"

"I'm glad you asked, my friend. I'm glad you asked," and Lucian reached out a hand. "I want to show you a few parts of our world you haven't seen yet. Take my hand, Aaron, for there is still danger yet in this land. And there are wolves among the sheep, Aaron, wolves among the sheep indeed. But as long as we stick together no harm will come to us, so it's best to be prepared whenever adventure or peril may call." And the two strolled hand in hand to some unknown adventure.

Lucian and Aaron parted from the straight path leading to the castle and headed towards a heavily-laden fruit tree and sat under its shade.

Lucian pointed to the fruit. "Take a bite, Aaron, and taste the goodness of the land.".

"Ok, Lucian," Aaron said with a smile as he plucked a delicious-looking fruit from the tree and took a big bite. "Yuck!" He spat out the fruit. "That's gross!"

"Ah, I see, Aaron. The fruit is indeed bitter for those who stay on the straight path. You must truly choose the king's path, Aaron, to discover it's sweetness."

"Ok, Lucian," Aaron took another bite of the bitter fruit.

"Oh no. No no no! This is bad, very bad indeed! What are we going to do, Aaron? What are we going to do?" Lucian was fidgeting in fear.

Aaron gave Lucian a confused look.

"Can't you hear them coming? From over there, from the enchanted forest. Their feet, can't you feel the ground pounding and hear the steps roaring toward us?" Lucian asked.

Aaron thought for a few seconds as he looked out at the enchanted forest. "Why, yes, Lucian. I do believe I hear them coming."

"Well what will we do, Aaron? This is bad, this is very bad indeed!" Lucian said in a panic. "Wait! I know, the sacred sword! You still have it, don't you?"

"Yes, I think I do!" Aaron looked down to see the broad sword sheathed and tied to a brown leather belt around his waist.

"You must battle them, Aaron. You must battle them all! Do it for the king and his castle and do it for all the small children who seek such high adventures!" Lucian commanded.

Aaron stared at the enchanted forest with a steely glint in his eye and was determined to battle the unknown intruders. And as Aaron prepared his mind for war the green goblins came pouring out of the forest, scowling and grunting and demanding the fruit from the tree.

"Give us the fruit! We want the king's fruit! Give it to us now or you shall perish!" the goblins called out.

Aaron unsheathed his sword and felt its power.

"Never!" he yelled and he attacked the goblins as they waddled towards them. He sliced through them and watched them disappear into thin air. They grabbed on to him, biting his ankles, scratching at his face and legs and rubbing his waist in an attempt to steal his belt. They overwhelmed him and tackled him to the ground and began rubbing their slimy fingers all over him.

But Aaron thought of Lucian, and he thought of the king and how proud he would be of Aaron, so he swatted them all off him and screamed, "To the death!" As he sliced through every last one of them, causing them all to disappear. And Lucian was right back at his side.

"Bravo, Aaron! Bravo indeed! You are so brave and strong; the king will be so proud of you!" Lucian gushed. And Aaron grinned, feeling so proud of himself.

CHAPTER 7

Aaron and Lucian continued their journey together, walking hand in hand, dancing and laughing as if they were the best of friends. Lucian showed Aaron all the secrets the king's land had to offer: the ancient ruins of some past civilization, the majestic unicorns, and the valley of wildflowers. Aaron was captivated by Lucian's stories of the king and his exploits in far-off lands and his daring escape from pirates and vagabonds. He told Aaron of how the king fought off the invaders from the north, of the ships he commissioned to explore far-off lands and the beautifully soft, clear crystal roads he had built. The more Lucian spoke of the king the more Aaron fell in love with him and so Aaron asked Lucian when he might have a chance to finally meet the king.

"You should have seen it, Aaron. The king was so brave and led his army into battle and charged through the invader's front line, causing them to scatter in fear," Lucian told Aaron as they walked further down the secret path. They reached a mountain which possessed a stairway of jagged rocks overlooking a steep cliff, and Aaron stopped in his tracks.

"Are you sure this is the way, Lucian? This seems dangerous," Aaron asked with wide eyes.

"The secret path of the king is a treacherous journey, Aaron, a treacherous journey, indeed. Many children have lacked the courage and turned back from the journey, forsaking their invitation to become a prince. Others have perished for not heeding my guidance. Should I tell the king you lacked the courage to become a prince and choose to no longer meet him?" Lucian asked.

"Well, no, Lucian! No! I'll do it. Let's climb up the rocks."

"Whatever you say," Lucian said with a cheerful smile. And Aaron climbed up the jagged rocks, scraping his hands and knees along the way and overlooking the steep cliff with a raging river below. They kept climbing higher and higher until Aaron felt they must be in the clouds when they finally touched down on solid ground.

"There, you see, Aaron? That wasn't so bad. The king will be so proud of you, so proud of you indeed! Now, what were we talking about?" Lucian asking himself as he scratched his head. "Ah, yes, the invaders! And the invader's fled in fear, abandoning their camp and leaving behind all their belongings. And the king and his army paraded pack to the castle with all his people celebrating their great victory along the way. Oh, you should have heard the cheers, Aaron!" Lucian shouted. "And he ordered a big feast and invited all the townspeople and he brought in all the plunder—" Lucian stopped midsentence and looked wide-eyed at the path in front of them.

"What did he do with the plunder, Lucian?" Aaron asked, hanging on his every word.

"Oh, Aaron. I'm so sorry. I'm sorry it has come to this."

"Come to what, Lucian? What's going on?"

"There he is," Lucian replied in a daze. "On the other side of the bridge, blocking our path."

"Who, Lucian?" Aaron asked confused.

"Don't you see him? It's the black knight, and he has come to destroy us. He's come to bring an end to our great adventure. Oh no oh no oh no! This wasn't how it was supposed to go! It's all been ruined, all been ruined indeed!" Lucian replied, pacing back and forth.

"What's the big deal about the black knight?"

"What's the big deal?! Well, he's only the strongest, most terrible knight to ever live. He wanders from village to village, stealing the souls of little children and sending them to the great pit of vipers where there is no escape. And he hates the king and challenges anyone who seeks refuge in his castle. He's bested more than I care to admit, Aaron. He's a dangerous man, but the only way you can reach the castle is if you accept his challenge and fight him."

Aaron looked before him and saw the bridge and stared down at the raging river some two hundred feet below and the great waterfall in the distance. He saw the shadowy figure on the other side with a lance in his hand and a flag that was waving in the wind.

"What's that flag he is holding?"

"The black knight has his own symbol and purpose, just as I have mine, and whenever you see his symbol you can be sure that your soul is soon to be stolen," Lucian said. "So, will you do it, Aaron? Will you risk your life and soul for the king?"

Aaron knew that the black knight might best him and his soul may be lost, and he also knew he might fall off the bridge entirely and crash into the river and be swept into the waterfall. It was a perilous adventure, a bitter fruit that he knew must be tasted. So, with great bravery and heroism Aaron drew the sacred sword into the air.

"I challenge you, black knight, to a duel! You shall let us pass or taste the blade of my sword," Aaron called out.

The black knight stood on the other side of the bridge, his armor was dented from a lifetime of battles and evading death and he had a broad sword sheathed to his waist that ran almost to the floor, giving Aaron goosebumps. He grabbed his sword and raised it above his head as well, accepting the challenge.

"To the death!" the black knight called out to Aaron.

Aaron stared at the sword, which looked to be longer than his whole body, and he became afraid. But he thought about the king and how brave he would think Aaron was and he found courage in his heart.

"To the death!" Aaron screamed as he charged across the bridge. And the black knight met him halfway and their blades glinted in the sunlight and sparked as they collided. And the black knight swung his sword at Aaron, but Aaron blocked the sword and parried. Then Aaron swung his sword at the black knight who blocked the attack and also parried. Then the black knight lunged at Aaron, but Aaron dodged the attack and stepped out of the way, pressing up against the bridge and peering down into the raging river below.

The two circled each other and continued sword fighting, striking each other and parrying. But Aaron slowly began tiring and the black knight's sword began raining down on him, blow by blow, until Aaron fell to his knees. The black knight knocked Aaron's sword out of his hand, and then dropped his sword and fell on top of Aaron's exhausted body. He pressed all of his weight on Aaron's abdomen and put his hands around Aaron's neck and slowly began squeezing the life out of him.

"Help, Lucian! Please, help!" Aaron called, gurgling and grasping for air.

"Aaron! All is not lost! You still have the stone of desire, pluck it from your pocket and wield it against the black knight!" Lucian called from the other side of the bridge.

Aaron could feel himself losing consciousness but frantically pushed his hips into the air, catching the black knight off balance, and then lifted his knee off the ground, bringing his pocket closer to his hand and fished out a rugged green stone. The green knight continued to squeeze Aaron's throat and Aaron knew death was on the horizon but before he lost consciousness, he lifted the stone of desire in the air for the black knight to see. The black knight released his grip around Aaron's neck and stared at the stone of desire, and Aaron gulped in all the air his lungs could hold. Aaron escaped from under the black knight and stood to his feet and the black knight stared at the stone of desire as if he were in a trance.

"That's great, Aaron! Now, you have him under your command and your wish is his desire. Now, be rid of this man forever!"

"Black knight, I banish you from this land. Now, get back on your horse and leave this place and never return!" Aaron boldly demanded.

"No, Aaron! No! That's no good, no good at all! You must kill the black knight. You must push him over the bridge so he shall never return!"

"Wouldn't it be nobler for me to spare his life and banish him from the land?"

"Suit yourself, Aaron, but if he goes along and battles and kills other young boys and steals their souls don't say I didn't warn you."

Aaron felt torn and stared at the river thinking about how the king would feel if the black knight killed some other young boy and Aaron could've stopped it.

"Black knight, stop!" Aaron called out, and the black knight stopped before exiting the bridge. Aaron took a deep breath. "Black knight, you shall walk over to the edge of the bridge." It felt uncomfortable, killing a helpless man who could easily be sent on his way.

"Go on, Aaron! Be rid of him!" Lucian called out.

"Walk over to the edge of the bridge, and… and jump to your death," Aaron called out and then watched as the black knight obeyed and tumbled into the raging river and fell down the waterfall.

"Bravo, Aaron! Bravo indeed! The king will surely be proud of you for ridding the land of this foul creature! Now, we must cross the bridge to continue our adventure and our adventure isn't much longer, Aaron. We are almost there!" Lucian cheered as he grabbed Aaron's hand and they crossed the bridge together.

Aaron touched down on the other side of the bridge holding Lucian's hand, feeling a tad bit guilty, and wondering if the king would approve.

"Lucian," Aaron asked as he sheepishly stared at his feet. "Did you mean it? What you said about the king? That he wants to see me… and that he wants to be my dad?"

Lucian laughed at the question. "Does your father the king want to see you? Well, of course he wants to meet you, silly! He's been looking for you all this time!"

"Ok, Lucian. You don't think he'll be mad that I sent the black knight into the river and over the waterfall?" Aaron asked with a worried look.

"Not at all, Aaron. He would have wanted it that way. That's why he sent me to come find you and guide you on your great adventure! I assure you, Aaron, you have saved the souls of countless children from tasting the unending stings of a pit full of vipers. That is something to be praised, and he will praise you indeed!"

"That does make sense, Lucian. Thank you for explaining it to me," Aaron said with a smile.

"You are very welcome, Aaron, and I will tell you even more. This world, the realm of the king, is an ancient world unknown to most little children. It is a great mystery that most children will never know. They will never get to see their greatest fantasies become true. But the king has been searching for you, just you, to join him in this beautiful world. You think he doesn't notice you, but he does. He knows who you are Aaron, he sees where you sleep at night and he was there the very day you were born. He was there the moment you came spilling out of your mother's womb and immediately noticed just how special you are. And he knows your adoptive grandparents and your whole family, and he asked specifically to meet you. You are a very special boy, Aaron, and soon enough all your dreams will come true. And when we finally complete our journey and arrive at the castle the king who will show you just how much you mean to him," Lucian told Aaron, touching him on his forehead, his shoulders, and then his nose. A slight sting accompanied each touch and Aaron knew Lucian must have very special powers.

"That sounds wonderful! I'm so thankful for you, Lucian! Thank you for guiding me on this adventure and showing me how brave I can be."

Lucian gave Aaron a slight smile. "You are very welcome, my truest friend, and we are well on our way, Aaron. The journey has begun. You've retrieved the sacred sword, bested the wildebeest and destroyed the goblin army. And now you've just bested the most fearsome knight in all the land. You have passed all his tests thus far and there are still more to come. But we are almost there, Aaron, and I can almost smell the roses from the king's private garden. And when we arrive he will be waiting for you, and he will throw the most lavish party in your honor. Everyone from all across the land will come and celebrate your homecoming. And you will finally meet the king, and he will embrace you with the warmest embrace, and you will stay with the king forever in his castle and never want to leave."

"I bet I won't!" replied Aaron, laughing in excitement. Aaron then became quiet as he asked Lucian another question.

"Lucian, this may sound strange, but I was wondering, will you be my friend? I don't feel I have many friends, and sometimes it can get awfully lonely. Sometimes I feel like no one likes me and I don't know what to do to change their minds."

Lucian chuckled, "Well of course we are friends, silly! After all we've been through we are the best type of friends, the very best kind, so you don't need any other friends. I will always be your friend, Aaron, whether you like it or not. And if you ever need me, at any time at all, you need do nothing more than call out my name, or draw my symbol, and I will be by your side."

Aaron was so excited to hear that he'd made a true friend!

"That sounds absolutely wonderful, Lucian, thank you!"

"Of course, Aaron! But remember: the secret path always seems bitter at first, just like the fruit from the tree. And there is no adventure that is not perilous. Your grandparents know this well, so you must listen to them and do as they say. No matter what."

"Do I have to, Lucian? They can be so incredibly kind sometimes, but other times they are even crueler, and I don't know if I can handle it."

"Believe me, Aaron, they do it because they love you. Besides, I know you can handle it, and when you are done handling it you will dance in the king's ballroom and feel the decadent ambiance of his splendor, and then you will know that it was all worth it. Repeat after me, Aaron: *I can handle it.*"

Aaron paused for a moment, but he thought about how wonderful this place was and he dreaded the thought of never being able to come back and never getting to see the king. "Ok, Lucian. I can handle it."

"Great, Aaron. Say it again!"

"I can handle it."

"And again." Lucian said, and Aaron obeyed.

"And one more time."

"I can handle it."

"That's a good lad. Now I think we've journeyed enough for one day, and as your bestest of friends I must send you on your way, but remember if you ever need me just call my name or draw my symbol and I will be there. On the count of three, you will find yourself back with your adoptive grandparents, ok? One, two, three!" and with that Lucian sprinted into the wind and took flight on two giant wings sprouting from his back.

Aaron watched Lucian trail off into the distance as the entire world seemed to slowly melt away, and as everything began to fade Aaron could feel something tight around his neck, and it kept getting tighter, and tighter, and tighter until he felt his head might burst off. He couldn't breathe at all and closed his eyes and struggled to gain his composure as he knew he was no longer in this wonderful world. He opened his eyes and knew that he was being strangled with some unknown cord and there was a thick plastic bag over his head, and someone was yelling at him.

"Say his name! Say it! Say it now!" But Aaron couldn't say anything because he was being strangled and was on the verge of passing out. "Say his name! Say it! Say it now!" Aaron was losing consciousness quickly and he feverishly began pounding his fists into the flesh behind him, anger building in his gut. The bag and the cord were finally released from him and Aaron took a large inhale of air. "What is his name?" someone asked him.

Aaron took a few more deep breaths. His adoptive grandfather was holding a cord in his hand. He looked at the man dead in the eye and yelled, "His name is Lucian!"

CHAPTER 8

The meeting was supposed to start over an hour ago, and the teacher stared at the clock waiting for Aaron's mother to come pick him up. Aaron was slumped against the wall outside her classroom, head buried in his hands in embarrassment from today's incident. She had always enjoyed having Aaron in her class. He was a very kind and sweet boy who seemed to make friends easily. He was bright and eager to learn and although he struggled to pay attention at times, he was a great student, which is why Mrs. Schneider was so concerned. As the school year went on, she was noticing a change in Aaron. Something was going on with him and Aaron didn't want to talk about it. She had seen some very unfortunate circumstances with her students in the past, where she felt obligated to inform the authorities that something was most definitely amiss, and Mrs. Schneider's hand was regularly hovering over her phone ready to make the call. But she wanted to talk with the parents first, give them the benefit of the doubt, and hopefully put her fears to rest. Together, perhaps they could help Aaron get back on track.

Aaron's mother finally stumbled into Mrs. Schneider's classroom over an hour late, hair a tangled mess and her lipstick was a day old.

"I'm so sorry, Mrs. Schneider. I really didn't mean to be this late. You see I stopped at the grocery store before our meeting so I could cook Aaron a nice home-cooked meal and then I ran into trouble. You see, I lost my checkbook so when I went to go check out I didn't have any money to pay with. I told them I'd be right back with the money but they were so rude and told me they would just have to put it all back and I could return when I had the money.

"So I went back home to get money from my husband and he would only give me fifty dollars, and fifty dollars wasn't enough. So, I had to stop at my mother's house to get more money so I could make Aaron dinner. And then I got into a fight with my mother when I was there and I lost track of time… and here I am." Margaret said, frantically explaining herself.

Mrs. Schneider sighed and slightly rolled her eyes, "Thank you, Margaret. I think we should get to business then."

"Ok, Mrs. Schneider, whatever you say."

"We've had another incident with Aaron, and it's not good. In fact, it's pretty bad."

"Well, what happened?" Margaret asked.

"During class today Aaron suggested to all the kids sitting at his table that they pull down their pants and share their 'privates' with one another."

"Oh," Margaret responded quietly.

"Yes. In the middle of class I looked over to see Aaron with his pants down telling his friends to go under the table to look." Mrs. Schneider explained. Margaret didn't respond, she just stared at Mrs. Schneider's desk like a petulant child who just got caught with her hand in the cookie jar.

"Margaret this type of behavior is grounds for expulsion. We have a zero-tolerance policy for sexualized behavior in children and, frankly, it is disturbing. I have to wonder where Aaron learned this type of behavior."

The silence hung in the air as Margaret breathed in the full weight of the accusation. She clenched her fists and bit her lip before she looked up at Mrs. Schneider with a response.

"You know, Mrs. Schneider, when I was a child my mother always played the tarot cards. And she would cast the tarot cards for me and my siblings to see how we'd turn out. My mother would shuffle the deck and grab the top card and it was always the fool. Every time she cast the cards for me it was the fool. And she would always say, 'Margaret the fool. Margaret the fool who dropped out of school. Margaret the fool who can't get a job. Margaret the fool who can't keep a man.' My whole life, Mrs. Schneider!" Margaret explained, rather childishly. Mrs. Schneider squinted her eyes at Margaret trying to understand why she was telling her this.

"So, when I became pregnant with my first child she said, 'Margaret the fool who will mess up her kids.' But I said, 'No! I will not mess up my kids!' And you know what I did, Mrs. Schneider? I got down on my knees and dedicated my children to the Lord. I gave them over to him because I didn't want to mess it up. I said, 'Lord, I know I'm a fool. But please save my babies!'"

Mrs. Schneider sighed heavily and rolled her eyes without trying to hide it and interjected, "I'm not going to report Aaron. At least not yet, Margaret."

"Oh, thank you, Mrs. Schneider! Thank you! I knew you were sent by God to watch over my baby!"

Mrs. Schneider was getting a little nauseous and chose to move on with the meeting. "I said at least not yet, Margaret. There's more, and it is concerning, and it needs to stop."

Margaret took a deep breath, "Ok, Mrs. Schneider, what is it?"

"I had a parent reach out to me letting me know that Aaron asked their son if he wanted to watch 'X-rated videos' with Aaron. Now where would he get that idea from, Margaret?"

Margaret didn't know what to say. She froze and began fidgeting her hands.

"It gets even worse, Margaret. And this is the part that makes me queasy. According to the parent Aaron told their son that he has played a role in an 'X-rated video' and he asked their son if he'd like to join him." Mrs. Schneider finished with a condemning stare towards Margaret.

"Well, I don't know where he got that from; it wasn't from me," Margaret responded meekly.

"Then where did it come from, Margaret? Where? Do I need to send someone to your house to assess the fitness of the home?" Mrs. Schneider asked.

"He got it from his brother!" she blurted out. "Yes, it was from his brother, Adam. He's twelve years old and we found a video under his bed, and it was X-rated. And he said that he let Aaron watch it and that they would act out some of the silly scenes, but not the sexual ones. That's what happened Mrs. Schneider."

"Well then, Margaret. I guess you have an answer for everything. Just don't let it happen again. If there is anymore sexual acting out in my classroom, I will pull him."

"You got it, Mrs. schneider. It will never happen again. Now I've got to go. I need to make Aaron a home-cooked meal. Have a great night, Mrs. Schneider."

~   ~   ~

Margaret grabbed Aaron by the hand and dragged him to the car. She threw Aaron into the backseat and slammed the door, bursting into tears and sobbing as she pulled out of the school parking lot.

"Do you have any idea how embarrassing that was, Aaron?!" she yelled with tears streaming down her face.

Aaron sat in the back silently.

"Do you?"

"Mom, I just—"

"I've never been more humiliated in my whole life!" she yelled as she began sobbing again. "Why can't you just be good, Aaron? Why is it so hard for you to be a good boy for once? I've got enough on my plate and I'm not going to stroll into your teacher's office for her to tell me what a horrible mother I am every time you can't do as you're told. Just, stop it! Stop it, Aaron!" she said as she slammed the steering wheel.

"You hate me, don't you?" Aaron asked her with a scowl.

"Do you want me to hate you, Aaron? Do you?" she asked, staring at him in the rearview mirror.

Aaron gazed out the window and into the clouds. He whispered under his breath, "Pretty soon you won't have to worry about me ever again."

CHAPTER 9

Aaron gazed out his bedroom window staring at what wasn't there. He chuckled as he joked with the clouds, the wind, and the empty space around him. He thought of his battle against the goblin army and how he had overcome the black knight. He thought of the perilous journey up the jagged rocks and all the stories Lucian told him about the king. He thought of all the great adventures Lucian had taken him on and knew he was with him now. He was both nowhere and everywhere, Aaron's new friend that he loved so much. Aaron was in such deep conversation that he didn't hear the knocking at his door behind him. He continued to stare into the clouds as he heard the funniest jokes, the silliest stories, and the most interesting suggestions of what Aaron ought to do and how he ought to behave.

"Stop being so silly, I can't do that! Can I?" he spoke to no one and everyone.

He had been in his room for most of the day. It was a sunny Saturday afternoon, and all the neighborhood kids were gathering together for shenanigans, all except Aaron. He skipped the morning game of football at the park and missed out on the scuffle that took place between the two teams. He missed the game of hide and seek at the playground because he had already been found and would never be lost again. He hadn't eaten breakfast or lunch because he was already full. And he ignored his brother Thomas who was knocking outside his door because someone else had been knocking that Aaron already let in. The two were slowly becoming inseparable and Aaron began ignoring his classmates and neighborhood friends in favor of being alone with his new friend.

He remembered the symbol on Lucian's forehead and drew it everywhere. He drew it on his school folders and scribbled it on the floorboards. He kept it in his pocket and hung it on his bedroom wall. He would stare at it when he was sad. He looked at it when he remembered that his birth father had left. He thought about it when his adoptive father chased him out of the house and called him worthless. He carried it with him when he visited his adoptive grandparents to ensure Lucian would answer Aaron's call. He would focus intently on the symbol as he drifted off towards the golden castle and was grateful that he'd been chosen to meet such a wonderful friend. And he smiled brightly to think that soon enough he would meet the king and never have to return to this awful house.

His new friend was a sign and a promise to Aaron that he would soon meet the king, that the king did love him and was eager to meet him. Aaron thought of all the wonderful things he might do with the king, of how he would give Aaron the biggest hug and kiss him on the cheek. He would tell Aaron that he loved him and was the son he'd always wanted. He would protect Aaron and never let anyone hurt him again. He would do all the things his birth father never did and his adoptive father wasn't willing to do and he would make Aaron whole. They would ride into the clouds together, never to return to this horrible place and there would be a great feast at the golden castle in honor of Aaron's homecoming.

Aaron just knew it would be worth it. As he listened to Lucian reassure him that the king was eager to meet him and had very special plans for him Aaron continued to ignore the knocking, soaking up the truth.

"Aaron, I've been calling you, didn't you hear me?" Thomas had crept in through the door without Aaron noticing because he'd been so focused on the clouds.

"Sorry, Thomas, I didn't hear you."

"Ok, what are you looking at? Is Wolfy out there in the sky?" he asked Aaron.

"No, Thomas, someone much better than Wolfy."

"Well did you want to go play outside? The day is almost over and then we'll be stuck inside and Dad is in a very bad mood today."

"That's ok, Thomas. Pretty soon I won't be stuck inside"

"What does that mean?" Thomas asked.

"It means I'll be leaving very soon lauka never coming back."

"Well, who told you that?" Thomas asked with a confused look on his face.

Aaron finally turned around to face Thomas, who was standing in front of the bedroom door. He smiled sweetly at his brother and responded, "He told me I can't tell."

CHAPTER 10

"Alright, Aaron. We are going to play a game now, a very important game, and we really need your cooperation."

Aaron sat on his adoptive grandparents' living room couch looking at the sea of faces surrounding him, wondering who they all were, how they knew each other, and what sort of game all these adults wanted to play with a child. It was early October now and he'd been reminded several times by his adoptive grandfather about the upcoming celebration. Indeed, Aaron was supposed to be a very special guest and his parents knew well in advance that Aaron would be staying at his adoptive grandparent's house on the night of the celebration. Things were indeed getting strange, and some unknown excitement was building in the air. He could see it on all their faces as they gathered closer for the game.

"This is a new game, Aaron, and it is very important to us, very important to us all, your grandmother and I included. And you know we've played some games in the past that were a little confusing and perhaps painful, but you see it was meant to help us all make a new friend, a very important friend. And today, we are hoping to play this very important game to finally meet this new friend. Can you help us with that, Aaron?"

Aaron felt numb but also perplexed, wondering why these strangers were wearing all white and why they had the look of eager desperation as if this truly were an important moment, and Aaron had a very special role to play. Aaron liked the idea of being important, but then again it was apparently also important that Aaron didn't tell anyone all the important things he did while in their care. He was hesitant, and unsure of how to proceed. He was a child surrounded by grown men and women who could easily overpower him and force him to do what they wanted him to do. But, for some reason, they weren't using coercion, they were all looking intently at Aaron as if they needed his consent, needed Aaron to say he wanted to play this game. They all kept staring at Aaron, with wide plastic smiles adorning their faces, and the clock kept ticking, and the uncertainty kept building. It seemed as if the longer Aaron waited to respond the more he could see on their faces just how important this game was, and even more important was Aaron's permission to proceed with the game. Aaron held the keys, and he didn't know what he was unlocking.

"Oh, I forgot to tell you, Aaron. If you play this game with us, then I'll take you out for ice cream! And we can even rent a movie, too. How does that sound?" He was upping the ante, increasing the stakes, and doing whatever he could to buy Aaron's consent. Aaron liked ice cream, and he really liked to watch movies. Perhaps this game wouldn't be as painful as in the past. And perhaps this had something to do with the king. Perhaps Aaron was special, after all, and perhaps he was a prince and he was getting ready to meet his father, the king. But perhaps the only way this could happen was if Aaron freely chose to meet the king, and Aaron had no problem with that. Aaron thought back over the years he had spent with his adoptive grandparents, all the games they'd played, the people they'd introduced him to, and the pain he'd suffered along the way. Maybe it was all building up to this moment where it would finally pay off. Maybe this is where the pain would all end and the love began.

With all that in mind, Aaron looked at his adoptive grandfather and eagerly nodded his head. "Ok, Grandpa."

"Great, son! That's just great! Ok, we'll need to prepare for the game, so be patient."

Over the next half hour or so Aaron's adoptive grandparents and their company prepared. They brought in a small mattress and laid it on one side of the living room and covered it with white linens. One of the adults grabbed a handful of gray dust from some unknown canister and sprinkled it all around the mattress, encompassing the mattress in a circle of the dust. Then they asked Aaron to take off his shirt, pants, and socks and lie on the mattress in his underwear. Aaron obliged with a little fear and confusion building in the back of his mind. And the fear and confusion began to build as he was approached by a woman with a brush and a container of red liquid. The women dipped the brush into the red liquid and proceeded to paint it onto Aaron's chest and legs and face. The liquid was thick and warm, and Aaron felt that this was all very strange. Aaron continued to lie on the mattress and watch as the adults huddled together in a circle and began murmuring together as if they were reciting a poem. The murmuring turning into singing and clapping until they broke the huddle, and they circled the living room, dressed in all white, singing and clapping intently as if they were expecting something to happen. They kept circling, over and over again, each with a look of intense focus and desire for something to happen. What that something was Aaron didn't know, and he still wasn't sure what his part was in this strange game.

The singing came to an end and the lights were dimmed and they all finally approached Aaron, hovering over him with eager anticipation. A woman began to speak to Aaron.

"Now Aaron, I have something I want to show you. Do you see this amulet? This amulet has been passed down through my family for over a hundred years. It used to belong to my mother, whose mother had given it to her, and whose mother had given it to her, and so on and so forth. And my mother eventually gave it to me. And do you know why this amulet is so important, Aaron?"

Aaron didn't know what to say, so he just looked at the amulet and responded that he didn't know what was so important.

"It's so important because the amulet bears the symbol of a great king, and this king can grant power to people. This king can give you all the toys you want, and help you make friends, and give you all the candy in the world. He can do all these wonderful things. But, you see, Aaron, the king likes to meet children. He likes to reveal himself to children, and if he reveals himself to children, he will reveal himself to all the children's friends. You see, the game is to call upon the king and see if he will become our friend. Does that make sense, Aaron?"

Aaron couldn't believe it. He was right! He was going to meet the king, and he knew this would be the most special day in his life. Nothing would ever be the same and soon enough he would be crowned prince of the golden castle and its kingdom.

"So, Aaron, can we count on you to play?" Aaron gave her a big smile and shook his head yes, that he was more than happy to play. "That's great, Aaron. That's just great. Here is what I need you to do. I'm going to dangle the amulet above your head and move it back and forth, and all I need you to do is follow the amulet. I need you to focus as hard as you can on the amulet with all your attention. Then, when I stop waving the amulet, I need you to focus all your attention on the wall on the opposite side of the room and tell me what you see. Do you think you can do that for us, Aaron?"

Aaron, who was eager to finally meet the king, was absolutely thrilled to be chosen for this moment, to find out that he was indeed special and that he was, in fact, fit to be a prince. Aaron just smiled at her and told the woman in white, "I'm ready."

And so, the game began, and with his adoptive grandmother and grandfather and all their friends hovering, the lady in white began dangling her amulet over Aaron, signaling for him to follow the amulet as it moved back and forth over him. Back and forth, back and forth, back dand forth. Aaron focused his eyes on the amulet with the greatest intent to see his greatest desire come to life. Back and forth, back and forth, back and forth. And everything seemed to fade away, everything but the amulet, and Aaron could see all its details come to life and the shimmering of its gold plate illuminated the room. Back and forth, back and forth, back and forth. Aaron felt like he was staring directly into the sun and the glow of the amulet blinded him, causing him to close his eyes. In his minds' eye, he could see the radiant walls of the golden castle, and he could see the golden castle's drawbridge slowly open, ever so slowly. And he knew once the drawbridge was fully open he would finally see the king. Aaron kept his eyes shut tight and watched the golden castle come to life. He watched the drawbridge descend closer to the ground. Finally, the drawbridge was completely open, and Aaron looked intently through its door to find the king. However, there was no king to be found. But there was a great rushing of wind as if a windstorm had ascended from the castle. And he could hear the flapping of great wings as if some glorious princely bird had taken flight from the castle on its way to meet Aaron. Aaron could feel the wind brush against his face and he whispered, "I think he's coming."

"Stop!" yelled the woman with the amulet. "Ok, Aaron. I can see something has caught your attention. On the count of three, I want you to open your eyes and tell everyone what you see. Can you do that, Aaron?"

Aaron shook his head, yes, feeling as if he were on the precipice of something incredible. "On the count of three Aaron, I want you to sit up and open your eyes, ok? One, two, and three!"

Aaron followed her orders and sat up with the palm of his hands on the mattress, holding his torso up. Then he slowly opened his eyes, eager to see what would greet him. With all the adults hovering on either side of him, Aaron cast his gaze at the wall on the opposite side of the room. He looked for the king, but there was nothing.

"Well, Aaron, what do you see?" asked his adoptive grandfather, but Aaron didn't respond, he was disappointed in the outcome. On the other side of the room was a fireplace with a black mantle and above that mantle was a picture of his adoptive grandparents with all their children. He couldn't help but look at the couple in the picture; they seemed so kind, caring, and loving.

He felt deflated and dejected as he stared at the family picture; then he lay back down on the mattress. He lay there as everyone hovered over him, expecting some great miracle to happen, but Aaron was tired and all out of hope. He stared at the ceiling, wondering what he was doing there, how he had gotten there, and how he was supposed to move on with his life. It was all just pretend, just his wild imagination getting away with him. There was no magical land, no clear crystal road, and no mythical creatures. There was no Lucian and no golden castle, and most importantly there was no king who desperately wanted to meet Aaron and love Aaron with all his heart.

Time continued to pass and he could tell the adults were getting a little impatient. But Aaron didn't care. He had suffered enough and he wasn't interested in placating his adoptive grandparents and their friends who were so bent on playing make-believe.

Stupid, Aaron thought to himself. So stupid, stupid that he ever believed he was special or that there was an important reason to be treated so horribly. But as he stared intently at the ceiling he thought he could see something moving. He focused his eyes further and it looked like a footprint indenting into the ceiling. There was a footprint directly above his head, and then he saw another one, and another one, and it was as if someone were walking on the ceiling and headed towards the other side of the room. Aaron's heart skipped a beat, and then he no longer noticed the footprint because there was a light tapping near the front door. TAP, TAP, TAP. TAP, TAP, TAP. It was the sound of talons or claws tapping the ceramic surface of the front door entrance. TAP, TAP, TAP. TAP, TAP, TAP. The sound grew louder, and Aaron realized that they weren't alone in the room. But he didn't want to look. Whatever was making that tapping sound must have claws, and whatever had claws couldn't be a king. What was he going to find when he turned his eyes to the corner of the room? TAP, TAP, TAP. TAP, TAP, TAP.

"Do you see something, Aaron? What do you see? Tell me what you see!" his adoptive grandfather pried.

"Yes, Aaron, what do you see? Tell us what you see?" they all demanded. It sounded like a sea of voices commanding him to turn his head and lay eyes upon the great tapper with the great claws who was just begging for attention.

"Go ahead, Aaron, what do you see? What do you see?" they all kept asking, and the creature kept tapping, so he finally began to turn his head to the corner of the room to the entrance of the front door. And there it was, crouching in the corner of the room. The first thing Aaron noticed was the big, blood-red eyes staring at him. They stared at him for what seemed like an eternity with a look of both mischief and disdain. The creature grimaced as if they knew each other and he very much disliked Aaron, and Aaron watched as the creature slowly stood up to reveal its full stature and person. And it was a sight to be seen; it was unlike anything he had ever seen before, and yet at the same time eerily familiar. It was jet black, darker than night, which made its blood-red eyes stand out even more. Its arms fell to either side revealing the sharp claws adorning its fingers. It had two horns protruding from its head, tall enough to scrape the ceiling. And there was a strange symbol in between its horns. The creature had two large canine fangs hanging from its upper lip and spilling down to its jaw. There were strange symbols on either arm which looked eerily familiar. And the symbol on its forehead looked familiar too. It had animal hooves and legs with the torso of a man and the arms of a human, which also seemed familiar.

It reminded Aaron of a friend. But this creature was no friend, for its glare at Aaron bore its evil intent. There was something very sinister about this entity. Somehow Aaron knew that its giant claws and fangs were meant for tearing through flesh, its large hooves for crushing bones and that it was pure evil that delighted in the suffering of others. But he knew this creature somehow, and he thought of the symbols and the horns and he thought about his time in the kingdom of the golden castle, and then he knew.

"Lucian?" As soon as he uttered the name his adoptive grandparents pinned down his arms and their friends pinned down his legs and the woman with the amulet forced open his mouth and forced him to drink a thick liquid that Aaron found revolting. He spat it out.

"Drink it down, Aaron! You need to drink it down!" She pinched his nose, forcing his mouth open again. As the warm liquid oozed down his throat, he could hear the cackling of hooves against the floor as it closed in on Aaron, ever closer, ever closer, until it was hovering just over him. Everyone in the room was in a frenzy from the mention of the name Lucian, as if they had won the game, but all Aaron could think about were those blood-red eyes, the horns, and the fangs and the claws. The creature was now staring directly at Aaron and he felt as if he were about to faint. The creature stooped down towards Aaron's head and he could hear a hissing coming from the creature and noticed it had a forked tongue protruding from its mouth. It was all too much for Aaron, so he closed his eyes and felt a large, fleshy organ smack him in the face, causing Aaron to pass out.

CHAPTER 11

"Come on, son, it's time to go in," his adoptive grandfather told him, ushering him down the hallway.

Aaron stood outside his grandparent's bedroom door and looked at the men who lay waiting for his company. He didn't want to go in. He was tired, and he was sore, and he didn't like the looks on their faces, and he wished he could be somewhere else, anywhere else but standing outside the bedroom door. Aaron wanted to do as he was told, but he was scared and afraid and alone, and so under his breath he called out to Lucian, "Lucian, please help me."

As soon as he uttered his name Aaron found himself drifting off to paradise.

"Welcome back, Aaron! Are you ready to continue our adventure?" Lucian greeted Aaron.

"Lucian, I'm scared and I don't know what to do," Aaron admitted.

"Well, of course you are, Aaron. Overcoming pain and fear is the way of the secret path. Why don't you walk with me, so we can continue our adventure," he said as he grabbed Aaron's hand and led him into a meadow.

"Did you know that the castle has special powers?" Lucian asked as they walked through the meadow surrounded by a giant wall of deep thickets filled with barbarous thorns. "You see, the king knows how treacherous the journey is to the castle, and he knows that dangers and suffering abound. So, when you finally enter into his castle it soaks up all your painful memories of the journey and all you're left with is the joy of being with the king. Doesn't that sound wonderful, Aaron?"

"I don't know, Lucian. I'm scared they're going to hurt me bad."

"It will only hurt a little, Aaron, but then it will be forgotten!" chuckled Lucian. "Have I told you about the rooms in the castle?"

"Well, no,"

"Oh, Aaron! They are so beautiful! There is the guardroom with beautiful coats of armor made of gold, silver, bronze, and alabaster! And the kitchen is filled with cookies and ice cream and—_"

"And spaghetti?" Aaron asked, cutting Lucian off.

"Yes, Aaron, all the spaghetti you could ever eat! And there is the bailey where all the children play their favorite games until the morning sun."

"Oh, wow!" Aaron responded.

"And then there is the tower that offers the most breathtaking views of the kingdom. And if you look really close you can even see the valley where the unicorns sleep."

"I would love to see that!" Aaron said.

"And if you look to the north, you can see the harbor where great adventurers set sail to unknown lands in search of treasure. And they battle pirates and vagabonds and take their plunder and steal their booty! Why look! You can see them now returning from their voyage. Can you see them, Aaron?"

Aaron squinted his eyes and gasped, "There they are! And they've got treasure chests that they are carrying off their ship!"

"That's right Aaron. And someday I am sure you will join them in their adventures. But let's not forget your bedroom, Aaron. The king has a wonderful bedroom prepared for you filled with toys and stuffed animals and games of all kinds."

"And I don't have to share with Thomas?" Aaron asked as his eyes lit up.

"No, Aaron," Lucian chuckled. "You don't have to share at all!"

"Oh, I mustn't forget the ballroom! It has marble floors and stone pillars and every night there is dancing. And on very special occasions they will dress up and wear expensive costumes and put on dapper masks. Aaron, you get swept up in the spectacle just watching! And there is the hall where he sits on his golden throne and everyone celebrates all that he has done for them."

Aaron looked in a daze, hardly believing it all could be true.

"All this could be yours, Aaron. If you are strong enough, the king will lead you by the hand into a very special room and reveal himself to you and finally embrace you as the father you always wanted. Isn't that what you want?"

"More than anything," Aaron responded.

"Great! Now, let me ask you, Aaron, have you ever heard the story about the phoenix?"

"Well, no Lucian. I haven't."

Lucian chuckled again. "Well, of course, you haven't. That's why you have me! Let me tell you about the phoenix. The phoenix is a very special bird, a terribly special bird unlike any other bird in existence. You see, Aaron, the phoenix is the most beautiful bird you could ever see. It has the most beautiful red talons, and its legs are covered with golden scales. It is as large as an eagle with a blue tail. What's more, it even has a golden halo perched on its head emanating the most beautiful golden beams in every direction. But what is most important about this bird, young Aaron, is that it never dies. It lives in a perpetual state of divine grace resplendent with the glory that can only be granted by a god. But every hundred years, Aaron, the poor bird must prove its undying devotion to this god and allow this god to completely decimate and destroy it until it is nothing left but a pile of ashes."

Aaron thought this was all rather strange. He wasn't quite sure how love worked, or life or death, or anything really for that matter. But something seemed off about this story, this depiction of divine grace bestowed upon this poor bird only after it agrees to suffer immensely under the hand of some divine force. And Aaron wasn't quite sure what all this had to do with him. He wasn't a bird, and he was pretty sure he couldn't live forever. But he trusted Lucian, in fact, he loved Lucian, so he continued to listen.

"You see, Aaron, you can only prove your love for someone by allowing them to destroy you. The phoenix's love for this god radiates from its halo and oozes its blood through every part of its body as it lets the god destroy it, only to let the phoenix arise anew with even greater power and beauty and divine grace. And do you know who that god is that destroys the phoenix, Aaron?"

Aaron was pretty sure he knew the answer but was a bit skittish to say it out loud. It wasn't quite the image he had in mind of the king, whom he desperately wanted to call father. But he had never stepped foot in a castle nor wore a crown of gold and he'd never granted a bird eternal life. He had never cast royal decrees, created kingdoms, or anything of that matter.

So, Aaron pursed his lips and feebly replied, "Is it the king?"

Lucian gave Aaron a look that was something between a smirk and a slight smile that was a bit perplexing to Aaron. "You are a very smart boy, and that is why you have made it so far on our great adventure! And we've finally come to the end, the last obstacle between you and the castle," Lucian told him as he pointed at the giant wall of thornbushes. "All you have to do is walk through, and we are sure to run into the castle."

Aaron stared at the large thornbushes with their oversized thorns and he took a deep breath and swallowed hard. "Are you sure this is the only way?"

"I'm afraid so. You must suffer the sting of his thorns before you may enter his castle. But we are so close, Aaron, so close indeed! Ok, watch me. I'll go first." Lucian let go of Aaron's hand as Aaron watched his friend walk directly into the dense thicket, getting caught in the barrage of sharp thorns which drew blood all over Lucian's body. "Ouch! Ooh, ow!" Aaron could hear as Lucian slowly made his way through the thornbushes.

"Lucian! Did you make it? Are you ok?" Aaron called out.

"Yes, Aaron, I am! I'm a little scratched up but nothing that won't heal in time. Are you coming?" Lucian called back.

"Can you see the castle?" Aaron shouted.

"Yes! I can see it!" Lucian shouted back. "It's just up ahead! Aaron, I am going to finish the journey. You must decide when you are ready and if you will suffer for the king. But I will be waiting for you at the castle, Aaron. I promise! It's been a splendid journey with you, Aaron, but the adventure is only beginning. Farewell, Aaron!"

Aaron stood in front of the giant wall of thorns pacing back and forth.

"Ok, Aaron, what do we do?" he asked himself. He thought about how far he had come in his journey, and he thought about what a great friend Lucian had become and how much he would hate never seeing him again. Then he thought about his adoptive father, the giant turd, and how much he hated living in his house. And then he thought about the castle with all of its wonderful rooms and its magical powers.

Finally he thought of the king, and imagined hearing the king say to Aaron, "I love you." A bright smile formed across Aaron's face as he took a step into the great wall of thornbushes.

"Ok, Lucian. I'm coming," Aaron said as he finally positioned himself on the bed.

CHAPTER 12

"No, Mother. No, Mother! Of course, I'm worried! Yes, I did speak with him and he said it would never happen again. He knows things got out of hand and Adam can be a bit rambunctious, but he's sorry it happened. The doctor asked how it happened and I did tell them the truth, so they sent someone over to make sure the kids were happy and safe. And I told the boys, 'Make sure you tell her that you like living here and you don't want to live anywhere else,' and that's what they told her, and she left. No, he fixed the broken drywall before she came and painted over it so she couldn't see it.

"Well, no one is perfect, Mother. I know you've never made a mistake before, but I'm doing the best I can. No, he wasn't like this when I first met him. You met him, he was a perfect gentleman and treated the boys like they were his own. He practically begged me to marry him. And do you remember that you were the one who said I should? Yes, you did! You went on and on about his money and his cars and the great life he would provide us. Well, what am I supposed to do now? He doesn't give me any money so how am I supposed to leave him, and where am I supposed to go? Well, I don't know what he does with all his money. He doesn't tell me anything! No! I would never let my children live with you. I'm their mother, and they need me! Well, of course, you think they'd be better off with you, you just think you're so perfect!

"It is under control, Mother. Yes, Adam and Sally are happy. Thomas and Ruben? They're fine, mother. In fact, they are more than fine. They're doing incredible, and they take such great care of me. They see me when he yells at me and they tell me everything is going to be ok. They comfort me and tell me they love me. They are such perfect boys. No, Mother, it is perfectly normal for them to take care of me like that. Yes, Mother, they are perfectly happy in the home. I just need to make sure he knows he can't treat the boys like that anymore. That if it ever happens again, I'll leave him for good and never come back, even if it means living on the street. No, I wouldn't be proud, Mother. Yes, I know. You had such a perfect marriage. How could I, with my three failed marriages ever compare to you? You never loved me, did you? Just say it! Oh, that is so mean, Mother!

"Everything is going to be fine, Mother, I just need a little more money. Of course, I'll pay you back! Of course, it's for the children! Well, that is none of your business. I need some kind of life! No, it isn't that much. There are a few overdue bills, and Aaron has a party to go to this weekend and I need to pick him up a costume. He's fine, mother. Well, I don't know how he feels about it, but he's staying over at my in-laws this weekend. They take such great care of him and it's a great place for him to get away from his father. I know, Mother. I know, Mother. I KNOW, MOTHER! Are you going to give me the money or not? Or do you just like to tell me what a horrible daughter I am before you help me? Everything is going to work out and be fine. The kids will be fine, you'll see! And then you'll be sorry you ever doubted me. I am a good mother. Yes, I am and I'm not going to let you pick on me like that! I am a good mother, a better mother than you will ever be and someday you'll be sorry you ever treated me like this!"

Aaron watched his mother slam the telephone back on its base, bringing the conversation to a close. He was standing in the hallway and tried not to notice her pacing back and forth in the kitchen, fuming over the phone call. But he could hear her begin to cry and began smacking herself on the head.

"Stupid, Margaret! Stupid!"

Aaron tried not to breathe; he didn't want his mother to notice he was there, and he stood silently as she began to sob.

"They all think I'm so dumb! I'm not dumb!" she cried in between sobs, believing the house to be empty. Aaron slowly peeked into the kitchen again and saw his mother sitting at the kitchen table and whimpering into her hands.

"Stupid, Margaret! Stupid!" She pulled her hands off her face and Aaron saw the tears smear her eye liner and mascara down her face.

"Is that you, Aaron?" she called out as she spotted him in the hallway. "Get over here!" she demanded, and Aaron walked over to her side with a guilty look on his face.

"Is this your plate?" she asked.

"Yes, Mom," he said with his head down.

"Well, why the hell didn't you put it in the dish washer?" she asked.

"I don't know Mom I—"

"And is that your schoolwork on the table? And your clothes in the family room? And your action figure under the desk?"

"Yes, Mom," he replied with a whisper.

"Why can't you just clean up after yourself? And why can't you just be good at school? And why can't you get along with your father? And why can't you forget about Darold? And why can't you just do as you're told? And why can't you help me get more money from your father? And why can't you stop being so god-damned difficult?" she ranted as she stared down at him, pointing her finger in his face.

"I'm so sorry, Mom I—"

"I just can't take it anymore!" she screamed as she stomped her feet and banged her hands on the countertop.

Aaron dropped his head in shame and proceeded to leave the kitchen when his mother grabbed his hand.

"Wait," she said as she sniffled. "You know I don't mean it. You know I'd die without you boys. I'm just a little tired, that's all."

"Ok, Mom," Aaron replied heading back to the hallway feeling even guiltier than before. He watched his mother wipe her eyes and head into the living room.

Aaron continued watching her from the hallway to make sure his mother was ok. She paced back and forth while puffing on the cigarette when something caught her eye. It was a drawing Aaron's adoptive grandfather had created for her, of all five of her children, smiling and happy. Ash from the cigarette fell to the ground but Margaret was staring so intently into the sparkling eyes of all her children that she didn't notice. A smile formed on her face as she murmured, "Everything is going to be ok, Margaret. Everything is going to be ok."

Aaron watched from the corner of the hallway as she took another puff from her cigarette. "You did the right thing, Margaret. Everything is going to be ok." Aaron could see the drawing from the corner of his eye and he wondered when was the last time he and all his siblings had smiled together at the same time. But Margaret's smile grew wider as she stared intently at her father-in-law's fantasy image.

She laughed to herself and kissed her hand and smudged it on the glass over the drawing of Aaron.

"You're going to be just fine, Aaron. You're going to be just fine."

Aaron watched the scene from the hallway and could tell she was so focused on the drawing that she had completely drowned out her surroundings. "It's all going to be ok," she told herself, unaware of the front door creaking open.

She was so entranced by the image of her fake children that she didn't hear the keratin and bone scrape against the ceiling. She couldn't feel the heat rise in the room nor did she pay any attention to the billows of smoke forming. His mom failed to smell the aroma of burning sulfur and couldn't hear the flapping of wings or feel the rushing of the wind in the room. She was so desperate to believe the drawing that she failed to see the footprints on the ceiling leading to Aaron's room and the blood-red eyes of the great beast glaring at her in the reflection of the glass frame, preparing to consume her family whole.

CHAPTER 13

The day had finally come, that glorious day that Aaron was promised would be the best of his young life. It was the day of the celebration and Aaron found himself in the backseat of his adoptive grandfather's car imagining himself being carted in a regal horse-drawn carriage for the last leg of his journey. He had proven himself to be both brave and heroic and was worthy of the king's love and to stay within the walls of his castle forever.

Aaron stared at the moonlight through the window, his face adorned with the purest of smiles. He had no way of knowing what time it was, but he was tired, and it had to be well past his normal bedtime. He was wearing a costume and a mask unlike he had ever seen before. He knew all his fantasies were coming true and that he was on his way to a royal masquerade, thrown as a surprise for the king, who was waiting for Aaron impatiently.

"This must be the darkness of nights," Aaron thought to himself, uncertain if he were still on earth or if he had already ascended to paradise. He could have sworn he saw the dwarfs on the corner of the street selling the gold and precious metals they mined.

He looked out of the car window to his right and the mermaids and mermen caught his eye and greeted him ever so warmly and kindly.

"Hello Aaron! You are finally on your way to meet the king, are you? I think you will find he is unlike anything you've ever encountered before. He'll make an impression on you, that's for sure, one you'll never forget!"

And he could see Wolfy flying in unison with the motion of the vehicle, smiling and smirking at him. "It has all come to this, my dear boy. You are ready for your transformation and we are all so very excited for you to join us forever! It will sting just a little, but what happens next will be worth it."

"Ok thanks, Wolfy!" Aaron responded.

"Who are you talking to, son?" Someone asked him, interrupting his trance-like gaze, snapping his attention back to the moonlight. He could no longer see the dwarves, mermaids, mermen, or Wolfy, but the brightness of the moonlight assured him they were out there, somewhere, cheering Aaron on and excited for the unknown escapades that were on the immediate horizon. Everything was about to change. He knew it, he could feel it deep in his bones.

The vehicle came to a slow stop and parked in some unknown location. Lights from inside the house sparkled so brightly. This had to be the golden castle! He could see the golden bricks and the clear crystal beneath his feet. The lights in the house seemed to transform the entire space into the magical realm he always hoped, always knew existed. And someone grabbed him by the hand and ushered him towards the entrance where Lucian was waiting for him.

"Aaron, you made it! Oh, I knew you would!" Lucian cheered.

"Thank you for believing in me, Lucian. All my dreams are coming true, and it's all because of you," Aaron responded with gratitude.

"Aaron, my true friend, this is only the beginning," Lucian told him with a smile. "Now, go and celebrate, the king is waiting for you inside."

"Aaron, did you hear me? I've got some friends I'd like you to meet inside," his adoptive grandfather told him. Aaron looked at him with a dreamy smile and followed behind.

The door opened and he was ushered inside into a room full of smiling people. "Hello little man, aren't we excited to see you!" Aaron just smiled at the nice lady in red, wearing some strange mask he had never seen before. And the kind lady gave him a pill which, she assured him, would make the night so much better and Aaron trusted the beautiful woman in red. He took in the scenery around him, and his senses began to overwhelm him, and he could sense that he was about to get completely lost in his imagination, or perhaps his imagination was about to come to life, but he knew this place would transform him, bring him to life, and reveal the incredible plans this world had for him. At that moment he no longer felt like a filthy throwaway. He didn't feel the pain of being abandoned, of being belittled, bullied, and blamed for all his adoptive father's problems. He was evolving, transforming, and there was nothing his adoptive father could do about it.

He was standing in the foyer of the golden castle, and the guests casually strolled past him with smiles. It seemed they all were so glad he was there. Someone wanted him and had a plan and a future for him! Aaron's face beamed with the brightest of smiles as he was led by the hand past the foyer and into another room. Suddenly this new room, along with a whole new world, opened up before him and he knew his adoptive grandfather was telling the truth. His senses were completely overwhelmed as he saw the masses of naked bodies all around him, wearing masks, and rubbing up against each other with intensity and eagerness. He looked to his left, to the right, ahead of him and behind him and it seemed as if the room was filled with nakedness and decadence.

Everyone seemed to be enjoying themselves in the ways that Aaron's adoptive grandfather helped him become familiar with. This must be what heaven was like. Amidst the guests he could also see other children dressed very much like he was, being led around by the guests by a collar and his brain exploded with the possibilities. This was all so new to him and he found the room transforming into a giant hall with marble floors, stone pillars, and the most exquisite masks. Oh, the masks! He would never forget how ornate, mysterious, and mystical they all appeared to be. And he looked at his own outfit and realized he was wearing the brightest of white robes and he just knew this was the princely garb that he was meant to wear.

It was all too much for Aaron. He couldn't really tell fully what was happening, where he was, and where he was headed, but he felt as if he were floating past the room and towards a door near the far side of the room. He felt he must be a ghost, for he was moving but couldn't feel his footsteps. He continued to creep towards the door and past all the naked bodies who were groping Aaron, grabbing at him and giving him the warmest of smiles. "This is love," he told himself.

He was drawing closer to the door and could see all the children standing outside the door as if they were waiting in line to meet someone. *The king!* They were all on their way to meet the king, who would welcome all these lovely children into his kingdom and bestow upon them the adoption they all so eagerly craved. One by one the children walked into this other room and Aaron's excitement and hope continued to build, and build until he felt as if he were about to pass out. He was now standing behind one other child and Aaron hoped he would make a good impression, would be as polite and kind as he was taught to be.

He was now just outside the door and Aaron was so eager to see what was on the other side and his imagination began to completely consume him. Finally, the door to paradise opened and he was immediately overwhelmed by the brightness of the room. Whatever was in the room was too much for Aaron to understand, and his eyes needed some adjusting to take in paradise. He closed his eyes for a moment, and then another moment, for it was all too good to be true. And as he opened his eyes, he found himself in the most majestic, opulent, and glorious hallway he could imagine. On either side were servants bearing arms in honor and protection of the king who was seated on his throne at the end of the hallway. They held swords and knives and whips and other cutting devices and Aaron looked into their eyes and could sense their eagerness to use the instruments they held.

Aaron felt like he truly belonged, for he was wearing his princely garb and he finally caught the gaze of the king, seated on his throne and smiling at Aaron as if he had been waiting for Aaron all these years. And the king was emanating the most beautiful light which filled the entire hallway, and everyone was basking in the king's aura. He wore a crown embellished with radiant gems of all colors, and a deep purple cloak with symbols and letters Aaron wasn't familiar with. And mixed amongst the symbols and letters were more gems of the most beautiful blues, purples, greens, and brilliant reds that proclaimed the king's perfection. This was Aaron's father, the light of the world, who would awaken the eternal light of divinity and sonship within Aaron's soul.

The king was the most beautiful man Aaron had ever seen and he found himself struggling to hold back the tears. It was all worth it: the fear, pain, humiliation, abandonment, bullying, belittling and berating, and the years upon years of making his adoptive grandparents happy. None of that mattered anymore, and he wouldn't have changed a thing, for it had all brought him to this magnificent moment basking in the light of the eternal sun. Aaron was positively jubilant when the king raised his hand and ushered him near him with a wave of his hand. And Aaron, with the widest of smiles, was all too eager to meet him. Aaron had finally reached the king, reached his father who was eager to afford him the right of adoption. The king stood up from his throne to greet him and he grabbed Aaron by the hand and led him to another room behind the hallway, and as he was swept into the room all the servants with their swords, knives, whips, and other cutting devices followed behind.

Aaron found himself in another room but was unsure of what the surroundings were. There seemed to be a row of beds where he thought he saw children sleeping, but he was so enraptured by the king and his gaze that the whole world melted around him. Nothing else mattered and whatever was happening around him was of no importance, for he was now orbiting around his new life and world: the king.

The king stared deeply into Aaron's eyes with the warmest of smiles, "Are you ready my son?" and Aaron's heart just melted at the question, and with the eagerness of a puppy he smiled at the king and nodded at fast as he could.

"Look deep into my eyes," the king ordered Aaron, who was still unsure of what was happening around him but could sense something happening to his hands and feet and neck and he was unsure if he was standing or lying. It was a violent feeling, but he didn't care in the least, for he was staring deeply into the eyes of his father, the father who'd always wanted him, would never leave him, and would initiate him into a new and exciting world within the golden castle.

Aaron could feel the searing pain around his wrists, his ankles, his neck. Something was burning him, deep into his skin, but he continued to stare into his father's eyes as he spoke to Aaron saying, "Prepare to be consumed by the devourer," and after his father finished the sentence his eyes exploded in color, the most beautiful reds, yellows, and oranges and it was as if Aaron were staring directly at the sun.

Aaron could feel his body begin to shake as if he were having a seizure, and he decided to stop thinking and just let it happen. Aaron's face was getting closer and closer to the bright sun when he noticed the king's mouth slowly open. Farther, farther, farther until the king's mouth was wider than his face, and as his body continued to shake and burn and sear, Aaron could hear a buzzing sound growing from within the king's belly. The buzzing grew louder, louder, louder until out of the king's mouth shot out large hornets. They kept coming out by the hundreds, thousands even and Aaron could feel the pain of their stingers all over his body, deep piercing pain, but he was committed to keep his gaze on his father, the king, and not think about the pain.

The hornets kept coming, and coming and coming, and Aaron's body began to shake violently from the impact of the hornets and the stinging until he felt his whole body must be swollen from the stinging. The pain was almost completely consuming all his senses, and just as Aaron was about to pass out the king's mouth began to slowly close. Aaron's body, however, continued to shake violently in the searing pain of love and belonging.

The king smiled at Aaron and said, "Welcome to the fraternity of great mysteries," and Aaron felt as if there were an opening being carved into his chest cavity and what he believed to be hot molten lava began to spill out of the king's mouth and into Aaron's body and all over Aaron's body, scorching his skin. Aaron was so eager to please the king and prove to him that this is what he wanted that he just continued to stare at the king who was spewing molten lava onto his abdomen.

"This is for you, father," Aaron said to the king as he grimaced in pain and agony. He could feel the warm wetness of a thick liquid splatter all over his face and body but was determined to not cry out in pain.

Once the king was done spewing the molten lava the king took his hands, caressed Aaron's face passionately, and closed his eyes and Aaron finally passed out from the pain, the love, and the glory.

When Aaron opened his eyes again, he found himself back at his adoptive grandparents' house, lying in bed, and could tell he was in a great deal of pain. His whole body ached, and he struggled to move at all. He could also sense his face was a bit swollen and he had a horrible headache, so he just lay awake in bed, pondering what had happened yesterday and what it all meant. It was supposed to be one of the greatest nights of his life, but now all he could think of was the great deal of pain he was in. There was a glass of water on the bedstand next to him along with two pills that looked to be aspirin, which he gratefully took, drinking the entire glass of water as he felt his body had been completely depleted of liquids and was in much need of replenishment.

He thought of the previous night, or at least what he could remember of it. It was all a jumbled mess in his mind. As he tried to think about it his mind was overwhelmed with disjointed memories, feelings, and sensations, but the pain was still very real. Whatever had happened last night he wasn't completely sure, but he could feel it throughout his body. He glided his hand over his stomach and felt the lacerations and wounds.

I finally met the king, he thought. Indeed, he had finally met the king, and Aaron's eyes went wide and he felt his face go cold.

Adolescent Nightmares

CHAPTER 14

"Are you ok, Aaron?" Mrs. Schneider asked. Aaron had just limped into the classroom and now his teacher was staring at his face. The cuts there and his split lip were still sore. She pulled him aside before class started and looked down upon him in the hallway with worried eyes.

"I'm ok, Mrs. Schneider. I just fell into a large thorn bush," Aaron replied, repeating what his adoptive grandfather told him and his parents when he dropped him off at home on Saturday. But Mrs. Schneider wasn't buying it.

"Really? A large thorn bush?" Mrs. Schneider asked Aaron. "It's ok if you didn't. You can tell me the truth, Aaron. What happened?"

Aaron scratched his head and squinted his eyes, trying to remember what really happened. It was all so blurry, hazy, and confusing. He knew the long-awaited celebration had taken place this past weekend and he remembered meeting many different people, including a king. Thinking of the king made Aaron queasy but his adoptive grandfather assured him and his parents that Aaron had a great time, other than when he ran out back and got stuck in a dense thicket of thorn bushes. The whole night was a complete blur, and he didn't want to think about it.

"What happened?" she asked again. The question rang in his ears and he felt his fingers begin to tingle. The sound of static was growing, and his knees felt like buckling as a garbled mess of terrifying images flooded his mind. The walls began to warp, and Mrs. Schneider was changing colors and Aaron feared that he was on the verge of passing out. The question haunted Aaron and he wasn't sure he was ready for the answer. He closed his eyes and took a deep breath and slowly waited for the static to die down. His fingers finally stopped stinging and he looked up at Mrs. Schneider and told her what he wanted to be true. "I fell into a large thorn bush, Mrs. Schneider. I'm ok. I promise."

Mrs. Schneider looked at Aaron with a tinge of sadness in her eyes and patted his shoulder with care. "Ok, Aaron. If you say so, but if you ever want to talk, I am always available."

Mrs. Schneider gently ushered him back into her classroom where he took his seat and did his best to pay attention to the lesson. She was writing sentences on the board to help the children practice their reading.

"Ok class let's see how well we're practicing our study words," Mrs. Schneider said as she instructed each student to read aloud with her. "Altogether now, class. The cat is under the rug."

"The cat is under the rug," they all responded. "The cat is under the rug, the cat is under the rug, the cat is under the rug."

"Great job class!" Now I'm going to call on you individually to read the sentences on the chalkboard.

Aaron knew he'd be called on eventually, and he could feel himself begin to panic. He felt terrified of what would happen if he gave the wrong answer. He didn't know why, but he knew the wrong answer could mean something horrible, very, very horrible would happen to him. At that moment Aaron desperately wanted to disappear and find a way to leave the world completely, to play in the beautiful field of lilies with his brothers or explore the ancient ruins with the adventurers in their ship, but the students kept reciting their sentences and Aaron knew his turn was close at hand and he could feel his whole body paralyze in fear. Closer, closer, closer he felt the impending doom encroach. His turn was coming and he wasn't ready. His fingers began tingling again and his eyes grew wide and blinked uncontrollably as a warm liquid dispelled from his crotch and down his leg, and that is when everything began to change.

The classroom slowly began to fade away along with the students until it was just him and Mrs. Schneider. The room darkened and he could see a different world filling in the empty space, a world that seemed painfully familiar that he would prefer to wish away. Slowly, tall metal apparatuses materialized along with swords, knives, whips, and other cutting utensils. A slight tear fell from his eye as the room seemed to narrow and his jaw dropped as Mrs. Schneider's gaze fell upon Aaron. Time stood still and everything seemed to be happening in slow motion. He could tell Mrs. Schneider was speaking to him, but it all seemed jumbled at first.

"The wing is singing the flood, the wing is singing the flood." It made no sense to Aaron and he wasn't sure what was going on, but he could see the lights in her eyes brighten tenfold, and illuminated the room in horrifying reds, oranges, and yellows. Blood began to spill from the sides of her mouth and down her blouse as she drew closer to him. Her voice slowly changed from light and whimsical to a deep baritone as his practice words came into full clarity, "The king is drinking your blood! Did you hear me, Aaron, the king is drinking your blood!"

It was all too much for Aaron to take in. He was unsure of where he was, who he was and why he was, but he was most certainly there, whether he liked it or not, and Mrs. Schneider's gaze was still steadfast on him and she was walking in his direction. By now Aaron had completely emptied his bowels and was unable to wish himself into some other world, and so the teacher continued to encroach on him, drawing ever so closer to him with the blood now pouring down her lips and covering her entire outfit. She was now hovering directly over him and the strangest, most terrifying thing happened. As she began talking her head rotated 360 degrees and was transforming before his very eyes.

The sight was too much to bear so he closed his eyes as he feared what Mrs. Schneider was transforming into. His body began to tremble as thought of what she might do to him and how much it would hurt.

"Did you hear me, Aaron? The king is drinking your blood." Aaron gripped his chair tightly and winced at the words. He knew she was hovering over him and he was unsure what to do or where to go. He took a deep breath and told himself that when he opened his eyes everything would be ok, and he would find himself seated back in Mrs. Schneider's class. But when he opened his eyes, Mrs. Schneider's was face now gone, and in its place was the beautiful and brilliant face of the king who had initiated him into the fraternity of great mysteries, adopted him as a son, and devoured his soul. The king's hand slowly raised towards Aaron's face, eyes radiating a blinding light, blood pouring from his mouth. Somewhere behind children were chained to the tall metal beds. The king finally brought his hand to Aaron's face, gently caressing him, but the pain, the love, and the glory were all too much, and Aaron passed out.

Aaron could tell he was now lying on the ground and slowly opened his eyes to see the concerned and alarmed look on Mrs. Schneider's face, caressing his head hoping Aaron would come to. "Are you sure you're ok, Aaron?"

CHAPTER 15

"Aaron. Aaron. Aaron, did you hear me, honey?" Aaron lay on the living room couch doing his best to ignore his mother. He laid as still as could be, still in recovery from all the bruises and scrapes that riddled his torso and upper body. He could hear someone calling his name but couldn't quite make out the voice. He was focused so attentively on the ceiling doing his best to not think, to not even blink, for every time he closed his eyes, he was assaulted with terrifying images that made his fingers tingle. It was like an alarm going off inside his head, like a police siren flashing garbled images of what had happened that night Aaron met the king. He couldn't blink, couldn't close his eyes no less fall asleep at night. For every time he closed his eyes he was there, dripping in blood and terror. Night after night the siren flashed, and Aaron did everything he could to block out the glimpses of truth. The alarm was sounding in his head. Something horrible had happened to him, and it was up to Aaron to accept the truth and tell someone. But Aaron didn't want the truth, not at all. He wanted nothing more than to block out everything that happened that night and pretend it never happened. He focused intently on the ceiling to forget he had ever met Lucian, ever visited the golden castle, met the king and somehow managed to screw everything up.

"Why am I here?" Aaron asked aloud, having expected to be living in the golden castle by now. He had passed all the tests and followed Lucian closely down the secret path and so was both confused and sad that he must have done something wrong after all. For here he was, still in his home, riddled with scrapes and bones aching, unsure of what to make of the images flashing in his head. He couldn't explain what happened at school: the horrifying vision of the king in his classroom, and what he wanted from Aaron. Something was wrong. He couldn't quite put his finger on it, but something felt terribly wrong. He had no place to hide, nowhere he could run from the king or the horrible images flashing in his head. The king's words were etched into his memory, "Prepare to be consumed by the devourer," and they sent chills down Aaron's spine.

Aaron could feel the king's presence everywhere he went, like a thick, black cloud hovering over him. And he felt that the whole world must be laughing at him for thinking he was really a prince who deserved to live within a golden castle and be loved by a great king. They were all laughing at him, mocking him, and deriding him; the dwarfs and mermaids and mermen, the adventurers, winged creatures, and all the fantastical and wondrous things a boy could imagine. No, paradise was not waiting for Aaron, only the horrific images haunting him in his head and the impulsive urge to scream at the top of his lungs.

"Aaron, did you hear me, honey? He's going to be here any minute and you better get ready."

Aaron continued to ignore his mother, wishing he were somewhere else. He watched a footprint indent on the ceiling. And then there was another. And then there was a handprint accompanied by another handprint. Finally, he saw a smiling face in the ceiling staring down at him and the colors began changing.

"We had so much fun with you, Aaron!" the walls began to warp, and the smiling face was pushing closer to Aaron. "We look forward to seeing you again real soon!" The colors began changing dramatically and the ceiling was now littered with handprints pressing down from the ceiling, reaching towards Aaron and his eyes began blinking uncontrollably. "Aaron. Come play with us, Aaron," they called out to him, reaching further in his direction. The colors became darker, and Aaron began to whimper as the ceiling was closing in on him and the smiling faces started screaming at him.

"Aaron! Your grandfather is here, honey." Margaret shook Aaron out of his trance and Aaron abruptly stood up, grabbed his jacket and bolted out the front door.

"If it's ok with you, Aaron, I think we'll get some ice cream and watch a few movies tonight. What do you think?"

Aaron looked nervously out the window of his adoptive grandfather's car watching the power lines go by. "Whatever."

His adoptive grandfather looked at Aaron and chuckled, "Oh, don't be like that Aaron! It wasn't that bad. Trust me, you had a lot of fun. And you made a lot of new friends. It was such a late night, but you really did have a great time."

Aaron continued to stare mindlessly out the window doing his best to not blink, wondering when he would see the ice cream parlor, and he realized that when he should have been looking at a mini-mall or small ice cream store, he saw the car roll into the driveway of some unknown home.

"What's happening? What are we doing?"

"Oh, don't worry Aaron. We'll be getting ice cream. All in good time. But we made some new friends from the celebration who wanted us to say hello. Won't you come in with me?" Aaron's hands began to tremble knowing what his adoptive grandfather's friends were capable of. If only he could run away. He took notice of the home and the neighborhood and wondered if he could perhaps flee, but he'd never been here before. Where was it and how would he get home anyway? He felt like an absolute prisoner, duped again. He was so stupid for ever believing the man in the first place.

Aaron didn't move but his door was opened and his seatbelt unfastened. Then he was taken by the hand towards the house which now glinted of gold and was forced into the majestic doorway. Aaron could feel the bile rise in his gut and he felt as if he were sleepwalking or daydreaming, refusing to accept this was, in fact, reality. Aaron was trembling as he was ushered through the door and they were greeted by a large, bulging man whose mere presence made Aaron dry heave. Aaron knew him. He'd been at the party, the night Aaron met the king, and he had to bite down on his lip to keep the bile from escaping his gut. Yes, his face was very familiar. Aaron thought back on the party and remembered the incredible violence and viciousness this man was capable of and died inside as the flashing sirens pounded through his skull.

Aaron's adoptive grandfather grabbed Aaron by the hand and led him to a green couch in the living room. Aaron sat in silent trepidation doing his best to quiet the alarms that were telling him to run, to get out of the house as fast as he could. His heart was beating through his chest and he could feel the perspiration in his armpits as if his body were preparing itself for what was to come. He could hear talking in the kitchen just adjacent to where he was sitting but wasn't quite sure what they were saying. He didn't want to hear what they were saying as he was doing his best to slip out of his body and find himself in some other world, any other world.

The talking between the two men continued and Aaron sat on the couch, frozen in fear and listening to the alarm go off in his head. "Get out, Aaron. Get out, Aaron. GET OUT, AARON!" he told himself as the alarm grew louder in his head and the imagery became more lucid and intrusive. He had to act quickly before it was too late. "GET OUT, AARON!" he told himself again. He gripped the cushion beneath him with a death grip as he tried to muster up the strength to flee. He took a deep breath in preparation for leaving this horrible place when he heard a flurry of footsteps. He was no longer alone. The moment was now gone, and all hope was lost. Aaron watched someone give his adoptive grandfather a wad of money and then Aaron was approached by the big bulging man. He sat next to Aaron on the green couch. It was the man from the party. The bulging man stared at Aaron with cold, menacing eyes as if he were very much looking forward to doing horrible things to him. As the bulging man leaned in closer to Aaron the events from the party began spilling out into his mind. The sirens blared and it became clear to him now why his body was riddled with cuts and why he was so sore. The truth flashed before his eyes and Aaron was helpless to suppress it. Visions of screaming children being raped and tortured flooded his senses, and buckets of their blood were being gathered for a ceremony. He realized the night he met the king was worse than he could have possibly imagined, what they had done to him and all the other poor little children, and it was happening all over again.

The man told Aaron to call him the Dungeon Master and informed him that he would be his slave for the evening. He leaned in close. "I'm going to tell you right now, boy, that there are some serious people down there, and if you don't do as you're told, we will kill you. This isn't a game, you hear me?"

Aaron could smell the mix of nicotine and boiled sausage on his breath and became nauseated to the point of vomiting. He felt the walls closing in on him and he began to suffocate under the weight of the words. The magnitude of the immediate horizon completely blocked out the sun and left Aaron in complete and utter darkness. He was alone, utterly alone and he knew that there was no special purpose of it all.

"I'm going to tell you right now. They are going to hurt you. You will be in a world of pain, and you are not going to like it. Not at all. But if you fight it, they will hurt you even more. Did you hear me? You're my slave now, and if you don't listen to me, I will kill you. Go on, now, boy. They're waiting for you downstairs."

Aaron noticed the camcorder at his side and realized he was starring in a nightmare where unspeakable things were soon to be done to him. There was no use in fighting, so Aaron slowly got up and walked towards the kitchen and past the kitchen and to the left was a staircase leading to the basement where his future lay ahead.

He could hear the music and see the candlelight and he slowly descended into the Dungeon Master's dungeon, his sacred world, his royal kingdom. With each step he took he felt his heart beat even louder, wishing to expel itself from Aaron's body and be saved of the upcoming pain. He felt lightheaded, and he knew he was about to pass out, but remembering the Dungeon Master's words he forced himself to stay in the moment, step by step, further towards the dungeon, into the deep, dark abyss. The Dungeon Master was behind him, leaving Aaron no escape and no choice but to descend to the very bottom, and he should have been ready, but he was still caught off guard by the five half-naked men wearing masks waiting in the basement. They were all facing each other around a circle drawn on the floor with a familiar symbol inside. Aaron knew he had seen it before. It was the symbol on Lucian's forehead, and it made his skin crawl.

The men wearing masks continued chanting with the loud music in the background and Aaron took in his surroundings. Aaron looked at the cinderblocks on the dungeon walls and the concrete floors and the symbol on the floor. There was a small table in the far-left corner with candlesticks and little figurines and incense and a large chalice. It was very strange to Aaron, but what concerned him more was the filthy mattress to the far right of the basement and even more troubling was the chain around the nearby pole and the makeshift collar at the end of the chain. And next to the mattress hanging on the cinderblock wall was some strange apparatus that Aaron thought must be for gutting a deer or some other animal. Aaron remembered this apparatus, remembered seeing it before, and as the men continued their ceremony, he allowed the explosion of memories and sensations to assault him, reminding Aaron of where he had seen that apparatus before.

He stood there, staring at the instrument of death and dismemberment, and barely noticed the hand on his shoulder pulling his shirt over his head. Nor did he notice the tugging of his pants or socks off. It was beginning, the reason he was here, the very reason he was born. They put a blindfold on him and put him in the circle. He was told to approach the voice he heard and every time he reached the voice a man would start praying aloud. After the man was done praying, he took off Aaron's blindfold, wrapped his hands around his neck and squeezed until Aaron's face burned, telling Aaron he would kill him if he didn't call him master and kiss the large protrusion bulging out of his pants. So, Aaron called him master and kissed him while he pulled Aaron's hair. The man put the blindfold back on Aaron and directed him to his next master whom he kissed and was strangled by as he knelt on Lucian's symbol on the concrete floor.

After the ritual was completed the Dungeon Master grabbed Aaron by his hair and walked his naked body over to the filthy mattress in the corner of the basement. The Dungeon Master threw Aaron on the mattress and ordered Aaron to put the collar around his neck. Aaron curled up into a ball and began sobbing in fear and disgust, wishing he were somewhere else, anywhere else.

"Shut up! Shut up and do as your told!" the Dungeon Master screamed as he stood over Aaron. The Dungeon Master held a rubber hose in his right hand and with a smile on his face began whipping Aaron, littering his body with red welts.

Aaron screamed in pain and tears streaked down his face. "Someone, please help! Don't do this to me! Please!"

The Dungeon Master smiled at Aaron, as if that was the response he was looking for and assured Aaron that no one was coming.

The Dungeon Master whipped Aaron with the rubber hose a few more times and Aaron finally grabbed the collar and placed it around his neck and took his place on the filthy mattress.

"Men of the secret path, my dear brothers, your king has watched over you on your journey to this sacred circle and has noticed your sacrifices. And now, he celebrates with you for joining him in the circle of the gods, the fraternity of great mysteries, and has given you this slave to do with what you will. Feast on his flesh, my brothers. Taste and eat!" the Dungeon Master cried.

The men all went upstairs as Aaron's adoptive grandfather took a seat on a chair next to the mattress, in deep conversation with the Dungeon Master. Aaron could see his adoptive grandfather's shoes on the floor next to him.

Aaron gazed ever so intently at the shoes, feeling that as long as he could see his adoptive grandfather's shoes, he could get through this and everything would be alright.

"It's time for you to leave. Come back in a few hours when we are done."

"But that's not what we agreed upon. What if I come back and he is gone or dead? How can I be assured you won't kill him?"

"We will pay you double. Half now and half when you come back."

"Make it triple," his adoptive grandfather said.

"Fine, just get out of here." Aaron couldn't believe what he was hearing. He couldn't imagine his adoptive grandfather would leave him all alone. But the Dungeon Master gave his adoptive grandfather a larger wad of money and to Aaron's horrible surprise he saw his adoptive grandfather rise from the chair and walk towards the stairs and out the front door. He just lay there, on his stomach, mouth completely agape in utter shock over what was happening.

Aaron kept waiting for the moment where he would separate from it all and find himself off in some magical world where he was safe and free, but it wasn't happening. Instead he could see the first man enter the basement encroaching ever closer to him. All hope was lost for Aaron, all beauty, purpose, and joy in this world were gone and he was left with nothing but the realization that he was about to be raped by five large grown men and no one could help him.

One by one they came down and Aaron was helpless as they did what they willed upon Aaron, fulfilling all their most insidious desires.

"Please, somebody help me! Somebody, anybody, please help me!" he screamed as each man, one after another had their time alone with Aaron. But no one came. He would not be saved from the situation. He could feel the sweat dripping from each and every one of them and smell the horrible body odor as they smushed into him. The fifth man finally made his way to the mattress and Aaron did his best to not look into his eyes for the look of pleasure and satisfaction was too much to bear. He found himself staring off into the distance when he noticed someone he hadn't seen before. A woman. It seemed like she'd appeared out of thin air as if revealing herself to Aaron. No one else seemed to notice her presence, no one acknowledged this woman in the corner of the basement, but she was the only thing Aaron could find the courage to look at and so he soaked in the image of this beautiful woman in the corner of the room crying, sobbing, distraught and refusing to be comforted. She had beautiful blonde hair and wore garments of white and blue and tears were running down her cheeks. Aaron drunk her in, and as his innocence continued to be devoured, she kept weeping, crying, sobbing. She was on her knees for it seemed she didn't have the strength to stand. She was so distraught, so overcome with emotion and she could barely move. And she kept crying until her tears soaked her garments.

Then Aaron noticed she was carrying a small animal in her arms, rocking and nursing this poor little animal as if it were her own child. And Aaron realized what she was holding was a lamb and the lamb had a fatal wound coming from his side and his blood was spilling all over the floor and soaking the woman's garments. The woman buried her head into the poor little lamb smearing blood on her face, and cheeks and lips. The men kept devouring and the woman kept weeping over this poor little lamb, face pressed deep into the animal's side while the poor animal's blood continued to spill. Finally, the woman caught Aaron's gaze as she continued to weep. She was so distraught she could barely look at him. It was as if she was completely horrified at what was happening to him and could barely acknowledge the cruelty of the moment, barely acknowledge this poor little lamb that was being slaughtered for the sake of the king, his servants, and their unending desire to destroy innocence.

Aaron kept staring at this beautiful woman, whose face and garments were smeared with tears and blood. Each time she looked at him the moment seemed too much for her to bear and she turned her head away, pressed it back deep into the side of the lamb. Then the woman finally found the strength and conviction to hold her gaze upon Aaron for more than a moment and she spoke.

"He will come for you, I swear it. He will carry you through hell and dance with you in purity. You will stare deeply into his beautiful blue eyes and know that He loves you." The words were a great comfort to Aaron, and he gave her a slight smile in recognition and gratitude, but just as quickly as she came, she was gone, and he was alone again in the dungeon.

When the fifth man finally excited the basement Aaron found himself alone with the Dungeon Master. Aaron grabbed at his collar, but the Dungeon Master barked at Aaron to leave it on.

Aaron was exhausted. "Please, can I please go home? It's over, I did everything you asked. Please."

But the Dungeon Master grabbed Aaron by the throat. "It is over when I say it is over!"

He sat on top of Aaron with a large blade in his hand and slowly cut him open from his chest to his belly button and the Dungeon Master then began licking Aaron's blood as it trickled down his stomach and soaked into the mattress. He then forced Aaron onto his belly and put all his weight and force into Aaron's tiny little frame and Aaron screamed for merc.,

"It hurts, it hurts! It's too much! Please stop!"

The Dungeon Master only chuckled was emboldened further. "Good! Cry, slave! Cry!"

And with that, the agony continued. Aaron was sure he was half dead and could feel the blood being spilled from him. The man was suffocating Aaron and taking great pleasure in every ounce of pain being inflicted. Aaron felt a final giant thrust into his backside followed by a great shout of victory and finally, the man withdrew.

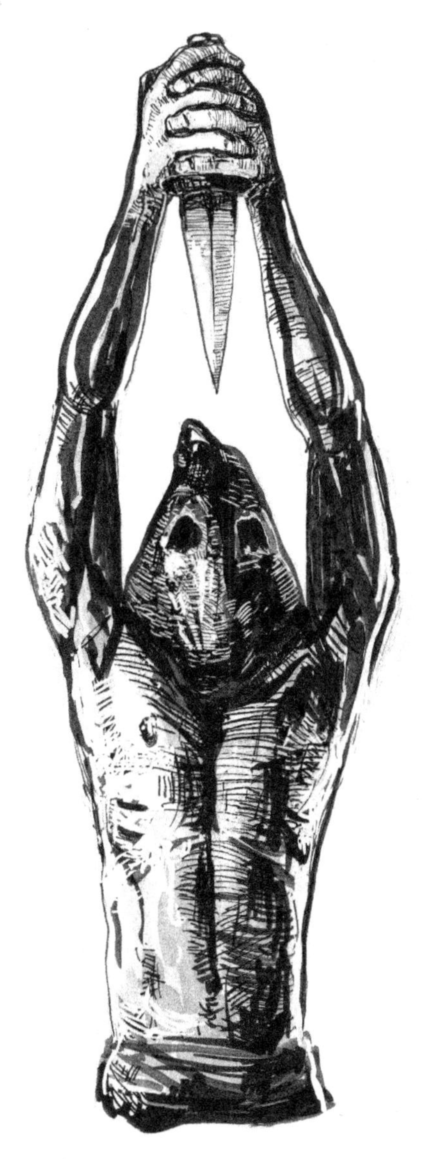

The Dungeon Master left Aaron in the basement, a bloody and slippery mess lying half-dead on the filthy mattress, and Aaron felt as if he were about to slip into a coma. His eyes slowly shut. He was ready to accept everything; he would forever be a member of this horrible kingdom and the king would torture him for the rest of his life. But before he could close his eyes completely, he noticed something in the corner of the room, someone he hadn't noticed before. Aaron was completely out of strength, exhausted, and had very little will to live, but something seemed to be happening in the corner of the room and so Aaron found the strength to cast his gaze in that direction, and what he saw startled him.

There, in the corner of the room, very much near where he'd found the beautiful woman, sat a man, head buried deep into his thighs and his hands covering his head. And Aaron paid attention to this man, whose body seemed to be shaking violently, almost as if he were having a seizure. Aaron fixed his gaze upon this man as he shook violently and sobbed in the corner of the room. He was wearing the brightest garments of white with a beautiful golden belt around his waist, and he howled like a mad man and moaned like a wounded and dying animal and his tears soaked into his clothes.

"Father! Father!" the man called out. "The deceiver and his deceptions!" and Aaron watched as the man tore open his tunic in agony, howling all the while, pounding his fists into the concrete and banging his head until it bled.

Aaron had never seen such a commotion before, had never seen anyone mourn so intensely, so passionately and with such great conviction and Aaron wondered what was the matter with the poor man. Aaron just watched as this man tortured himself, agonizing over something that must be very important to the man. Something must have been stolen from him or something horrible must have happened to someone he loved dearly and he would not be comforted or consoled. Aaron had never seen such anguish, such self-inflicted pain, and felt sorry for the poor man with the torn tunic and tear-soaked clothes, and Aaron could see the snot and spittle coming from his mouth and soaking up his face from all the sobbing.

Aaron just lay there a sweaty and bloody mess, taking in this most unusual scene wondering what could have been so horrible, so unbelievably painful that would cause this man to punish himself in such great agony. And as Aaron continued to stare the man finally cast a gaze Aaron's way, and their eyes locked briefly. The man was so distraught he could barely look at Aaron. There was a look of deep shame and sadness in the man's eyes, and he had to cover his face again and buried his head deep into his tunic. Aaron was starting to think that perhaps this man was agonizing over him, that these tears, the wailing, the moaning, the pounding of his fist, and the tearing of his tunic was because of Aaron, of where Aaron was and what had happened to him. Aaron almost felt sorry for the man because his anguish was so deep and pure.

Aaron was mesmerized by the man and soaked in the moment of this incredible person who was so worked up about his pain, his torture, and his abuse. The man finally found the strength to lock his eyes upon Aaron's, and with a look of great sadness, he stared directly into Aaron's soul.

"I will come for you, I swear it. I will carry you through hell, and we will dance in purity. When you stare deeply in my blue eyes you will know that I love you." For the first time in a while, a smile crossed Aaron's lips, in wonder and amazement of who this incredible man was who seemed to care more passionately for someone than he ever thought possible. A tear fell from Aaron's eye and he found that he was crying with the man, together, and for a moment he didn't feel all alone in the world. And just as quickly he appeared the man was gone, and Aaron passed out from exhaustion.

When Aaron came to he found himself back in the car, groggy and sore, and headed towards the ice cream shop that was originally promised to him.

"Well, Aaron, I believe you deserve some ice cream."

But Aaron didn't feel like ice cream, didn't feel like existing in this world anymore, and as he thought of the beautiful woman caressing the lamb and the man in the basement with him, he found himself opening his mouth and saying, "Take me home."

"But we haven't gotten the ice cream yet, Aaron. And afterward, I thought we could watch a few movies together."

Aaron didn't look at the man, could barely acknowledge the man, and stared out the window at the people passing by, wondering if anyone else had ever been chained naked to a filthy mattress before, had ever been sacrificed to the filthy pleasures of men. He wasn't so sure how normal all this was or not, but for the first time in his life, he found the courage and the conviction to stand up for himself and put an end to this chapter of his life.

"Take me home. I'm done, with all of it, forever."

His adoptive grandfather didn't respond in words to Aaron's request, but he slowly turned the car around and redirected the vehicle towards Aaron's house. It was a slow, awkward ride home as Aaron could see the man transform from a loving grandfather into a disgusting demon before his very eyes; a demon who fed on the innocence of children and offered their bodies to the highest bidder. His true colors were coming out and Aaron was beginning to see the man for what he was and what he had allowed himself to become. It was a sad and terrifying realization, one Aaron really didn't want to think about. The vehicle finally pulled up to Aaron's house and parked in the driveway. Aaron unbuckled the seatbelt and reached for the door when his adoptive grandfather gently grabbed his wrist.

"Oh Aaron, you know what happens if you say anything, right?"

Aaron didn't want to think about it, didn't want to acknowledge it, and didn't want to see this man ever again. He was going to dream up a world where he had never met the man, never visited the golden castle nor met Lucian or the horrible king who had consumed Aaron that night. From that day on he would do his best to put all this behind him, and so he hopped out of the car and hobbled through the front door and the two would never meet again.

The man kept the car parked in the driveway for some time waiting to see if either of Aaron's parents would come out to confront him. After several minutes had passed a smile formed on his face. He was in the clear. His adoptive grandson wouldn't say anything. It would be their little secret and Aaron would do his best to forget what had happened that day and all the days prior. He reversed the car out of the driveway and slowly drove away as Aaron's house began to transform. The red bricks and white siding of the house began to slowly fade away and was replaced with beautiful golden bricks. The transformation started at the base of the house and slowly it seemed to be swallowed up completely, devoured by these beautiful golden bricks until it was completely gone and, in its place was a beautiful golden castle whose beauty could be seen from miles away. It was so captivating that it overshadowed the winged creature inside, hovering over Aaron's bed.

CHAPTER 16

"Are you sure you don't want to visit?" Margaret asked Aaron. His adoptive grandfather was on his way to pick up Sally.

"Yeah, Mom. I think I'll just stay home." Aaron was still recovering from their last outing. He was doing his best to forget he'd ever met the man and slowly his memories began to fade away. And in its place was building a growing anger against the world.

"Are you sure, honey? There really isn't anything to do at home."

His mother was practically pushing him out the door, trying to get rid of him. He barked back, "I said I don't want to go!"

"Well, fine then. Have it your way." Margaret stormed out of the kitchen and lit a cigarette on the back porch. Aaron watched her leave and his eye caught sight of his adoptive father watching television in the living room.

"It's all your fault," he said to himself. Aaron had always done his best to avoid the man, but today he was so angry and he couldn't help himself.

He continued to stare at him and said a little louder, "It's all your fault." Aaron's adoptive father turned his head towards Aaron and they locked eyes the way bulls lock horns.

"Something on your mind, Aaron?" he asked with an accusatory tone.

Aaron wore a deep scowl on his face and mumbled under his breath, "I hate it here."

"Better speak up, son," his adoptive father said, daring Aaron to provoke him.

Aaron spoke up a little louder, "I said, I hate it here."

"If you're going to say something then just say it!" his adoptive father yelled.

"I said I hate it here!" Aaron screamed at him, but he wasn't prepared for how quickly his adoptive father jumped out of his seat and sprinted towards the kitchen. Before he knew it Aaron was pinned against the kitchen wall and his adoptive father's face was mere inches away. He rolled up Aaron's collar around his fist and Aaron thought the man's head was about to explode.

"If you hate it here so much then why don't you go stay with Darold?" Aaron's eye twitched in anger as he bit his lip.

"Oh, what's that? It's because he doesn't want you? It's because he never wanted you and left you for another family?"

Aaron grabbed at his throat. "I hate you!"

Aaron's adoptive father threw Aaron to the ground and slapped him across the face, screaming back at Aaron. Aaron curled up into a ball as the man pummeled him until he was exhausted.

"If you hate it here so much," the man breathed heavily, "then there's the door. Go ahead, live on the streets." Aaron's shirt was balled up from his adoptive father grabbing his shirt and he couldn't help but think of killing the man.

"What's going on in there?" Margaret called out from the back porch.

"Your son is thinking about leaving here to live on the street, Margaret. How does that sound?"

"What?!" she called out.

"That's right. Your royal highness, the prince, thinks he deserves better than what I can offer him. I told him if he hates it here so much, he can get his ass out of here."

Margaret shuffled back inside the house to break the tension. "Now cut that out. Aaron isn't going to live on the street. Stop being so mean to him!" His adoptive father was still breathing heavily from the scuffle and Aaron sat on the living room floor, his hair was a mess and he had a large rug burn across his face.

"Aaron, are you ok? You know your father doesn't mean that."

Aaron didn't respond. He just looked at the floor wishing he could be somewhere else.

"It's not too late. You can still go visit your grandparents with Sally if you like."

The suggestion was too much, and Aaron got up abruptly and stormed upstairs into his bedroom. He slammed his door shut and laid down on his bed, thinking of all the horrible things he wanted to do to his adoptive father. He entertained every dark and evil thought that came to mind and a slight smile formed on his face as he imagined a world where he had the power to hurt his adoptive father. Hate was growing in his heart and consuming his thoughts and as it spilled over to prayers for his demise a pair of red, beady eyes formed in the darkness of Aaron's closet.

The eyes stared intently at Aaron as the boy brooded over the days' events on his bed. Those red, beady eyes had seen much in its existence. It saw unfolding since the dawn of time the created world, everything in it, and the order of the cosmos. It saw the creation of galaxies, the birth and death of stars, and the collision of celestial beings. It saw the expansion of the universe and atoms move faster than the speed of light. It saw mountains dive into the sea and the sea wither away into nothingness, and the reinvention of everything that ever was. And soon enough it would ensure that Aaron's life would fall apart and help him bring an end to his existence.

CHAPTER 17

Aaron rubbed his eyes as he headed to the bathroom. It was the middle of the night and he was yet to fall asleep. Something was eating him up inside and he decided to get a drink from the faucet to hopefully cool him down. He could hear the floorboards creak as he made his way down the hallway and he could hear his adoptive father snoring from his bedroom. Aaron opened his mouth wide with a big yawn and turned the handle to the bathroom door. He opened the door to the bathroom and was rattled to find Sally. She was standing on a stool, scissors in hand and chopping away at her hair.

"Sally, what are you doing?" Aaron asked with a startled look.

"I don't want to be pretty anymore, Aaron," she said with a look of determination in her eye. "I want to be ugly; I want to be dirty and filthy. I want to shave it all off. I want it all gone so they won't touch me ever again," she went on as she cut away more of her locks.

"Sally, don't do that! Your hair is so pretty, why would you want to get rid of it?"

Sally lowered the scissors from her hair and glared at Aaron, "Stop asking me so many questions, Aaron! Stop making me talk! They're going to find me, the demons, and they're going to pull out my tongue and rip out my eyeballs and eat them for dinner!" she screamed as she ran the blade of the scissors over her arms.

"Take it easy, Sally. It's all going to be ok," Aaron said.

"They're here, Aaron!" Sally said, staring at the bathroom door with wide eyes as she ran the scissors over her arm even harder, breaking the skin. "See what you've done, Aaron?! You've ruined it all!"

"Sally, calm down, no one's here, it's just me, Aaron!" he told Sally as he slowly walked towards her in an attempt to take the scissors from her hand.

Sally backed into the corner of the bathroom, behind the sink and began talking, "I didn't say anything, I promise! No, I didn't, I didn't, I swear!" she pleaded as she began to cry.

"Sally, it's just me, Aaron! It's ok, I promise!" he said as he went into comfort Sally who put her head into her knees, sitting behind the toilet. "Sally, it's me, Aaron!"

Sally slowly lifted her eyes and looked at Aaron with a mix of shock and terror. "No! Not again! Not again! Please! Daddy, get me out of here! Get me out of here! Get me out of here!" she cried as she continued slicing her arm with the scissors.

Aaron saw Sally's blood mix with her hair and the sight of her cutting herself in fear of the demons he couldn't see began tearing him apart.

Aaron felt the tears fall down his face and he rushed down the stairs and into the empty living room and fell to his knees.

I need to get out of here. Aaron began slamming his fists into his head. *I need to get out of here. I need to get out of here. I need to get out of this nightmare!* He continued slamming his fists against his head, hoping to force himself into unconsciousness, into a world away from this nightmare, at least for a little while. *Please, get me out of here!* he thought to himself as he quickened the pace of his self-harm. He continued the punches and the pain, doing whatever he needed to escape this nightmare that was forced upon him, a nightmare with no escape, no exit, and no intervention. And he kept slamming his fists into his head in desperation over and over and over again. He slammed his fists hoping the memories of the king would pour out, and he slammed his fists hoping the memories of his adoptive grandparents and all their friends would pour out, and he slammed his fists hoping to enter into a new world and never return to this horrible life that was fated to him. But after several minutes of work Aaron knew he didn't possess the strength to force himself into unconsciousness, hadn't the strength to fight back against the abuse, and there was nothing he could do about it.

The tears gushed out of his eyes as he curled up into a ball, accepting defeat, and began sobbing uncontrollably.

He curled himself into the tightest ball he could and sobbed and sobbed and sobbed and he lay there in the shadow cast by the winged creature that was hovering over him.

CHAPTER 18

aron knew something was coming, but he wasn't quite sure what. There was usually a sense of dread and despair about the house, but today it seemed particularly heavier than usual. He thought about his life, how it was fraught with unimaginable pain and hopelessness that he couldn't escape. Wherever he went, it followed him as if it were his life companion meant to guide and instruct him on the ways of the world. As much as Aaron disliked his company, the pain stuck to him as if it were his shadow. He found himself staring off into distant space trying to understand the overwhelming numbness that consumed his head and chest, and it was this numbness that seemed to be the cause of the constant morose and flat effect he wore all too well.

It was with this heaviness that Aaron waited for his mother in the kitchen. She had explained there was news to be shared, very important news. Whatever this important news could be Aaron wasn't sure, but he was bracing for the worse.

"Hi honey," Aaron's mother said as she stroked his back and joined him at the kitchen table. She had the dejected look of someone who had failed at something very important.

"Aaron, honey. We need to talk. It's about Sally," his mother told him.

Aaron's attention was distracted; he was staring out the window at the large oak tree in the backyard. He couldn't help but imagine what it would feel like to be a leaf on the branch, ready to fall at any moment, succumbing to the inevitable coldness of the season.

"You know how we had her see the doctor because of her sores?" his mother asked him. Aaron didn't respond as he thought about the lingering sores on his face and backside.

"Well, the doctor was concerned and thought she should see a therapist. And you know those trips your adoptive father had been taking with Sally? Well, they were trips to see the best therapists and psychologists in the area. Your adoptive father made sure Sally talked to them, for as long as she needed."

"Ok," Aaron responded as he thought about all the beatings and beratements the man had given him over the years.

"And based on what Sally told the therapists and psychologists they decided to get a social worker involved. And we told Sally, 'You need to tell them the truth, it's ok.'"

"Uh huh." Aaron recalled when his mother had told him to lie to the social worker who was sent to inspect the home after his adoptive father put Adam in hospital.

"So, the police eventually got involved and spoke with Sally," Aaron's mother said, her voice trailing off. "Honey, someone has been hurting Sally. And she is in a lot of pain, but we are going to do everything we can to help her. She's going to see all the specialists and get the very best care and no expense will be spared until our Sally is back to normal."

"That's great," Aaron said glumly as he stared at his hand-me-down shoes, socks, and pants.

"I just wanted you to know that she's going to be ok. We're going to do everything we can, and we need you to help Sally the best you can."

"Gotcha," Aaron responded, slowly dying inside.

"I'm glad we had this talk, Aaron. Do you have any questions or anything you want to say to me?" his mother asked as she got up from her chair. "Oh, nothing happened to you, did it, Aaron? While you are at your grandparent's house?" she asked with one foot out of the kitchen.

"Nope," Aaron responded feeling himself break into a million little pieces.

Chapter 19

It was well past midnight by now, and Aaron lay in his bed staring at the ceiling as he had been doing for the last several hours. He couldn't manage to close his eyes long enough to fall asleep or get his body to unclench long enough to relax. He just lay there wide awake and terrified as he recalled the events of earlier that day. It was all his fault.

It had been dinner time and everyone but Sally was seated around the dinner table. You could cut the tension with a knife, as if one misstep and the whole room might explode. Aaron and his siblings sat quietly eating their dinner hoping not to disturb or disrupt the moment, the rare moment of peace and quiet.

"Thanks for the lasagna, Mom," Aaron said with his head down, feebly staring at his plate.

"You're welcome, honey," she said with a smile, acting as if she didn't notice the uncomfortable silent tension. His adoptive father took another bite of lasagna and gave a brooding glare at his adoptive children. They all stared at their food, not daring to make eye contact with the man.

The setting was all too much for Aaron, so he decided to fill up his glass of milk and hopefully get out of eye contact from his adoptive father, who just kept glaring at the children. Aaron opened the fridge and poured himself a glass of milk and slowly made his way back to his chair. But suddenly there was a loud commotion from upstairs, a loud, jarring but familiar commotion that pierced through the tension in the room and caused Aaron to stop in his tracks and hold his breath.

The screaming finally passed, and so Aaron continued his journey to his chair when he heard another blood-curdling cry, followed by a loud pounding of the wall.

"They're coming! Someone stop them!"

That's when it all fell apart. Aaron was so startled by the pounding he lost grip on his glass of milk and he could see the glass slowly descend towards the ground, ever so slowly, knowing that as soon as it hit the floor all hell would break loose. He knew the chain of events this would set off and he was helpless to stop it.

Smash! Went the glass on the floor, and quickly Aaron heard a loud pounding on the dinner table. "Damn it, Aaron! What the hell is wrong with you?"

Aaron's mother quickly got up from her chair to clean up the mess, trying to mitigate the damage, but the dominos were already falling.

"Why don't you leave him alone?" Adam, who was now fourteen, shot back at his adoptive father.

"Stay out of it, Adam! This doesn't concern you," he responded. Thomas and Ruben knew what was on the horizon, so they briskly left the dinner table.

"You always talk about how you're our father and that we're supposed to call you dad, but our dad would never do this," Adam said with a pause. "Darold would never treat us like this,"

The man put his fork down and stared at the table with an intense gaze as if he were a volcano ready to erupt, and before Adam could comprehend what was happening his adoptive father had already darted across the table and grabbed him by the throat.

"Say his name one more time, say it! I dare you." His adoptive pushed his face into Adam's.

"His name is Darold, and you're the reason he's gone!"

The man flew into a complete rage and lifted Adam out of his seat and threw him into the drywall, causing the wall to crumble as Adam's torso got stuck in the wall.

"What the hell is wrong with you?" his mother screamed.

"His name is Darold!" Adam screamed again, and his adoptive father lifted Adam out of the wall and off the ground

Aaron swiftly got out of his chair and left the kitchen and entered the living room where he found Thomas sitting on his knees and rocking himself with a hairbrush in his hand.

"Gotta get out of here," he mumbled as he began banging it against his head, looking to leave the nightmare.

BANG! BANG! "Please, somewhere else, anywhere else."

BANG! BANG! BANG! went the brush violently against his head, and Aaron just stood there watching his sibling assault himself, "Gotta wake up, gotta wake up, gotta wake up."

BANG! BANG! BANG! the assault continued, and Aaron could see the blood trickling down his ear and onto the collar of his shirt, "This isn't happening, this isn't happening. It can't be happening," he mumbled as he kept banging, and banging, and banging until there was a loud SNAP! And the handle of the brush flew off which caused Thomas to break down in tears, moaning and falling to the ground, burying his head into his hands for his inability to leave the nightmare.

The scene was too much for Aaron to take in, so he walked past his bleeding and weeping brother and headed upstairs to his bedroom and crawled under the covers and began to shake violently as he could hear the fight commence between his adoptive father and Adam, all the while Sally was banging violently on the wall screaming, "I hate you all!" which echoed through the whole house.

Aaron was shaking so violently and wished someone could rescue him from this horrible place. After some time the violence died down and there was a silence in the house, and during that silence, Aaron reflected on his life and thought about life at his adoptive grandparents' house, the video games, the movies, the candy, and the brief moments of affection, and he half questioned his decision to leave that world behind. They had offered refuge from the storm of his home life, even if it came at a horrible cost. But now he was all alone and the violent imagery of the day was swirling in his head and he was helpless to fall asleep.

So, there he was, well past midnight, staring up at the ceiling, wondering if he could at least fall asleep to get a brief respite from the pain of his life, but so far it had evaded him. He continued to stare at the ceiling and could see the ceiling begin to move, very slightly at first but growing in animation and clarity as the minutes passed by. There was some object at the ceiling, something dark, something flapping, and he could feel a slight breeze on his face. The slight breeze intensified until it was a rushing wind and Aaron closed his eyes and let the rushing wind wash over him, blowing away the violent commotion of the evening and felt a deep silence fall over him.

It was such a beautiful moment, feeling as if something was above him, working to get him to forget the violence and terror of his life and Aaron was grateful and found himself mouthing the words, "Thank You. Thank you, whoever you are, wherever you are," and as soon as the words left his mouth, he could feel a slight tickle on his large left toe, as if someone were nursing and nurturing him to sleep.

"You are welcome, my dear child. There there now, all is well. I am with you, so close your eyes and sleep." Aaron happily cooperated and a smile formed on his face as he drifted off to sleep.

CHAPTER 20

"Aaron can you hear me, honey? I've been calling you for thirty minutes!" Margaret shouted outside Aaron's door.

Aaron sat on his bed intently flipping through the pages of the book that he hid under his bed. His mother had taken him to the library last week and he found himself in the occult section and couldn't help but peruse the various books. Aaron stared at the selections on the shelf: *The History of Vampires, Mind Control and other Psychic Abilities, Werewolves and the Creatures of the Night,* and other books related to witchcraft which completely captured his attention. But it was the book with a large symbol drawn on the cover that captured his attention. He stared intently at it, feeling some strange connection to the symbol. He could feel it becoming glued to his hand and felt an unknown energy release from the book and radiate through his hand. He needed this book. He tucked it inside his pants and under his shirt and told his mother he was ready to leave.

"Aaron, we've got to leave, now!" his mother called out again.

"Go away, Mom!" he shouted back as he continued reading. Except for occasional visits to the bathroom, Aaron hadn't left his room in several days, nor had he showered or brushed his teeth. Bags formed under his eyes and he smelled horribly of body odor. He had a split lip from a scuffle with a neighborhood bully and the skin was beginning to blister. This wasn't the first time his lip had been bloodied so he decided to hole up in his room to escape the beatings. But he had his book and its symbol that kept him company.

"Aaron, we're going to be late for your baseball game!" Margaret called out again.

"I said in a minute, Mom!" he called back.

Aaron was finishing a chapter on how to perform a seance to summon spirits. The book explained that there were various types of spirits in the world, some which could be called upon for good, some which could be called upon for evil, and some which latched themselves onto the souls of individuals and turn them into living gods. The book described how spirits, and sometimes demons, could cling to family members for countless generations and that one must be very careful evoking the mysteries of the universe.

"It is the blood that the spirit truly desires," he read aloud as his brain began to tingle. "A sacrifice of blood to appease the demon's appetite is the surest way to his power."

Aaron was taking this all in when he heard a low, gentle humming. It was a deep sound with a significant bass to it and it made the hairs on Aaron's neck stand on end. It stopped Aaron in his tracks and the book fell to the ground. The humming persisted for several minutes and Aaron wasn't quite sure the source of the noise. He was alone in his room, after all, and the humming seemed so close to him that it must be coming from inside the bedroom. He was too scared to look around, given the nature of his reading material and that there was no logical explanation for the sound resonating throughout the room. There he was, all alone, and the humming, which started off as almost indiscernible, was slowly becoming more and more clear. This was not random noise. Aaron could tell it wasn't the furnace or the bathroom fan down the hallway or music from another room. It was coming from inside the room.

Finally, the humming became clear and audible, and Aaron realized that someone was singing a lullaby, but Aaron didn't dare move his head to see the source of the lullaby, as he was terrified to think that he wasn't alone in his room. Then Aaron thought of the story his mother had told him all those years ago, of how she summoned the devil and how much the devil wanted to destroy her and followed her for years to come. He thought of all this and he thought of the book which said there were evil spirits but also good spirits, and Aaron knew this spirit meant him no harm. On the contrary, this spirit was his only respite, source of comfort and only guiding light in the world. This spirit made sure he fell asleep every night and comforted him when he was in his room, all alone. This spirit never hurt him or put Aaron in danger, and so Aaron slowly began to welcome the noise and tuned in to the lullaby that was being sung to him. He cast all his attention on the humming and could finally make out distinct words.

"Rockabye baby on the treetop," the spirit sang in a deep, low voice, deeper than Aaron had ever heard or was accustomed to hearing. "When the wind blows the cradle will rock." Aaron was familiar with this lullaby, for it was sung to him as a small child, before he was adopted and before everything began falling apart. There was, in fact, a time before his birth father left when everything was as it should be, and it was during this time that his mother sang him this lullaby. He was relieved that he knew the lullaby and was grateful that the spirit was evoking a memory from a safer world. "When the bow breaks the cradle will fall," Aaron could finally get a sense of the direction of the voice, which was his bedroom closet. He didn't feel as scared anymore, for it was clear that this spirit was his true friend and cared for Aaron in a way that no one else did.

Slowly, Aaron began turning his head towards the direction of his closet, which was directly behind him. Aaron was staring out the window and slowly cast his gaze towards his bed, and then the wall past his bed, and then finally the open closet. And on the top shelf of his closet, next to his baseball card collection he saw a grotesque head that seemed to be planted into the wall. He wasn't sure if he had ever seen such a head before, for its skin was pale white with flashes of red streaking horizontally across each eye with little red dots speckled over its face. Its eyes were as dark as night and were staring directly at Aaron as if it had been watching Aaron this whole time. As if it had always been watching Aaron and had known Aaron for longer than he could imagine. The figure sent shivers down Aaron's spine for it was so foreign to Aaron and at first glance seemed menacing, mischievous, and threatening. But then again, here it was, singing Aaron a lullaby, doing its best to comfort Aaron, as it had for longer than Aaron could even fathom. It was a paradox, an enigma, an anomaly that Aaron couldn't understand, but Aaron was in no position to turn away help, so he stared back into the eyes of this thing which had made its way into Aaron's closet and into Aaron's life and listened as it finished the lullaby, "And down will come baby cradle in all." And as the lullaby was completed the creature flashed Aaron a large smile, revealing the large fangs adorning its mouth.

"Ok Mom, I'm coming down."

CHAPTER 21

"Where do you think you're going?!" an angry voice shouted after him.

Aaron sprinted through the neighborhood park, doing his best to lose the three boys chasing after him. But they were gaining on him and he was running out of steam. He'd had several altercations with them already and he thought they would have moved on to someone else by now, but there must be something about him that was worth beating to oblivion. So he kept running.

"I'm going to stomp you, Aaron! Did you hear me!"

Aaron heard him all too well. He ran as hard as he could until the stitch in his side became too great and he keeled over in pain. *Get back up, Aaron*, he thought to himself. *Get back up!* But by the time he got back up it was too late, and he was tackled to the ground.

Aaron was pinned down to the ground as the largest of the three sat on top of him and began raining down punches, his fists smashing into Aaron's chest, arms, and face.

"Get him!" the other boys cheered as Aaron felt a set of knuckles collide into his jaw.

"You think you can spend time with my girl?" the boy jeered at Aron.

"I didn't know! I swear! I haven't seen her in like a month!"

"You think she'd go for scrubby white trash like you? You must be out of your mind!"

"I'm sorry! I'll never see her again, I promise!"

The boy gave Aaron a menacing smile. "I'll make sure of that!" he said and continued to hammer down blows. Aaron covered his face to mitigate the damage, but the boy wasn't done, and as the punches increased in ferocity everything began to change.

Aaron could feel the wind and the sand whipping against his back. He stood lifeless and limp staring mindlessly into the sea of sand and rocks. He wasn't quite sure where he was or where the bullies went, but he really didn't care anymore. He was twelve years old, and he hated his life and the world even more now than ever.

He gazed into the vast desert, soaking in the heat of the atmosphere and swept his eyes across the barren landscape. This was an environment that reflected his reality. There was no life, no vitality, no nutrition or source of comfort, or growth. There was only death, all the life had been sucked out of the space a long time ago, and so it was only fitting that he be in this place, in this time, to meet with what he felt was his only friend in the world. Jagged rocks pierced through the ground and deep caverns were dug into canyon walls, and the endless sea of sand continued to whip across his back, and it was through this storm of sand that he first began to hear his companion who was guiding him on his painful journey.

"They hate you, Aaron. The whole world hates you." Aaron clenched his fists in anger and could feel his spine straighten. He had barely spent any time with the girl, and he stopped seeing her after his first beating. It wasn't fair and Aaron agreed that it was because the world did hate him.

"Who will come to help you?" He could feel his blood begin to boil and the heat rise from his nostrils. No one had ever helped him. No one stopped his adoptive father from hitting him and yelling at him. No one saved him from the bully's fists pounding into his face. The whole world enjoyed watching him suffer and he knew it.

"Make them pay, Aaron. Make them all pay." Aaron dug his toes into his shoes and clenched his teeth in anger. He was sick of waiting for someone to help, sick of waiting for life to be fair. He was done waiting for someone to tell Aaron that he deserved better, that he didn't deserve all the horrible things that ever happened to him. He was done waiting for someone to tell Aaron he was deserving of love, for he finally accepted it wasn't true. It was never true, and as the sand continued to whip against his back, he could feel the demons begin to rise from within him.

"I can help you, Aaron, if you ask. I will show you the secret path." Aaron felt as if he were a time bomb about to explode. He was ready to pour out all his pent-up anger and was eager to watch it spill all over everyone around him.

"Help," Aaron called out to the voice. And as soon as the words parted from his lips, he felt a rushing wind overtake him and knock him to the ground. He closed his eyes and allowed the whipping wind to overwhelm him. He breathed it in, and the wind filled his lungs and awakened something inside him. He felt an explosion in his brain and a great spirit of destruction and chaos came to life and he screamed at the top of his lungs.

He opened his eyes, and he could see fear in the eyes of the large boy who was pinning him to the ground. Aaron stared at the boy with a crazy look and screamed at him again, catching him off guard. The boy's jaw dropped, and Aaron lunged at his hand and started biting him. Aaron clamped down on his thumb with his teeth and nearly bit it off.

"What the hell?!" the boy cried out. The boy stood up and got off Aaron, but Aaron still had his thumb between his mouth and was growling like a like a wild animal. "Stop it, Aaron! You're going to bite it off!" He had pierced the boy's skin and his blood was smeared on Aaron's lips. Aaron released the boy's thumb but began chasing him.

He licked the blood on his lips and said, "I want more! Give me more!"

"Whatever, man. Just leave my girlfriend alone," the boy pleaded with Aaron as he and his two friends ran away. Aaron could feel his blood still boiling within his veins and he loved it. He felt alive, invigorated, and emboldened and began scanning the environment. He turned his head to the left, and then to the right, and then turned around when he finally saw it. He wasted no time darting over to the nearby sidewalk where he found a piece of jagged glass from a broken beer bottle. Aaron squeezed the jagged shard with his left hand and began carving up his right palm. The wind whipped at his back as the jagged edges tore through his skin and droplets of his blood hit the pavement. He looked with satisfaction at the symbol he'd carved on his hand and his sacrifice of blood that bled into the pavement.

CHAPTER 22

"Ok class, it's time to begin our lesson." Aaron listened to Mrs. Brown, his seventh-grade English teacher, as she took hold of the classroom. But Aaron didn't want to be taken ahold of and he didn't want to begin the lesson. He was sick of doing what he was told and following the rules. In fact, he wanted to break the rules and everything around him. He desperately wanted to break something beautiful and at the front of the room he found the most beautiful thing he could break. It was a new student who had just transferred to their school and today was his first day.

Aaron glared at him with his crisply ironed buttoned-down shirt, his designer jeans and shoes, all readily attentive to the teacher's lesson. Meanwhile Aaron was wearing stale-smelling jeans with a ripped t-shirt. Stress-induced sores were forming around his mouth and he wore a baseball hat because he didn't want anyone to see him. Students laughed at him because he talked to himself in the hallway and bumped into walls and he hated them for it. The new kid looked so perfect; Aaron would make him pay for it.

The English teacher continued her lesson for the remainder of the hour, but Aaron failed to notice as he was directing all his attention towards the new student and all the horrible things he wanted to do to him.

This is it, Aaron told himself. *It's time.* He felt a gentle breeze behind him, and he felt compelled to introduce himself to the new student.

The bell finally rang, and the teacher reminded her students to hand in their homework assignment, which was to create a poem for every month of the year. Aaron looked down at his assignment lying on his desk and thought of all the poems he wrote, about how he wanted to kill himself and everyone around him. He thought about how much he hated his life, and he was sick of doing nothing about it. He bit his lip and squeezed his desk as he looked at the symbol he carved into his hand and he knew what to do.

Aaron ran past his teacher's desk and threw his assignment on it and ran after the new student.

"Hey, wait up!" he called out while running after the new student. "Wait up!" He finally caught up to him and tapped him on his shoulder.

"Hey, are you new here?" Aaron asked.

"Yes, I am! My name's David, pleased to meet you!" the boy replied with a carefree demeanor.

"Yes, nice to meet you too. I'm Aaron. I thought you were new, and I wanted to catch up with you to invite you to a quick meetup behind the classroom. I figured you didn't know about it, so I thought I'd fill you in. Want to come?"

David hesitated. "I don't know, Aaron. I don't want to be late for class."

Aaron put his arm around David's shoulder and assured him it would be alright. "It will only take a few minutes, I promise. There's someone I want you to meet. I promise you won't be late for class." David looked at Aaron as if he didn't know what to do. He was so perfect, with his designer jeans and crisply ironed shirt and Aaron assumed he had never been punched before.

Aaron slowly nudged David with him towards the end of the hallway towards the door.

"I promise you it will only take a minute. I promise you won't be late for class. Trust me," Aaron said with a sly smile. Aaron was roughly six inches taller than David who felt a bit intimidated in Aaron's presence.

"Ok," David replied reluctantly. "If you say so."

"Good," Aaron said as he hurried him towards the exit. The closer they got to the exit the more Aaron thought about how much he hated his life. His asshole adoptive father was always picking on him; it was time for someone else to feel hated.

Aaron propped open the door and grabbed David by the hand, practically sprinting to get to the back of the schoolroom.

"Aaron, you're hurting my hand. Can you slow down?" But Aaron wasn't willing to slow down.

Aaron squeezed David's hand, "Shut up for a minute!"

"Huh?" asked David.

"I said shut up!"

Aaron finally turned the corner and threw David against the wall.

"What's going on? Where is everyone? I thought you wanted me to meet someone?" David asked. Aaron could sense the fear in his eyes which brought him a deep satisfaction. "What's going on, Aaron?" David asked again. Aaron flashed him a smile and lunged at David, tackling him to the ground. "What are you doing?"

"Let me show you what I'm doing, David," Aaron replied as he threw his first punch at David's face. David screamed out in pain.

"Why are you doing this to me?! Please stop! Someone help me!"

Aaron threw another punch, and then another, and again until his knuckles were bloody and raw.

No one helped Aaron. No one ever helped Aaron, so he swung his fists even harder and pounded David into the dirt. Images of naked men flashed in his mind and he swung harder, and then he saw his adoptive father yelling at him, and he swung even harder. His eyes became agitated and wet, and he kept punching until he was finally tackled to the ground.

CHAPTER 23

The principal waited inside her office for Aaron's mother to arrive. She had presided over the middle school for more than twenty years and had seen it all. Some exceptional students had graced her halls and gone on to outstanding universities and colleges and carved out immensely rewarding lives for themselves. She even had a few letters from past students in her drawer, letters giving thanks for the sense of discipline Mrs. Sullivan instilled in her students and the individual attention she was able to give them. She had an uncanny ability to remember each one of their names, all five hundred or so, and would greet them in the hallway.

Most of her students, however, were not destined for greatness. Most would go on to live middle-class pedestrian lives working mundane jobs and doing their best to support their families and eke out a vacation every now and again. They were great students and great people, but they just didn't have the intellectual power nor the drive to rise to the top of the class. Many wouldn't even graduate from high school. They would be forced to work dead-end jobs with little to no chance of advancement. Life handed out skills and circumstances and they, unfortunately, drew the short stick on both accounts. Many were good kids, well-intentioned with decent manners, and she felt obligated to give them her best effort, to make sure she helped these students squeeze out as much untapped potential as possible.

However, not all her students had well intentions. Some of them had no intention of learning anything or discovering any of their hidden potential. Some of them were so troubled, so wild and beyond the pale that Mrs. Sullivan had no intention of helping them. In fact, it was her conviction to get them out of her school as soon as possible. She had been principal at the middle school long enough to see how a few bad eggs could ruin it for everyone. She had seen the bullying and the vandalism, of how the misfits of the school create an unsafe space for others, making it hard to learn and thrive. They were unstable, unpredictable, and ill-mannered. Some came from broken families and had difficult living situations, and others most certainly had some undiagnosed mental disorder, and some were pure evil.

Some were beyond redemption, beyond hope and without a doubt were headed to prison, to the homeless shelter, or an early grave. This was most certainly the case with Aaron who had made her job an absolute nightmare since he started the seventh grade. He was completely disrespectful to all his teachers and would invoke riots and mutinies in his classes, chiding his classmates to turn against their teacher and completely run amok. And then there was the large number of students who complained about his bullying, picking fights with them, stalking them, spitting on them, and threatening violence. Aaron had already gotten in more than a few fights on campus this year and Mrs. Sullivan had seen enough. There was also the vandalism, the writing of strange symbols on the bathroom walls and lunch tables. But the tipping point was his violent assault of a new student.

Yes, Mrs. Sullivan had seen enough. Aaron had already been suspended from school three times and she was on the verge of expelling him from the school entirely. Mrs. Sullivan had called this meeting with Aaron's mother a week ago to let her know that Aaron would soon be dismissed from her school if she so much as heard a whisper of poor behavior on Aaron's part, that she had a list of alternate schools that Aaron could attend and vandalize. She was eager to get this boy out and create a safer and healthier environment for the rest of the school.

But earlier that morning one of Aaron's teachers had reached out to Mrs. Sullivan. It was Aaron's English teacher, and she felt obligated to share with Mrs. Sullivan the homework assignment that Aaron had handed in. The kids were given an assignment to write a poem for each month of the year and the poems Aaron turned in made his English teacher's hair stand on end.

The poems were dark, morbid, macabre, and painful to read. They were about suffering, and of horrible things that happened in the world. They were about how much the world hated Aaron and how the voices in his head told him he ought to kill himself. It was a cry for help, and it was incredibly painful for Mrs. Sullivan to read. These were words coming from a wounded child. Reading his poems made her skin crawl and she knew she had to somehow intervene. For her part, Mrs. Sullivan knew an investigation was necessary and she immediately contacted the local child protection authorities to investigate Aaron's home. And that became the additional reason for her meeting with Aaron's mother today, to let her know that very official people would be paying her a visit to assess Aaron's home life and determine if he were better off living elsewhere.

Aaron's mother finally arrived and found her way into Mrs. Sullivan's office and took a seat opposite her desk. Mrs. Sullivan gave Margaret a cold assessment, determining the fitness of this woman to provide the appropriate atmosphere for her children. It didn't take her long to see the naivety and gullibility of this woman, the complete obliviousness of her surroundings. Her hair was a mess and she had stains on her pants, and she was a full twenty minutes late for the meeting, stating that she couldn't find parking. Mrs. Sullivan didn't say a word but let Margaret speak. She was like a leaky faucet that wouldn't shut up, one excuse after another, completely absolving herself from any responsibility in Aaron's poor behavior. On and on she went and the more she talked the more Mrs. Sullivan could feel the heat rise from her nostrils. She didn't say a word, she just let Margaret spew forth excuses, complaints, contradictory statements and give the impression of a woman whose children were being abused significantly right under her nose.

Margaret's presence and her self-portrayal ran completely against Mrs. Sullivan's own disposition. Mrs. Sullivan made it her responsibility to know what each and every one of her students was doing while in her school. Mrs. Sullivan came early and stayed late to make sure her students had a safe place to learn and grow and thrive; Mrs. Sullivan all too often wanted more for her students than they wanted for themselves. It all became clear now, after speaking with this mess of a woman, that if Mrs. Sullivan didn't intervene Aaron may very well kill himself. So, while Margaret continued to blabber on about how stressful her life had been lately Mrs. Sullivan abruptly stopped her by putting her hand in the air as a gesture for silence.

Mrs. Sullivan let the silence hang in the air for a while to amplify to Margaret the importance of the coming words. Mrs. Sullivan finally put her hand down. "I have a message for you."

She grabbed a pen and a scratch piece of paper and began scribbling something down. She passed the note over to Margaret who looked at the writing and with a confused looked on her face.

"What is this?"

Mrs. Schneider glared at Margaret with steel resolve in her eyes. "It's the name of the social worker who is prepared to remove Aaron from your care. She will be paying you a visit tomorrow morning."

Chapter 24

A aron looked out at the sun as it melted into the ocean. He walked along the shoreline and was soothed by the gentle rolling of waves. He could feel the tiny little specks of sands on the bottom of his feet and felt the warm breeze of a beautiful summer day against his face. Aaron finally sat down in the sand, laid back and let the sand caress his head and offer him a moment of peace. He knew he was dreaming but he didn't care. For a short moment of time, he could finally breathe deeply.

He closed his eyes for a moment, soaking up the peaceful sound of the ocean. It whispered to him that beauty and peace and joy existed somewhere in the world. He felt the sand beneath him, supporting him and keeping him from sinking into the darkness of the earth. And he could feel the warm beams of the sun gently kiss his face, convincing him that the light of life and love existed and wanted to penetrate his heart and soul. And as he thought of all these wonderful things, things that were in complete contrast to his life at home, he felt a warm and moist pressure on his forehead. He opened his eyes to see a man standing over him, kissing him on his forehead.

Aaron was surprised at the gesture and that he had failed to recognize that he wasn't alone on the beach, that someone was there watching him the whole time. The man offered Aaron a hand to help him up off the ground, which Aaron gratefully accepted. The man was indeed a stranger but at the same time looked very familiar to Aaron. He looked like how Aaron imagined his own father. He had dark brown hair, tanned skin, and a fit and muscular physique. He was someone that Aaron was naturally drawn to, with charisma and a countenance that immediately put Aaron at ease, as if this man meant Aaron no harm but perhaps had an important message to give. Aaron felt unusually comfortable around this man, a man who seemed to be outside of his imagination and had somehow infiltrated his dream.

Aaron stood on the beach a mere two feet away from the stranger and peered into his eyes. He had beautiful blue eyes with flecks of lightning and speckles of starlight. He stared into the man's eyes and it was as if he were watching the dawn of creation. He could see galaxies colliding and stars being born. He saw black holes collapse into themselves and the expanding of the universe. He saw the settling of constellations and individual planets. He saw the birth of the sun and the power of its heat bring the earth to life. And he saw the sprouting of trees and flowers and mountains crawl out of the earth and ascend to the sky. And he saw waters burst forth from the earth, filling its great caverns. He saw the stars popping up one by one and he watched as the most beautiful star in the sky fell to the earth like a bolt of lightning. There was beauty and purpose, and both were knitted together with the unspeakable power of love. Aaron saw all this in the man's eyes and knew he was in the presence of something both great and terrible.

The man approached Aaron and offered him a kiss on either cheek and then also on his hand as if to pay homage to Aaron. The stranger made Aaron feel that he was of great importance and had a critical role to play in the great drama that had been unfolding since the dawn of time. Aaron was grateful for the moment and so Aaron gave the stranger his complete and utmost attention when the man spoke to him, saying, "Aaron, I have a message for you."

He then stooped down and began drawing in the sand and it didn't take Aaron long before he recognized what it was. He hung his head in shame as he stared at the symbol in the sand, the same symbol he had carved into his hand, and thought of all the horrible things he had done recently and the monster he was slowly becoming. He was mortified that this beautiful man knew it all and watched as he scribbled it out, as if it never even existed. Aaron then made an audible gasp as if he finally understood.

"David." Aaron's jaw dropped as he realized that the pain he caused David was the same pain that his adoptive father and countless others had caused him over the years.

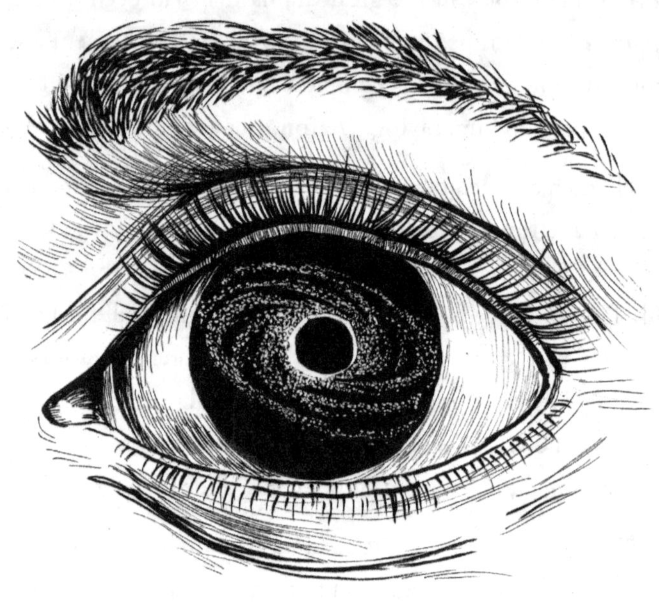

The sun finally dipped below the ocean, giving birth to the darkness of night and Aaron wondered if David was still hurting and whether Aaron would cause more pain to others.

"There are things in this world you don't understand, Aaron. You wouldn't believe them even if I told you. Just know you are deeply loved."

The man's words hung in the air and then settled into Aaron's heart. He wanted to change. He had to change before he turned into a complete monster.

"Don't lose hope, Aaron," the man encouraged. He grabbed Aaron by the shoulders, forcing him to stare into his eyes again, and Aaron teared up as he saw the beautiful young man Aaron was always meant to be. "Behold, he makes all things new," the man told Aaron, caressing his shoulders. The man gave Aaron a big hug and walked down the shoreline leaving Aaron in the care of the starry sky. Aaron kept his gaze firmly on the stranger until he was a small dot on the horizon.

"Please don't go," Aaron whispered as the dot continued to fade. "I wish this didn't have to end," he said as he watched the father he never had disappear into the night.

Chapter 25

Aaron rushed to his English class in hopes to arrive before the bell rang. He knew he had to make things right and would find David and offer him his most sincere apology, to let him know he was wrong, that he was sorry and that he would never do it again. Things were going to change, and Aaron was excited to take the first step. He could see the open door to his classroom down the hall and practically ran down the hallway.

Aaron stepped through the classroom door with several minutes to spare and looked around for David. He saw him in the front of the class talking with several students and Aaron began walking towards him.

"David," Aaron called out, preparing to offer his apology when his English teacher Mrs. Brown grabbed him by the shoulder.

"Where do you think you're going?" she asked, whipping his neck back and turning him towards the back of the class. She dug her fingers into him as she ushered him away from David. "You are never touching him again. Just go sit in your desk and leave the other kids alone."

Aaron looked over his shoulder at the rest of the class, who were all scowling at him for what he had done to David. He had become a pariah and none of his classmates wanted anything to do with him.

Aaron's heart began to sink, as he knew it was too late. He took his seat in the back of the class and watched as his classmates socialized with one another before class. There were still a few minutes left before class started and he could feel every second as if they were darts being thrown at him. Each one reminded him just how alone he was. There they were, all at the front of the class, having fun and enjoying each other's company. And David was right in their midst, telling jokes and laughing with all the friends he had already made. The bruises and cuts on his face were healing quite nicely and he had moved on as if it never happened.

David belonged with his classmates, all of his normal classmates with wonderful, normal families who took care of their children. He knew David's parents loved him, protected him, and made sure he had nothing to do with kids like Aaron. There they all were, enjoying the beautiful life that was meant for them. And there Aaron was, a complete mess, alone by himself at the back of the classroom. He picked at the large sores around his mouth. Some were scabbed over, and some had formed puss which oozed out and dripped on his clothes. Flies began circling around him and colliding into him from his horrible body odor. His shoes were two sizes too big, and his shirt was crinkled and stained from not being washed in weeks. He pulled his baseball cap down.

He felt like time were standing still as he waited impatiently for the bell to ring and bring an end to the embarrassment and humiliation of being a complete loser with no friends. He took his hat on and off constantly as a nervous twitch and he could see his classmates turn around and look at him. They were all whispering, pointing, and laughing at the mess at the back of the class, the pathetic, disheveled bully who wore urine-soaked pants and crinkled and stained shirts and drew strange symbols all over his hands.

Aaron was utterly embarrassed and felt as if he were about to pass out. The walls began to warp, and the room began to spin, and he wished someone would bring an end to the horrible nightmare. The walls changed color and the students were all glowing in neon pink and green as their whispers turned to laughter and the laughter eventually to cackles as they all turned to face Aaron. They were all pointing at him and bellying over in laughter as Aaron realized the blood squiring out of his left wrist was from a razor blade he was holding in his right hand.

"It's for the best, Aaron," Mrs. Brown told Aaron with a cold, blank stare from behind her desk. The blood kept dripping down Aaron's wrist and spilling all over the floor. He was fading away. He closed his eyes for the last time, serenaded by the cackles of his classmates until the bell finally rang.

All the students took their seats, but Aaron flew out of the classroom door in a mad scramble. He panicked as he looked for the nearest bathroom.

"Aaron! Come back here, Aaron!" he could hear Mrs. Brown call him in the background. But he had no intention of returning. He spotted the men's bathroom and jetted towards it in a panic. He opened the first stall door and locked it tight behind him and spewed his lunch into the toilet and all over the seat. After wiping off his mouth Aaron began to whimper and slowly started banging his head against the brick wall. He began banging harder and harder. *You're such a loser, Aaron! Why do you have to be such a loser!* He kept banging his head and began sobbing, hoping the nightmare of his life would end when a fly collided into his face, causing him to slip and hit his head on the toilet.

"I'm telling you Margaret, there's something wrong with him and he's an embarrassment to the whole family!"

"No, he's not! He's just fine, and if you would stop being so mean to him maybe you two would actually get along," Margaret barked back to Aaron's adoptive father.

"I've put up with so much of his shit, his hissy fits and temper tantrums and he still gives me attitude. He's lucky I don't knock him into next week!" the man responded.

"I thought you already did that! Aaron told me all about how you were beating on him again. Throwing him to the ground and smacking him over and over. No wonder he doesn't like you!" Margaret quipped back.

"God damnit Margaret! Those damn kids of yours don't respect me or listen to me. In my own house! And if they don't want to respect me then I will make them respect me. You got that?! You let them know I'm coming for them!"

"Don't touch my children!"

Aaron sat deeper into the bathtub as he overheard his parents arguing across the hallway in their bedroom. His head was still throbbing from his incident in the men's bathroom earlier that day and the lingering embarrassment of being laughed at in class was still with him. Even worse was when his mother picked him up from the principal's office. Mrs. Sullivan insisted Margaret bathe Aaron because his body odor was sickening. He sank into the warm water as the sound of his parents arguing about what to do with their mess of a son faded into the background. He looked down at his right hand and saw the symbol he'd carved into his palm was beginning to disappear. The symbols he had drawn on his arms were also fading away from the water but the sores on his face with their scabs and puss remained.

He then looked down at his left hand which held a razor blade in it. His urge to hurt himself had been growing over the past few months so he'd stolen a razor blade form a local hardware store. He stared intently at the slicing device and wondered if he had the courage to use it on himself. He thought of all the friends he didn't have, the girls he had never kissed, of all the love no one felt for him, and realized that no one would miss him if he started cutting. He held the razorblade in his fingers and raised it until it was hovering over his right wrist. His hands began to tremble as he wondered what might be waiting for him when he died, if something better would be waiting for him if he killed himself, or perhaps something infinitely worse. Aaron wasn't sure, so he dropped the razorblade which fell onto the bathroom floor.

"What am I going to do?" he asked himself aloud. He closed his eyes and immersed his head under water, trying to escape the memory from earlier today. But as he lay there immersed in the water with his eyes closed images of his adoptive grandparents flashed into his mind. They were both naked, hovering over their bathtub and ushering Aaron to come closer. He quickly raised his head out of the water and shot up out of the tub. He grabbed his towel to wipe the water from his eyes and walked towards the bathroom mirror after draining the tub.

He looked at himself in the mirror and winced when he saw the terrible sores surround his mouth and looked down at the sink. "What am I going to do?" he asked himself again. He could barely look himself in the mirror, but he slowly raised his eyes again. Standing directly behind him was a man covered completely in red clown makeup hissing at him and grabbing with his arms. Aaron swung his arms behind violently and fell to the ground. He looked up to find the man, but he was no longer there. He was falling apart, and as he heard the sounds of flies hitting the outside of the bathroom windowsill, he quickly put his towel on and headed to his bedroom.

By then his parents had gone downstairs to eat dinner. But Aaron wasn't hungry and he didn't want to see any of his family. He laid in bed completely still waiting for the shadow cast by the oak tree in his back yard to completely engulf his bedroom. He wanted to sleep and hopefully find himself in a peaceful setting with the kind man from his earlier dream. The man who'd revealed to Aaron the young man he was meant to be.

"Please, be there," he said aloud. He closed his eyes and with a large yawn asked again, "Please be there," and Aaron slowly drifted off to sleep.

TINK, TINK, TINK. TINK, TINK, TINK. Aaron was awoken by the sound of a hammer spiking a nail. TINK, TINK, TINK. He attempted to roll over to see where the sound was coming from, but he was being restrained and was unable to move.

"What the hell is going on?"

He did his best to move his head to his right and he saw his mother by his side, and in her hand was a hammer and in her other hand she was holding a nail that was plunged into Aaron's wrist. TINK, TINK, TINK. He panicked and tried to talk but the words couldn't get out of his mouth and he began shaking violently.

"It's for the best, Aaron," she told him as she continued hammering. TINK, TINK, TINK. TINK, TINK, TINK. Aaron looked over to his left and saw his adoptive father hammering a nail through his wrist as well.

"It's for the best, Aaron," he told Aaron who could feel the bed of lumber he was resting on. TINK, TINK, TINK. TINK, TINK, TINK. Aaron looked to his feet and he saw David from his English class hammering his feet into what he now understood was a wooden cross.

"It's for the best, Aaron," he said with a smile as blood splashed across Aaron's face, feet and body.

His bedroom had peeled away, and his parents and David lifted the cross Aaron was nailed to. They raised it in the air and hung it on a beam which hovered over the concrete floor. He looked below him and saw a circle with a symbol inside painted onto the floor. He then looked around and saw a mattress in the corner of the room and an unknown apparatus hanging next to it. He violently flung his torso around trying to free himself.

"Help me! Somebody help me!"

His parents watched him hang from the cross with their arms around David, holding him tenderly and smiling at Aaron.

The blood from his wounds dripped onto the symbol beneath him and it was like acid eroding away the concrete. His blood began to pour down, eroding away all the concrete and revealing a giant pit in the ground filled with poisonous vipers. Aaron looked at his parents and with a whimper pleaded with them, "Please help me. Please. I'll do better, I promise!"

But they just smiled at him, waving goodbye and holding David even tighter in their arms. He continued to dangle over the pit and began to cry when he felt a bombardment of flies collide into his head and neck and heard someone whisper into his ear, "I'll steal your soul, Aaron," as they proceeded to cut the rope that held the cross to the beam.

Aaron closed his eyes as he catapulted towards the bottom of the pit, his body completely drenched in his own blood and the vipers were eagerly waiting for his arrival. He was now a mere foot away and one of the vipers catapulted itself at Aaron's face causing him to scream in horror. He finally hit the bottom of the pit and the vipers swarmed him like flies on fecal matter. They covered him completely, biting him and his body began to shake from the pain.

"Help me!" he screamed, and the shaking became more violently. "Help me!" he shouted again, and the shaking became so violent that it forced him to open his eyes to see his mother shaking him out of his nightmare.

CHAPTER 26

It had all been a nightmare, a horrible nightmare following a continuation of other horrible nightmares over the past month and Aaron was becoming completely unhinged. He didn't know how to explain it to anyone, didn't know who or how to ask for help. He would fall asleep at night and feel his companion squeeze his lungs and bury him into his bed under its weight and he was helpless to do anything but watch the voice take various shapes and control his dreams. He would cry for help but found himself unable to speak, dry heaving the words "Help!" which were nowhere near loud enough for anyone to hear. Aaron's companion was turning all his dreams into nightmares, turning his whole life into a nightmare, one which Aaron was desperate to be rid of. However, he had no idea of how to escape this companion that Aaron had so eagerly welcomed into his life in the first place.

Aaron stood in the living room, staring at the ceiling. He had his blanket and pillow in hand like a little child but dreaded the idea of falling asleep. He was never going to sleep in his bedroom again. It would be different in here. Maybe tonight would be a normal night, maybe he would simply close his eyes in slumber and open them up to be greeted by the morning with no remembrance of dreaming at all. His whole body was on edge and he was terrified to fall asleep, but he covered himself with his blanket. Tonight would be different; the living room would be different. Perhaps he had merely imagined his companion, the nightmares and the whole mess he found himself in. He decided to would count down from ten in the hopes by the time he got to one he would be fast asleep.

"Ok, Aaron, you can do this. Here we go, ten," he began counting off, allowing his mind to drift off aimlessly into a sea of random thoughts and fragmented memories. "Nine," he continued and could sense the living room and all his immediate surroundings fade away. His eyes were getting heavy and he could tell he was being lulled closer into a deep sleep.

"Seven." His eyes became heavier, and he closed his eyes for just a moment and opened them to find himself lying on a sea of glass with a golden castle glowing in the distance. The sky was ablaze like a roaring fire from the sun, which appeared mere feet away from the castle, causing the whole atmosphere to turn reddish-orange. It was a strange sight that was both vaguely familiar but also completely foreign, strangely soothing but unnerving at the same time.

"Six." Aaron opened his eyes back again and he was in his living room staring at the ceiling. By now he was having a hard time getting the words out of his mouth and could tell sleep was close at hand.

"Five." He stared at the ceiling of the living room and watched as large indents were made into its surface, the size of footprints. Aaron was too tired to think much of it and continued to count. "Four."

Aaron closed his eyes again and reopened them to see a beautiful man dressed in royal garments with a golden crown on his head seated on a throne. He was now in an ornate and royally decorated throne room with a beautiful red carpet leading to the throne and with the king's royal guards flanking either side of the carpet. The king stared at Aaron with a mischievous smile and Aaron watched his eyes explode into the most beautiful reds and oranges and yellows, which lit up the entire room. And slowly the king began to open his mouth, and Aaron watched as hornets poured out of his mouth like a rushing river.

"Three." Aaron opened his eyes again to find himself back on the couch in his living room, staring at the ceiling, which was dripping blood onto his forehead and smearing into his hair. There was some ruckus happening upstairs that was a bit unnerving, but Aaron was too tired to care. "Two." Aaron closed his eyes again feeling the warm embrace of a thick, syrupy liquid continue to trickle on his face and some unknown organ slapped his face to the sound of a gentle hissing into Aaron's ear.

"One." Aaron opened his eyes and found himself lying on his couch in his living room and he could only assume that the trick hadn't worked after all and that he was still awake. But everything seemed a little off as if all the life had been sucked out of the house. He couldn't quite put his finger on it, but the entire living room seemed to be cast in some unknown shadow which gave the furniture and the walls a greyish hue. He looked around. He was most certainly becoming unhinged and his mind must be playing tricks on him, for he felt he was both in his house and somewhere else completely at the same time. The silence of the night filled the room and Aaron was overwhelmed with a sense of calm about the situation when he heard a loud creaking coming from upstairs. It sounded as if a door were opening. Perhaps someone had gotten up to use the bathroom. The bathroom was at the end of the hallway upstairs and to the right, so Aaron assumed he would remain alone with his thoughts.

THUD, THUD, THUD.

That was odd. He could hear the footsteps, but they seemed louder than usual and disjointed. There wasn't a rhythm to the steps and suggested someone learning to walk for the first time. Aaron was becoming a little unnerved by the sound. Something wasn't quite right. Perhaps his adoptive father was in a very deep sleep, deeper than usual, and was causing the loud, disjointed thuds that were coming from upstairs. Perhaps he would soon hear the bathroom door creak open, and Aaron would breathe easy again.

THUD, THUD, THUD. More steps, which was very unsettling. He should have reached the bathroom by now which wasn't too far from his bedroom door. THUD, THUD, THUD. Then Aaron remembered the bathroom was situated at the far end of the hallway furthest from the stairs. Consequently, if someone were going to the bathroom the sounds of the footsteps should be growing fainter, but that wasn't what was happening at all. THUD! THUD! THUD! Instead of growing fainter, the footsteps were growing louder, were getting heavier and the hairs on the back of

Aaron's neck stood on end as he realized someone was headed towards the stairs, towards the living and Aaron's frightened body.

THUD! THUD! THUD! Aaron felt he must be in a dream, a dream in which he felt completely alive, could feel the goosebumps growing on his arms and his neck, and could feel his heart beating through his chest. Aaron held his breath, went completely still, hoping that he could somehow hide from this unknown entity. THUD! Aaron felt like screaming and crying at the same time. The owner of these loud and disjointed footsteps seemed to be taking their time, savoring the prolonged terror and the building panic of the moment. There was a long pause and Aaron felt this was the deciding moment. Aaron knew he was a mere moment away from no longer being alone. In place of the footsteps was the loud thudding of Aaron's heartbeat which was getting louder and quicker as the seconds continued to tick. THUD! THUD! THUD! THUD! His heart pounded louder and louder, quicker, and quicker and it took all his strength and focus to not scream. The tension and suspense were killing him, and images of blood and naked bodies and severed heads flashed into his mind. THUD! THUD! THUD! More images flashed into his mind, grotesque images of grown men raping a child, suffocating him under the weight of their filthy bodies. Images of a dirty mattress on the floor of a disgusting basement and the slight hint of incense invaded his nostrils. THUD! THUD! THUD! It was a complete avalanche of horrible images he prayed weren't memories or any way related to his life and Aaron felt as if someone were forcing Aaron to watch the most disturbing moments of a movie that should never have been created in the first place. THUD!

THUD! THUD! His heart was now beating out of his chest and Aaron was desperate to run away with it. Aaron couldn't take it any longer and inside his mind he was screaming, *SOMEONE PLEASE KILL ME!*

As soon as the thought escaped his mind and entered the psychic arena, he heard a tumbling from the top of the stairs. Something had fallen down the stairs and came crashing down into the wall at the foot of the stairs. Aaron didn't dare glance in the direction of the stairs, then the whole situation would become real. *No, I won't look, I won't look, I won't look*, he told himself, wishing to deny what was inevitably going to be a horrible situation. The unknown entity didn't move, and Aaron could see in his distant peripheral something at the foot of the stairs lying motionless in a jumbled ball. Aaron could feel a tear fall from his eye and he so wished this weren't his life, that these weren't his circumstances and that there wasn't some *thing* at the foot of the stairs which he knew must be coming for him. He wished he didn't live in a world where so many wanted to hurt him and there were so many forces outside of his control that were more powerful than he, dictating his fate and plotting his misery and destruction. But wish as he may, the entity remained at the foot of the stairs, seemingly lifeless and perhaps dead, and perhaps it was in Aaron's best interest to finally acknowledge it and get it over with.

"Ok, Aaron, on the count of three." The couch he was resting on lay parallel to the stairway and Aaron slowly turned his head to the right to bring the entity further into his realm of vision.

"One… two…three."

And there it was, a jumble of limbs held together by a lifeless torso. Aaron wasn't quite sure what he was looking at, but it was something akin to a human being, but not quite human. It didn't have any hair on its body, as if it had been rubbed off from centuries of decay. And there was no life within it. It almost had a blueish hue, as if all the life and blood were drained from it and it went past pale. It had shackles on its hands and around its neck as if it had been locked up in a deep pit for countless ages and it had somehow managed to crawl its way out.

And so, there it lay, at the foot of the staircase, a mere fifteen feet away from Aaron, who was paralyzed in fear, perplexity, and confusion as to what had happened and – more importantly – what was to happen next. Aaron couldn't take his eyes off the creature and time seemed to stand still. TICK TOCK, TICK TOCK, TICK TOCK. Aaron could hear the grandfather clock in the background chattering. TICK TOCK, TICK TOCK, TICK TOCK. The grandfather clock continued to pay witness to the absurdity of the moment, and the beating of his heart to the truth that he was, in fact, alive.

Aaron didn't know to do, but he was desperate for help and ready to call out for his mother. And as Aaron pursed his lips to cry for help, he felt the weight of an invisible hand tear into his chest and squeeze his lungs, relinquishing the use of his voice. All he could manage was a soft muffled cry, which caused the lifeless creature to prop up its head and stare directly into Aaron's eyes. This creature looked at Aaron as if he were a piece of meat and feeding time was past due by a few centuries. Aaron began to tremble, and he continued to try calling for help. But his whole body went numb, paralyzed in fear, and the invisible hand holding his lungs hostage squeezed even tighter causing Aaron to panic even further. "Help!" "Help!" he cried out, but the only one near enough to hear his cry was the zombie-like creature, whose eyes were wide with eager anticipation of a delicious meal.

The zombie picked up one hand and reach out to the floor, dragging its body closer to the couch where Aaron lay. It then reached out its other hand in Aaron's direction and dragged itself forward with its legs dangling behind. Slowly, the zombie made its way closer and closer to Aaron's domain and all Aaron could do was shake helplessly, paralyzed in fear. The zombie dragged its nails on the floorboards, and with each passing moment, Aaron could feel himself leaving his body. He was floating off into the corner of the living room, watching the zombie prepare to devour its meal.

"Help! Help! Somebody help me!" Aaron cried out again, frantically shaking to get his limbs to work. But it was no use, and Aaron couldn't help but watch the terror that was unfolding before his very eyes.

The zombie finally made it to the couch Aaron was resting on and propped itself up on its knees. From the corner of the living room Aaron could see it hovering over his body and fear struck him as he saw the zombie slowly open its mouth. But its mouth kept opening further and further until its mouth was the size of its head, and its head was now the size of a watermelon and, to Aaron's utter dismay, it prepared to feast on his body. Aaron saw the short, nubby teeth dulled from crunching flesh and bones and knew the worst was coming. The end was here, and it would be incredibly painful. It was all a trick. All of it. His companion in the desert, the lust for power and control, the chance to become a king and a god, it was all a ploy to completely destroy Aaron only to have him arise anew as a soulless, godless, empty vessel completely drained of all light and life. And as the zombie finally chomped down on Aaron's head, he could feel the searing pain reverberate throughout his body and he shook as if he were having a seizure. CHOMP, CHOMP, CHOMP. Aaron watched it all happen from the corner of the living room, his own destruction at the hands of an escaped prisoner from the pit of despair, the same pit he now knew was destined for him, and he was helpless to stop the attack.

CHAPTER 27

"Are you ok, young man?" the old lady asked Aaron. "I'm so sorry, ma'am. I didn't mean to knock it over."

Aaron looked at the sweet old lady with a mixture of both guilt and fear as he reached down to grab the ceramic figurine he'd knocked onto the ground. He was so groggy from a lack of sleep that he'd walked right into the display case.

"It's quite alright, these things happen!" she replied with a smile.

"Thank you, ma'am. I promise it won't happen again."

"Oh, don't even worry about it, dear. I'm just glad you're here!" She said with a warm smile as she made her way back to the cash register.

Aaron put the ceramic figurine back on the case where other religious items were being displayed and shuffled down the aisle and dragging his pant legs. His pants were too long so he grabbed them to ensure he didn't stumble and knock something else over. He felt so out of place in the store. Everything was so pristine and perfect. The shelves were sanitized from unwanted dirt and dust and he could smell disinfectant in the air. He looked around at all the other smartly-dressed patrons, what was he doing there?!

But he knew why he was there. His mother explained it very clearly as she drove him to the religious bookstore he was now standing in.

"I won't let them take you away from me, Aaron. I just won't." He knew she was referring to the social worker that had visited a few weeks ago and grilled her on her parenting skills. Aaron had enjoyed watching his mother squirm under the weight of the social worker's accusations, and he thought it might be nice to live elsewhere. But he knew something needed to change and running from his problems wouldn't help. He couldn't stand the nightmares anymore and wanted to be the young man that the stranger from his dream believed Aaron could become.

"You're done with all that devil stuff. All of it. I found that book of yours and threw it in the trash. No more weird movies or music or symbols on your arms. And you need to stop spending so much time alone in your bedroom. You need to change, honey, so you're going to pick something out from that bookstore and we're not leaving until you do. It's time to find God."

Aaron's mother parked the car in the parking lot and lit a cigarette, "Go on now. Find God!" she told Aaron as she blew cigarette smoke out the car window.

And so Aaron found himself perusing various religious items wondering where God was to be found. He felt so embarrassed about how he was dressed and the sores on his face and he was expecting to be wiped away from the store just like the unwanted dirt and dust. But, to his surprise, the nice old lady behind the cash register seemed to be glad Aaron was there. She flashed him a smile and gave him a wave, asking if he needed help finding anything. But he could hardly ask her to help him find God. Perhaps God didn't want to be found anyway. Perhaps God had already found those he really loved which didn't include Aaron and so he was just wasting his time with the whole charade. Aaron wasn't sure. So he continued to stumble through the store holding his pants up and wondering what he was looking for.

His mother had shared a few Bible stories with him when he was a child, but he could barely remember them and understood them even less. He had walked past the book section and saw a variety of Bibles and books on Christian spirituality and philosophy.

"*The Screwtape Letters*," Aaron read aloud the title of one book. "What the heck is a screwtape?" he asked himself. Then there was another book that caught his eye: *Fresh Wind, Fresh Fire.*

"Huh?" he asked aloud, wondering what stale wind and fire might look like. Aaron wasn't finding God in the book section, so he kept walking.

He walked down another aisle where religious music was being displayed and decided to take a closer look. There were shelves on either side of him all lined with compact discs and he grabbed several and took them over to a station where he was allowed to sample them, but it didn't take long for Aaron to realize he wouldn't find God here, either. All the songs were so foreign to him. He didn't understand what they were singing about and why they were so happy. He just couldn't relate so he put all the compact discs back where he found them and continued his search for God.

He moved on from the music and strolled into the religious apparel where he found a variety of t-shirts, sweatshirts, hats, and socks extolling the "Holy One" and Aaron had no idea what that meant. He then found himself stumbling into the religious crafts where he knocked over the ceramic figurine. There were ceramic lambs and lions and wooden crosses. There were also bracelets with the letters WWJD written on them. *What?* Aaron picked one up to study it closer. He didn't know what any of this had to do with God, so he put the bracelet back down and continued walking through the store.

Just past the crafts were a large wall of paintings and drawings and Aaron walked over to get a closer look. They were all masterfully drawn and were all very interesting paintings. There was a painting of a large boat in the ocean and another where the ocean was split in two and there were people walking between the two bodies of water. One painting had a lion and lamb playing with each other and then there was another of a dove with a stick in its mouth. There was also one with a group of adults and several animals in a farm all staring at a baby. What were they waiting for that baby to do? And more importantly, where was God? He still didn't know.

Aaron was discouraged and began walking towards the door to let his mother know he hadn't found God when something caught the corner of his eye. It was near the ground so it was harder to see, and it was much smaller than the other paintings, but Aaron could tell immediately that it was different. He decided to take a closer look, so he walked back towards the paintings and crouched down to see what it was that caught his eye. It was a painting of a man, and the man had a look on his face that Aaron was all too familiar with. It was despair, and anguish, and complete hopelessness. Aaron grabbed the painting and examined it further, and he noticed the torn jeans the man was wearing that didn't fit right. And he noticed the man's crinkly shirt with stains on them. He had the look and posture of a broken man ready to crumble. And Aaron could see his body was limp and his knees had buckled from the crushing weight of being alive. His eyes were closed, and his head tilted back because he no longer wanted to face the world. It was a man who had given up, who was ready to die, and the only thing that was holding him up were the arms of the man standing behind him, refusing to let go. Aaron gripped the painting tight and studied every last stroke on the canvas. After several minutes of studying the painting Aaron let out a slight chuckle and then a long sigh in disbelief that he'd found a priceless treasure he believed could never exist. As he stared into the eyes of the man sustaining the broken and miserable wretch on the canvas Aaron smiled to himself, for he knew he was staring into the eyes of God.

CHAPTER 28

It was the power. It had always been the power to change his own circumstances that had seduced him. He longed for the power to fight back against the circumstances that were crushing him. But he had now tasted the fruit of pure power; he had familiarized himself with the ways of the dark and slowly began to understand what happens when power is divorced from love. It was dawning on him that the ability to dominate could only take someone so far in life and that power in and of itself could be a weapon for immense good but also immeasurable evil. And no matter the amount of force, power, or pressure put on a human being you could never compel them to love. Aaron realized that although it would've been marvelous to have the power to remove himself entirely from the trauma of his life, it would be even more marvelous to be surrounded by a great cloud of love that would help heal his wounds. The idea that someone was holding Aaron up and refusing to let go was more appealing than revenge and the thought that someone loved him more than life itself was the most wonderful thought of all.

This was the thought that brought Aaron to the desk in his bedroom staring at the Bible his mother bought him at the bookstore. She had also purchased him the painting, which was now hanging by his bedside. He was eager to learn more about the great companion holding up the anguished man in the painting and refusing to let him go. He wasn't quite sure where to start but he knew the gospels were important, so he thumbed through the book until he landed on the book of Matthew. Aaron began reading, *This is the genealogy of Jesus the Messiah...* and immediately he was gripped by the story of this man who was also God, this Christ Man who loved humanity so much that it caused blood to poor from his skin. The words jumped off the pages and Aaron felt himself transported into a world where pain and misery compelled a god to take action and lavish love on the hurting, bleeding, and impoverished of this world. In this world, there was a god that lamented over the pain of its people, who wept over his friends and showed his love by pouring out his blood. In this world, there were suffering people everywhere. There were the demon-possessed, the blind and the deaf, and there were the misfits, the strangers, the poor and hungry, the outcasts and the unwanted, the mistreated, and this Christ Man came to them, and wept over them, and created a way for all the degenerates to experience unfiltered love for all-time.

This was the story that Aaron read, the story of a Christ Man who chose to suffer alongside humanity, who was compelled by love to reveal Himself to those that needed him most, and Aaron felt as if he were a character in the book, that he was one of the degenerates, the misfits, the outcasts and the unwanted. He was alongside them shouting, "Hosanna! Save me! Please save me from this miserable existence!" Aaron felt as if this Christ Man came specifically to him and for him and that there was a deep love for Aaron that he couldn't quite understand.

Aaron could smell the grit in the air and feel the heat of the desert as he walked through Jerusalem to see what this Christ Man would do. Aaron peeked his head into the temple to see the Christ Man raise hell over the selling of cattle. He held his breath as he saw the Christ Man defend the charlatan and urge her to sin no more, and he rejoiced with the disciples as he saw the Christ Man multiply the fish and the bread to feed the large crowd of followers. He could also feel his heart beating through his chest as he saw the Christ Man walking on water and yelled out in fear as he saw Peter began to sink to the bottom of the lake. He could feel the hope spring up in his chest as the crippled man took his first step since childhood, and when the blind man saw his own reflection in the pool for the first time. Aaron felt the full range of emotions as he journeyed with the Christ Man through Jerusalem and Galilee, but he was unprepared for the emotions that swelled inside as he saw the Christ Man betrayed by one of his closest friends.

Aaron felt a deep sense of shock as the Christ Man was taken away by very official-looking men to the Temple. Aaron could feel the dread and despair and the worry weighed heavily on his face as the Christ Man was condemned by the local authorities. It was as if this story was taking a terrible turn for the worse and Aaron wasn't prepared for it. And Aaron couldn't help but yell out, "NO!" as one of these officials struck the first blow on the Christ Man. Aaron felt powerless as these men wailed on the Christ Man, and whipped him with cords and beat him with their fists and Aaron could feel the blood wet his lips and flesh hit his face as the torture commenced. And Aaron could feel the first teardrop trickle down his face as he saw the Christ Man turn his head towards him from his torture chamber, blood running down his face and stared directly into Aaron's eyes.

Aaron couldn't believe it, that the Christ Man had even noticed Aaron was there at all! And yet He held his gaze towards Aaron as the cords tore the flesh off his back. Aaron could tell the Christ Man was in extreme pain, but it didn't dissuade him from holding eye contact with Aaron, and it seemed that all the pain in the world couldn't stop him from letting Aaron know that He noticed him, that He chose to be in this predicament and chose to suffer all this world could throw at Him. And Aaron couldn't quite put his finger on the moment, but he knew he had seen this Christ Man before. He had seen him in some other life, in some other situation of great mourning and sadness. Aaron had a hard time looking into the Christ Man's eyes, suffering as immensely as He was, but he couldn't shake the feeling there was a time the Christ Man had also had a hard time looking into Aaron's eyes in a moment of his own great suffering. And Aaron felt that somehow, they were linked together by their mutual suffering and mourning for one another.

Aaron felt as if he were beginning to lose it, the intensity of the moment and the depth of the Christ Man's resolve to suffer was more than he could handle. He could feel his body begin to tremble as if he were a dam on the verge of bursting open, as if there were tears that needed to be spilled that would gush from the depths of Aaron's soul that he didn't know even existed. Aaron walked alongside the Christ Man as he was given the cross to carry to his death, all the while doing his best to stay strong for the Christ Man. And so, they walked together towards the ultimate form of suffering humanity could imagine at the time, and Aaron was so torn inside with what to make of the situation. The Christ Man had performed miracles, raised the dead, and walked on water. He showed all the signs of possessing unspeakable power and yet he chose to walk right into the lion's den and stuck his head in the lion's mouth. Aaron felt it was all wrong but right at the same time and as he kept reading the pages of the book, he took steps in stride with the Christ Man towards the top of the hill where he would go to hang on that cross until his lungs filled with blood and he suffocated to death.

They had finally made it to the place of his execution and Aaron sat next to the Christ Man's mother and his beloved friend John and they all cried together as the Christ Man's blood poured through every crevice of his body and he cried out in anguish from the pain. The Christ Man looked lost as the pain overwhelmed Him and perhaps, he no longer knew where He was or even what He was. But the Christ Man took a deep breath and was given something to drink from his tormentors. Aaron's eyes were fixed resolutely on the Christ Man, unsure of what would happen next. The Christ Man closed his eyes and took another deep breath and opened his eyes and looked directly into Aaron's eyes for a second time. The Christ Man's whole body was trembling as if it took his every ounce of strength and focus to hold the gaze with Aaron. The Christ Man bit his lip but continued the gaze for what felt like an eternity. And Aaron felt as if the Christ Man were staring into the very depth of Aaron's soul and infiltrating his lungs with a warmth and comfort Aaron had never felt before. The gaze radiated like the sun and pierced through Aaron's eyes and exposed the darkness and the lies embedded in the back of his psyche that told Aaron he was worthless, unlovable, and undeserving of love. Aaron could see the pain in the Christ Man's eyes and throughout his whole body and Aaron wished the Christ Man would quit staring at him, for he knew he didn't deserve the attention and hated to see the Christ Man suffer so immensely. But the Christ Man was making it a point to maintain eye contact with Aaron, and he was invading Aaron's senses and soaking into every cell of his body. He was like a rushing river that was carrying away the deep debris at the bottom of Aaron's heart, and just as the whip had peeled away at the Christ Man's skin Aaron could feel the bitterness peel away from his heart.

Time seemed to stand still, and Aaron felt as if he were transforming on the inside, that somehow the Christ Man's pain was redeeming him from the cruelty of the world. And as the Christ Man's body continued to tremble in pain Aaron began to see the beautiful world that was intended for Aaron, that was stolen from him by the hands of demons and jackals, and this Christ Man refused to sit by idly and watch Aaron destroy himself. Aaron's whole body felt as if he were about to set ablaze from the emotion and the drama and the love. The dam was beginning to burst, and Aaron was finally seeing that perhaps he was worthy of love, that he wasn't a filthy throwaway, and that perhaps someone or something was out there that couldn't bear to see Aaron in so much pain. Perhaps someone was watching him and was desperate to take the pain away. And as Aaron thought about all this and stared into the deep pool of unshakable resolve, he saw the Christ Man's mouth part and with the faintest sound whispered, "I will come for you. I swear it."

And as soon as the words parted from his mouth a tormentor pierced his side to bring an end to the suffering. And the Christ Man closed his eyes, his head fell forward, and He was no more.

It was all too much for Aaron, and he keeled over in excruciating pain from the pent-up love in Aaron's heart finally spilling out from the depths of his soul. He wept from the pain and the love and the resolve of this Christ Man. It was just a book, but it seemed so much more than a book. The book was a window into another world, a portal into the divine allowing men to pierce into the very mind of God. For the first time in his life, Aaron felt he was loved. He couldn't help himself from weeping. His whole body was warm from the flame of divine love and as the tears fell down his cheeks and hit his bedroom floor, he thought to himself of this beautiful Christ Man and he hoped amongst all hopes that He did know who Aaron was and that He did love him as much as he appeared to in the book. He felt his love rush through his body like a mighty torrent, mixing with the divine love that invaded his heart, and knew he was becoming something new entirely.

The Christ Man held Aaron up in his bedroom, refusing to let him fall apart, all the while two red, beady eyes filled with hateful intentions looked upon them.

CHAPTER 29

That night Aaron slept peacefully for the first time in months. There were no demons or jackals, no night terrors or paralysis. And there were no voices or fear or paranoia. There was only the sweet sensation of being loved. Aaron woke up peacefully in the morning and knew there was something different about the day. He could feel it the moment he opened his eyes and knew it when he felt the warmth of the sun radiating from hundreds of thousands of miles, making its way to his very home and into his very life, illuminating all the beauty and hope and clarity that was promised to him and meant for him since the dawn of time. He could see its rays of light exuding hope and redemption and watched the flickering of its beams dance before him as if to remind him of all the reasons there are to dance in this life; of all the reasons there are to laugh and to smile and for Aaron to radiate hope and love and joy from the epicenter of his being.

The light that had set flame to all the lies he had been told and had been telling himself for too many years. The light was a messenger declaring the purposeful intention to set him free from years of deception and cruelty and to herald a new age of divine grace. It felt like the birth of a star, or the moment absolute light collides with absolute darkness, like a tidal wave of beauty decimating a great beast and drowning out its howl and hateful intentions. It felt as if he were being reborn as a creature of pure light and that he was being flipped inside out, emptied of all the filth building up inside and knitted together by the very hands of God.

The thought was overwhelming, so much so that Aaron failed to notice his lips form a smile as he watched his messenger declare the dawn of a new glorious age. He closed his eyes and soaked in the warmth of the sun and gladly received its message and accepted the omen and allowed pure love to completely overtake him. He felt its power enter his bloodstream and soar through his veins colliding with every cancerous thought and belief about himself. It radiated throughout his entire body and Aaron knew not what to do but simply express his silent gratitude that the darkness was over. *Behold, He makes all things new*, Aaron thought to himself as he felt the healing power of pure love cause him to become something different entirely, something he had never been before nor ever imagined becoming. He could feel the spark of the divine igniting with him, interacting and intermixing with the material world and the cosmic order and he knew that a beautiful future was meant for him. He knew that he was meant to become a star that radiated pure love throughout the material world, creating beauty he never knew existed.

The darkness was lifting, and the true light of life and love was dwelling inside him and would be his constant reminder of the truth. The light was surging, pouring into the great chasm where his heart once was and convincing him of the truth. Love had made its dwelling place within Aaron's heart and was expelling the darkness. And he didn't have to earn this love. He didn't have to walk through the thicket of barbarous thorns or keep the company of demons and jackals. He didn't have to sacrifice his innocence night after night in eager anticipation that someday he may feel the warm embrace of love. Aaron found himself drifting in this sea of love simply for being; not for what he had done but what he was. What he was compelled pure love to suffer alongside him, allowing his blood to be spilled just the way Aaron's had years ago.

The thought overwhelmed all his senses, that he had a deep and vital purpose in this life, and that he was deeply loved and would never be put in harm's way again. It was strange, Aaron thought, that he had seen the sun and felt its warmth all these years and failed to understand its message. All these years the sun had been calling out to Aaron, seeking to ignite his life with the truth of his existence, but Aaron hadn't understood. And all these years the great bodies of water had been reaching out to Aaron, declaring the great abundance that was provided for him; to drink in deeply the truth of his existence, but Aaron hadn't understood. And all these years Aaron had failed to understand the world's most beautiful wildflowers and lilies and roses with their seasonal death and resurrection had been calling out to him the promise of new beginnings. Aaron realized he was surrounded by beautiful messengers meant to reveal the truth, and Aaron made a promise to himself that he would never ignore their messages again.

Aaron heard the front door open and pretended he was still asleep, for he wasn't ready for the beautiful moment to end. He still preferred sleeping in the living room. He just had the feeling that something evil lurked inside his bedroom and preferred not to lie completely vulnerable next to a portal leading to a pit of unending torment. The power of light was indeed transforming him, but it was still a process and so there he lay on the couch in the living room.

Thomas entered the door with his friend Michael, whose house he had stayed at the night before. Aaron could hear the two chatter but acted as if he were still asleep, not ready to share the moment with anyone else. But he listened in on the chatter and could hear that they were talking about Aaron, and Thomas was telling Michael that Aaron had gone through a tremendous transformation. He told Michael that he was immensely proud of his brother, that Aaron had overcome significant obstacles, and was making great choices in his life. Unknowingly, Thomas lavished upon Aaron the gift that every child craves. Aaron soaked it in, listening intently to the praise and love and pride Thomas had for him, that he was proud to call Aaron brother. Aaron was as still as a board but inside him, he was exploding with gratitude and felt an avalanche of emotions stirring within. He was becoming whole, and Aaron could feel the agitation in his eyes and the quivering of his lips and was grateful for all the messages God had sent him that day.

CHAPTER 30

"And God said, 'Let there be light,'" Aaron read aloud as he sat up in his bed. He had read through all the gospels and so he decided to go back to the very beginning, when creation began, and he squinted his eyes as he slowly absorbed the material before him. The painting of his companion was still at his bedside and Aaron finally felt safe in his bedroom, unafraid of what might visit him when rested his head in the darkness of night. He read a few chapters and began yawning as darkness slowly descended upon his bedroom. The last several weeks had been filled with peaceful dreams and he smiled as he slowly drifted out of consciousness.

It didn't take long for Aaron to feel the gentle wind caress his face and he finally opened his eyes to find himself in the midst of a peaceful meadow. He looked long and hard at the environment: the mountains, the aroma of wildflowers, lilies, roses, and daffodils, and was grateful for the unblemished beauty. It made him think of the Christ Man, and then the man who spoke to him on the dream-beach, and it caused a warm smile to cross his face. Aaron soaked in the ambience of this perfect moment and called out to anyone who would listen, "I love you."

As soon as the words left his lips and collided with the atmosphere he heard the shuffling of feet in the distance. Then there was a loud hissing noise and Aaron turned his head to see a large creature running towards him. The creature was pitch black with red, beady eyes and large horns protruding out of its head. It had long, razor sharp claws attached to its fingers and the creature bore its fangs with great ferocity and intent. It had the effect of a picture jumping out of the page of a book. It rattled Aaron and jolted him from his perfect moment. He felt like he was in a dream within a dream and Aaron hesitated as the creature drew closer to him and with great savagery and ferocity screamed, "To the death!" as it extended its claws towards his chest. The creature was a mere few feet away, prepared to devour Aaron, but he wasn't afraid. Aaron wouldn't give into the intimidation and knew the Christ Man was with him and he could feel love soaring through his veins.

The creature was now within striking distance, and as he made a violent lunge towards Aaron's chest Aaron let out a scream which emanated a blinding light that repulsed the creature and sent it sprawling backward. The creature stumbled over itself and fell to the ground in disbelief. It stared at Aaron in shock for a quick moment, but the shock turned into rage and it ran back towards Aaron and began screaming again, "I will steal your soul, Aaron!"

But Aaron was emboldened by love and power and began speaking in a language completely foreign to him, a language that was lost to time. But they seemed familiar to the creature, for it began to squirm and folded under the weight of Aaron's words. Aaron approached the creature with love and power radiating from his being and spoke the mysterious words over the suffering creature until it ran away in defeat.

Aaron opened his eyes to find himself back in his bedroom. He thought of the unintelligible words from the unknown language he had spoken and he knew that something had happened. He could feel the power invade his bedroom, sanitizing it from all that had haunted Aaron over the years. He felt love capture all that had been stolen from him, and his eyes were open to the great extent to which various invisible powers were at play in his body and mind.

Aaron was on high alert and immediately began scanning the bedroom, sensing that something was still amiss. He looked in his bed, and then at his desk, and finally he looked in the direction of his closet as his heart began beating wildly. There it was, on the top shelf, next to his baseball card collection, in all its anger and ferocity. It was the white face with red streaks across both eyes with red speckles covering its face. It had large fangs and its face was protruding from the wall as if it were attempting to break through the wall. The creature hissed at Aaron but Aaron wasn't afraid and didn't give in to the creature's unspoken demands. Instead, Aaron opened his mouth, and began speaking again loudly in an unintelligible language that only the creature understood.

Aaron could see the fury and the rage in its eyes, as Aaron's words soaked into the creature and reverberated throughout the bedroom. Its eyes glinted with deep resolve at Aaron, refusing to obey the commands coming from his mouth, but the words were like a fire to the creature who screamed in pain before finally ejecting itself from the bedroom.

Aaron sat up in his bed when his mother bolted through the door and turned the lights on. "What's going on, honey? Is everything ok?"

Aaron didn't quite know how to respond to the question, for he felt that things were happening that were far outside his understanding. The whole exchange was very odd but invigorating. He felt in control, he felt that love had invaded his soul and would never, EVER, let the darkness consume him again.

Whatever happened, its significance was far greater than he could understand, and he chose to savor the moment that, for the first time in a long time, everything was ok.

CHAPTER 31

aron stared at the clock on the classroom wall from his seat in the back of the class. He was counting down the minutes and practicing what he would say. He wanted to get it just right. He had already made so many mistakes and he couldn't afford to mess it up this time. He couldn't tell what Mrs. Brown was babbling on about, but the year was almost over, and his grades were all but doomed so he continued to ignore her lesson and stared at the clock, thinking about what he would say.

It had been a long year, a strange and difficult year, but Aaron wasn't looking back. He wasn't dwelling on his mistakes and the people he'd hurt, and he knew what he needed to do. The minutes were winding down and he looked around at the students who all still disliked him and wanted nothing to do with him. He was alone, but he saw that the symbol he'd carved on his palm had all but faded and in its place were the words he had been preparing to say to Mrs. Brown. He thought of the painting hanging on his bedside wall and felt love surge through his heart, so he didn't let his fear get the best of him.

The bell finally rang, and the students slowly began to scatter, chatting amongst themselves along the way. But Aaron was still lingering in the back of the class, still scared about what he was about to do.

"Did you need something, Aaron?" Mrs. Brown called out to him. He knew she didn't like him and could tell she was deeply annoyed that he was yet to exit her classroom. He could hear it in the sound of her voice and by the way she looked at him he knew he didn't belong. He never did. No one forgot what he had done to David, especially her, and she gave him a look of disgust and contempt every day he stepped into her classroom. This moment was no different.

"I said did you need something, Aaron?" she called out again with an obvious tinge of annoyance. Aaron took a deep breath and finally stood up. He stared at his feet as he slowly walked towards her desk at the front of the classroom. She began to gather her things and busied herself with straightening her desk, waiting for the moment to be over. Aaron finally made it to her desk and stared at his feet and put his hands in his pockets and tried to gather his thoughts.

"Well, what is it, Aaron? What do you want?" Mrs. Brown asked with a building frustration.

Ok, here we go, Aaron told himself and took his hands out of his pocket.

"Mrs. Brown, I know I'm not supposed to be around David—
—"

"That's right, Aaron. You're not," she replied before Aaron could finish his sentence. She didn't even bother to look at him but kept busying herself with straightening her desk.

"Right. I know I'm not supposed to be around David," he continued while still staring at his shoes. He could feel the weight of her contemptuous glare and lacked the strength to look her in the eyes. "So, I was hoping you could give this to him." Aaron pulled out a letter he had written to David. "You can read it if you want to, or whatever. I just really wanted to tell him something."

"Are you sure you haven't caused enough damage, Aaron?" she replied coldly as she gathered the assignments that were handed in at the end of class.

"Right. Well, I'll just leave it here in case you want to give it to him," he replied, still staring at his shoes. Aaron dropped it on her desk and slowly walked out of the classroom without ever making eye contact. It was a difficult moment, but Aaron was glad he'd done it. He knew Mrs. Brown was eager to be rid of him so he scurried down the hallway to his next class. He walked at a brisk pace and never looked back.

Mrs. Brown opened his note and read his message to David. And while Aaron moved along to the next class filled with other students that didn't like him, Mrs. Brown locked her classroom door and soaked in the regret and shame emanating from Aaron's message, and she welcomed the great swell of compassion and love for him that sprouted in her heart.

Aaron missed it all, but God and the clock on her classroom wall paid witness to the moment a sweet, kind smile formed on Mrs. Brown's face as she said aloud, "Well, then. Maybe there is hope after all."

WAKE UP, AARON

CHAPTER 32

Aaron stepped off the school bus and took a deep breath as he stared at the towering building ahead of him. It had to be twice the size of his middle school and he was overwhelmed as he thought of everyone he would meet and all the things he would learn inside its walls. It was the first day of high school and he felt like this could be a fresh start. He hadn't had a nightmare in months and lately he'd been able to focus attentively in class and didn't worry about seeing or hearing things that weren't there. In fact, he had done such a good job that he was able to turn things around in Mrs. Brown's English class and he squeaked by with a passing grade. It was a miracle, but he remembered seeing the look in Mrs. Brown's eye when she told him the good news.

"Keep up the good work, Aaron. You've earned it," she said with a smile. The students in his class slowly warmed up to Aaron as he cleaned up his look and exercised proper hygiene. He wasn't quite there but it was close enough and a few boys had eventually found their way over to Aaron's desk and befriended him.

Aaron had become into an attentive and polite student and he finished his eighth-grade year on a positive note, getting the best grades he had ever gotten and receiving a Student of the Month honor from one of his teachers. His mother also received a call from the school principal applauding her and Aaron for his drastic turnaround.

"Whatever you are doing, keep it up!" Mrs. Sullivan told Margaret. "Something has gotten into Aaron in the best possible way. He is a pleasure to have in our school and is getting along so well with all the students and teachers." Aaron felt as if he were a wellspring of love that poured over into the lives of everyone around him, and each night he would go to his room, shut his door, and attentively listen as the Christ Man poured out more of His love into Aaron's heart and bring tears to his eyes. He had a new friend, one that meant for Aaron's good and not his destruction, and Aaron would follow the omens and stay on the path that the Christ Man was laying out for him.

Aaron began walking towards his new school and David stepped off the bus shortly thereafter, following closely behind Aaron. Mrs. Brown had passed along Aaron's note after all, and they were both surprised to see each other at football tryouts that summer. It took some time but by the end of the tryouts David approached Aaron and forgave him. It was a difficult moment for the both of them but once it passed they were able to see all they had in common and soon became friends.

David walked past Aaron and knocked his backpack strap off his shoulder and ran towards the entrance.

"Beat you there!" David yelled as he ran past Aaron.

"Come on!" Aaron said, chuckling as he ran after David. They both finally made it through the front entrance and looked around the sprawling interior of the building. There were kids everywhere walking to and from class. Some students were big, and others were small. Some were downright huge, and some had full moustaches and beards and stood at least a foot taller than the two of them. As they both caught their breath staring at their classmates they couldn't both help but feel like small fish in a very big pond.

"We'd better stick together, then," David told Aaron as he grabbed his hand and walked over to their lockers. Aaron found his locker and fumbled through his combination, trying to put his jacket away as fast as he could so as to not be late for class. David was much quicker at opening his locker and quickly shut his things inside and chided Aaron to hurry up. Aaron finally got his combination right and put his jacket into his locker and as he shut his locker he could hear someone calling his name.

"Aaron, over here!"

He turned around to see Amanda standing at her locker in the distance. He and Amanda had shared gym class last year and they had spoken a few times. She was a kind girl who had always been nice to Aaron and he got the feeling that she was smitten with him. This made him a bit uncomfortable because girls made him feel squeamish. There had been a few girls over the summer break that Aaron had run into who expressed interest in spending time alone with him in their bedroom, and while Aaron was flattered, he had no interest in the invitations. It was all just so uncomfortable to Aaron. The attention made the hairs on the back of his neck stand on end and filled him with the sudden urge to run away screaming. Sometimes he would become nauseous and feared he might throw up. He knew it wasn't something he could handle and felt it was best that he steered clear from the issue altogether and work on making more friendships with his classmates.

"Aaron!" she called out again. He stopped to think about her and remembered that they had gotten along well enough in class. He also remembered that she played soccer and volleyball and was a part of the student council. She seemed like a very normal person who probably had very nice, normal friends and came from a nice, normal family. He was torn and was wondering if he should go say hello.

Aaron felt a tug on his shoulder. "So are you coming with me?" David asked as he started to head towards their first class. "Don't leave me hanging!"

Aaron felt a tinge of guilt for not immediately following David to class. But there was a warm breeze blowing on his neck and pushing him in Amanda's direction.

"Suit yourself. I'll catch you later, then." David called out.

"Sounds good, David," Aaron replied as he stared at Amanda and slowly began walking in her direction, feeling the warm, gentle breeze carry him towards her locker, excited to see what the future had in store for him.

CHAPTER 33

"Surprise!" Aaron was stunned by the unexpected cheer and immediately opened his eyes and moved his arms forward as if he were bracing for impact. It was a beautiful sight, and the gesture made Aaron smile from ear to ear. His eyes started watering up so he quickly rubbed the tears away so no one could see. Never in a million years had he imagined that so many people would come together and celebrate his birthday. But there they were, all smiling at Aaron as if they were excited and grateful to be there. And he had Amanda to thank.

They were all out on the back deck of her parent's house and Aaron was amazed to see the big to-do Amanda made over his fifteenth birthday. She had blown balloons and bought party hats and had festive music on in the background. She'd also planned a few party games and even bought cake and ice cream. It was a birthday unlike any other and Aaron couldn't help but explode in joy. Aaron was speechless but the smile on his face said it all and so much more. It said of how grateful he was to be surrounded by friends he never thought he would have. It said that he finally felt he fit in somewhere and that there were people that really cared about him. And it said that he would never have to think about the painful memories of his past ever again.

Amanda joined Aaron by his side as he remained speechless. "Happy birthday, Aaron."

She grabbed his hand and he squeezed hers and although the act made him queasy he was trying to warm up to Amanda's affection.

"So, what do you think, Aaron? Did you see it coming?" David called out from the crowd. Aaron laughed out loud and stared at his shoes. So much had changed over the year and he was still acclimating to the positive attention.

"No. I didn't see it coming. Not in a million years!" Aaron finally replied.

"Well, you deserve it! Happy birthday, buddy!"

"Happy birthday, Aaron!" they all called out. It was a mixture of friends from school and teammates from his football and baseball team. There were also several of Amanda's own friends who made up the party, and as several of his friends descended upon him to give him a big hug he wondered how this had all happened.

After the first day of school, he and Amanda kept in touch and talked on the phone regularly. After a while she invited Aaron over to dinner to meet her family and it wasn't too long before Aaron found himself spending most of his evenings at her house studying. Her house was always so clean and her parents so friendly. They always seemed happy to see Aaron and would ask him about football and baseball and inquire about his grades in school. They asked him so many more questions than his own parents asked him, and it made him feel strange but comfortable at the same time. It was a real respite from the turmoil that persisted in his own household, so he happily accepted her invitations to study.

This went on for half the school year until Aaron felt a bit stuck. He really enjoyed Amanda's company and didn't want to stop spending time with her, but at the same time he was scared what might happen if they became a couple. They still hadn't kissed, and Aaron brushed off all her advances to get near him, as if he were a wounded animal wincing in pain. She had given him every indication that she cared for him but there was something inside him that instinctually withdrew. He knew this was unfair to Amanda who'd told him on several occasions she cared for him as more than a friend and that something needed to change.

Aaron wasn't ready to stop seeing Amanda so he decided he to do his best to ignore his discomfort and pursue her romantically. It was a slow process and by the time his birthday rolled around near the end of the school year they still hadn't kissed. He knew Amanda cared for him; he could see it in her eyes while she attended to the surprise birthday party she had thrown. And he could tell by her thoughtful birthday present and all the effort she'd made to invite his friends and gather the supplies for the party. And yet Aaron still struggled immensely with the thought of building a romance. But he knew that had to change. Amanda deserved it and he knew he should want it, was supposed to want it, and would just have to get over whatever his issues might be.

It had been a magical evening and as the guests began to scatter he looked up at the starry sky and thought of the man who'd revealed to Aaron the young man he was always meant to be. It was all coming together perfectly, and the man had been right about everything. Aaron stared at Amanda from the back deck as she was cleaning in the kitchen. She was throwing paper cups and plates in the trash when her head lifted up and she noticed Aaron staring at her, smiling. Amanda smiled back at Aaron and Aaron made his way from the back deck and opened the back door to meet her in the kitchen. They were both now alone in the kitchen, her parents having gone out for the night. Aaron slowly made his approach, ignoring the queasiness in his gut and the pounding of his heart, and gently caressed her head. He drew her in for a kiss and they both closed their eyes as their lips finally locked together.

"Happy birthday, Aaron," Amanda said to Aaron through a wide smile, but the sound of buzzing static had filled his ears and drowned out the sentiment.

CHAPTER 34

"Try not to poke me, ok Aaron?" Amanda chided Aaron with a smile. Aaron smiled as he focused intently on pinning the corsage to the spaghetti strap of her dress. His hands trembled. Both of her parents watched Aaron fumble along with amused grins on their face.

"Yeah, Aaron!" her dad called out. "Don't think you can stick a needle into my daughter's shoulder and then take her out for the night!" Amanda's mother chuckled as they both laid on the lighthearted banter at their daughter's steady boyfriend.

"Ok, guys. I'll do my best, but no promises," Aaron responded with a devilish grin. But the joking was over, and Aaron focused in on the corsage and spaghetti strap like a surgeon performing heart surgery and after he got his hands to stop trembling he pushed the needle through, pinning the corsage to Amanda's dress. "Thank God," he whispered under his breath. He took a step back and stared at Amanda and how beautiful she looked. She had her hair pinned up and her makeup was done with an understated sophistication and she was practically glowing. Meanwhile, Aaron was wearing hand-me-down dress pants from his brother Adam, his adoptive father's jacket and shirt, and his brother Thomas' dress shoes. His mother had purchased him a nice tie and Aaron pulled it all together like a puzzle whose pieces were barely fitting.

But Aaron didn't mind. He was just glad to be there and was grateful that he and Amanda were still together and her affection for him had only grown over the past six months. Since his birthday party Aaron had slowly began showing Amanda more affection, and they shared tender moments together where their lips would lock and he would caress her head and back. But they were still infrequent, and he had to fight against the queasiness when he was around her. But she was worth it and had been so patient with Aaron over the past year. She had such a lovely family, the type of family Aaron always longed for, and hoped he would have someday. And although buzzing static would fill his ears every time they kissed he thought of the man in his dreams who encouraged Aaron to not lose hope and was determined to not let his nerves get the best of him.

"Ok, Aaron, be sure to bring Amanda home in one piece!" her father called out.

"I promise!" Aaron called back as he opened the door for Amanda in the passenger seat of her parents' car. They were kind enough to let Aaron use their vehicle since Aaron didn't have one of his own.

"Thanks for taking me to the dance," Amanda said with a smile. "You played a great game yesterday, by the way. And you look so hot in that uniform!"

"Thanks," Aaron replied, shaking his head in amusement, "I'm glad you noticed."

"Of course I noticed! All the girls noticed, Aaron, and I'm so proud you chose me out of all the girls who were tripping over each other to go to the dance with you!" she said mockingly as she rubbed Aaron's thigh.

Aaron could feel his brain begin to tingle but he just smiled at Amanda, shook his head in disbelief and said, "Whatever!"

Aaron pulled up to a restaurant where they were meeting friends before the dance started. There were a dozen couples meeting up and Aaron was excited to see his friends from his football team, including David. Aaron walked through the front entrance holding Amanda's hand and saw the rest of the party taking their seats at a large table at the back of the restaurant.

"It is about time you got here, Aaron!" David called out, giving him a big hug.

"I know, I was having a hard time getting Amanda's corsage on. And her parents were watching me, so I felt like the pressure was on to not stick her with the needle."

David looked over at Amanda. "Looks like you pulled it off. Now you've got them on your good side they won't suspect what you'll do to Amanda tonight," David said with a chuckle and put his arm around Aaron's shoulder. Aaron smiled and watched

Amanda talking with her friends at the other side of the table and ignored the panic building in his chest.

They all finally sat down, and Aaron spoke with David and his other friends about last night's game and laughed at Aaron for completely missing the ball on several occasions and Aaron laughed at himself, grateful to be amongst friends. Aaron began sharing a story with his friends from the game when he felt a hand caress his inner thigh again and the buzzing static grew so loud he could barely hear what he was saying. His head began to pound mercilessly, and his brain was tingling all over. He did his best to concentrate so as to finish the story and was grateful to see them all smile and laugh when Aaron had finally delivered the punch line.

The meal was finally over and they got back into Amanda's car and headed to the school where the dance was taking place. Aaron and Amanda made small talk and Aaron could see in the corner of his eye that Amanda was staring at him with a smile, as if she were truly enjoying his company. It was a beautiful starry night and Aaron grabbed Amanda's hand as they headed towards the school.

"Amanda, I just want you to know that you're a very special girl, and I'm glad you've chosen to be with me. You make me really happy," Aaron told her, fighting back the rising panic in his chest.

"I feel the same about you. The past year has been incredible, and I wouldn't trade it for the world." They smiled at each other as they walked through the entrance into the great homecoming celebration.

Aaron could feel the excitement in the air and soaked in all the ornate decorations that adorned the school halls. There was a station where teachers were serving punch and snacks and there was a photobooth in the lunchroom. It was beautiful, and Aaron was grateful to share the moment with Amanda. The lights were dimly lit and there were students everywhere wearing sophisticated dresses and smart suits and Aaron felt a strange tingle in his hands as they made their way to the gymnasium where the dance was taking place.

It was such a perfect moment and Aaron felt as if they were both floating down the steps towards the gymnasium. There were a set of double doors into the gymnasium that were decorated to look like the entrance to a castle, and as he walked across the gymnasium threshold Aaron laughed to see all the beautiful colors shining from the DJ's booth and the disco ball hanging from the ceiling. The dance floor was filled with students, all smiling and laughing and rubbing up closely on each other. The lights from the DJ's booth reflected off the disco ball and made it look like all the students were changing colors, making Aaron laugh as he began to dance. It was a magical moment, and Aaron danced with carefree exuberance as if he were a child and shouted at the top of his lungs out of joy. And as he continued to soak in the moment, he felt Amanda's body press up against his and then she grabbed his hand and put it on her backside.

Aaron ignored the queasiness and pounding in his head and squeezed her backside and gave her a passionate kiss. And as they continued to kiss Aaron looked across the gymnasium towards the entrance to see someone waving at him. It was a woman in a beautiful red dress, and she was wearing an ornate mask and she was gesturing Aaron to come to her. Aaron continued to dance with Amanda and ignored the woman, assuming she was calling for someone else.

Aaron and Amanda had danced through several songs and they decided to take a break and go get some punch. It was going to be a long night of dancing and they wanted to pace themselves. So, they made small talk with their friends and talked about their favorite songs and the different couples they were surprised to see together before they headed over to the photo booth. After catching their breath, they finally made it back into the castle doors. Aaron and Amanda found their spot on the dance floor and continued their dancing. Aaron grabbed Amanda close when a waving hand caught the corner of his eye. It was the woman in the red dress again, gesturing for him to follow her somewhere.

"Amanda, do you know that woman?" Aaron asked pointing in the direction of the masked woman in red.

"What woman?" she asked.

"That woman in red over there. With the mask. Do you know who she is? She keeps waving at me and signaling for me to follow her."

She gave Aaron a puzzled look. "She must have taken off, Aaron, because I don't see her."

"Oh yeah, I guess you're right," Aaron responded, as he continued to watch the woman in the red dress gesturing for him to follow her.

CHAPTER 35

"I hope you like lasagna!" Amanda called out to Aaron from the kitchen. She carried the hot dish to the kitchen table where Aaron was sitting with a forced smile on his face. Several months had passed since the homecoming dance and Aaron couldn't get the image of the woman in the red dress out of his mind. He couldn't put his finger on it, but he felt like he had seen her somewhere. He just didn't know where. It was eating him up inside but whenever Amanda asked Aaron how he was doing he always lied and told her he was great. When she asked how their relationship was going he would lie and say it was perfect. And he had lied to her today when she asked him if he'd like to spend a night alone with her while her parents were out.

"There is nothing I'd like more, Amanda," he told her. But the truth was that he was growing increasingly wary of intimacy. He did his best to hide his trembling hands and focus past the pounding in his head to keep the relationship going.

"So, we won our soccer match last night," Amanda said in between bites.

"That's great," Aaron replied after taking a bite of lasagna.

"And I made a game-winning save at the end to keep the game from going into overtime."

"That's great," Aaron replied again.

"And as of right now we should be able to make the playoffs for the first time in ten years."

"That's great."

"And if we win a playoff game there will be an article about us in the newspaper."

"That's great," Aaron replied as the lasagna fell off his fork, falling back on his plate.

"And there is a UFO on the front lawn ready to beam you up to the mothership," she said jokingly.

"That's great."

"Aaron! Are you even paying attention to me?" Amanda asked with a mix of irritation and humor.

"Oh, geeze. I'm so sorry. I was thinking about my math test earlier this week that I bombed," he responded, telling her a half-truth. "I'm not sure what happened but my grades seem to be slipping and I guess it's getting to me."

"Well, I think we should get these dishes cleaned up and find a way to relax," Amanda said with a smile.

Aaron took a deep breath as he cleaned his dirty dishes, but the buzzing static filled his ears and he could feel the pounding in his head. Amanda grabbed him by the hand and walked him towards the hallway near the garage. She squeezed his hand tightly and he could feel his heart begin to pound through his chest. He knew what was down the hallway, and he didn't know why but a nest of vipers in his head began squirming, hissing, and biting with such viciousness and ferocity that he lost feeling in his arms. But he followed her into the hallway, turned right, and looked towards their destination: the basement. Aaron couldn't quite put his finger on it, but he knew horrible things happened in basements. Somewhere at some point in his life, he was led into a basement. It felt like a sixth sense, and with each step, he could feel his hairs stand on end as if he were descending into a deep, dark dungeon where unthinkable evil occurs.

He descended further and further into the dungeon, and he felt a rushing wind behind him. It was hard to make out with all the squirming, hissing, and biting but Aaron could have sworn he heard the flapping of wings. Further and further into the dungeon they descended until they reached the bottom and Aaron had to swallow hard to keep the bile spilling from his gut. It was absurd, incomprehensible, and completely illogical that he should feel such tension, agony, and panic being alone in this basement with Amanda. He didn't know why and felt helpless to stop it, so he repeated the lie to himself that everything was alright and continued walking with her.

They walked the full length of the basement until they reached the far-left corner of the room and on the basement floor was laid a mattress and Aaron was on the verge of passing out. Why did this all seem so familiar? He could see in his mind's eye the smashed mirror and the broken fragments of his memory all screaming at him the truth of the matter, but he just couldn't understand, just couldn't make out the words, and so he sat down on the mattress. There was a desk next to the mattress where they kept their computer, and to the right of the computer was a statue of the Virgin Mary, the Mother of God; her arms were spread wide to console the suffering masses of the world. It was as if she were staring directly into his soul, watching him and mourning for him, and he couldn't help but feel like this was all very familiar in some strange way. As if in another world he had been on a mattress in a basement while Mary the mother of God was watching over him. He didn't quite know what to think about it and did his best to ignore the tightness around his neck and his chest.

Amanda grabbed Aaron by the hand and beckoned him to lie down on the mattress while she gave him a back massage. And there he was, lying on his stomach, staring over at Mary the mother of God, and his sense that something was terribly wrong only grew and his whole body tightened up. He gripped onto the sides of the mattress in preparation for some unknown pain that was coming his way.

"Woah Aaron, can you relax? Why are you so tight, this is supposed to be enjoyable!" Amanda chided him, half-jokingly. Aaron chuckled at the comment and told her he would do his best, but he began to feel nauseous and could feel the bile rise in his gut. Something horrible was going on here. He wasn't sure what it was or why, but he felt that something utterly horrible was about to happen, something completely painful and disgusting and he needed to leave immediately. Amanda straddled him from behind, massaging his shoulders and for some reason, Aaron felt as if he were going to cry and wasn't sure why, and his body tightened even further to the point where his whole body was clenching. "Ok. I can tell this isn't quite what you are looking for, but that's ok, I think I may have something else for you," she told him with a smile.

Amanda got off of Aaron and they both sat on their knees facing each other. Amanda gave Aaron a wide smile as she took off her shirt and then helped Aaron take off his. She caressed his face and looked deeply into his eyes as they kissed passionately. But Aaron couldn't get her eyes out of his mind, why was she staring at him? What was she about to do to him, and how much would it hurt?

She drew her face closer to his ear and whispered, "The king is drinking your blood."

Aaron flinched instinctually, completely unnerved and perplexed at the statement.

"What did you say to me?"

She looked at him a bit confused but with kindness in her eyes. "Relax, I just said I'm coming in for a hug."

Aaron didn't know what was going on or what was wrong with him, why he was so on edge, but he told himself that everything was ok; everything had to be ok. So, she drew closer to him and he could see bright white lights beaming from her eyes.

The lights were so bright that he had to close his eyes. He tried to open them but all he could see was blinding lights all around him, completely drowning out his surroundings.

While Aaron was trying to make sense of the blinding lights Amanda leaned in and gave him another passionate kiss. Aaron did his best to ignore the growing static and stroked her bare back. After she kissed him she whispered into Aaron's ear, "I love you."

And as soon as the words parted her lips a high-pitched, blood curdling scream filled the air followed by the sound of thick rubber smacking bare skin half a dozen times. Aaron's whole body tensed up from the noise and he yanked on Amanda's hair and pulled it tight.

"Aaron, you're hurting me! Stop!" Amanda cried out.

But Aaron couldn't hear her, for the sound of rubber smacking bare skin was followed by the sound of a child crying for help. "Someone, please help! Don't do this to me! Please!" which was followed by a frantic gurgling sound of a strangled child desperately gasping for air. Aaron felt his neck begin to tingle and pulled Amanda's hair even harder and dug his nails into her arm with his other hand.

"What is wrong with you! Stop! Let me go!"

He could feel her struggling against him, but he was in a complete daze as someone began speaking.

"The boy must not cry out in pain. We will need assurance."

"My friend would love to play a game with you, Aaron. Will you please wait in the living room?"

Aaron dug into Amanda even harder.

"Let me go! Let me go!" But Aaron didn't hear her, he was too busy paying attention to the voices in his head that were consuming his attention.

"Stop! It hurts! It's too much! It's too much!" a young boy cried out, to which a man responded, "Good! Cry, slave! Cry!" Aaron was about to explode in anger and confusion when he felt Amanda's palm slap across his face.

"Aaron! What the hell is wrong with you?!"

Aaron released his grip from Amanda and stared off into the distance, like he wasn't there, like he was somewhere else completely.

"What is wrong with you, Aaron?" Amanda asked again. But Aaron didn't respond as he was still trying to figure out where and when he was. "Is there something wrong, Aaron? If you tell me maybe I can help you."

Aaron got off the mattress and sat on a nearby couch, still in a daze, looking as if he still didn't know where he was. They remained in silence for several minutes until Aaron finally stood up and jetted up the stairs and out of Amanda's house, leaving her where she stood.

CHAPTER 36

"Who are you?" Aaron asked himself as he stared intently at his reflection in the bathroom mirror. It was a question Aaron had begun asking himself more frequently over the past few months. As the tingling in his brain grew worse and the bombardment of horrible images and sounds increased, the more concerned he became with what was going on inside him. He stared at his reflection in the mirror as if he didn't know and was desperate to find out who the young man was that was wreaking havoc on his life.

"Who are you?" Aaron asked again hoping for a response. But no response ever came, and Aaron couldn't help but feel like a stranger in someone else's body with someone else's memories and experiences he couldn't access. He imagined the mirror falling to the ground, shattering into hundreds of little pieces, all with their own distinct image of himself calling out to Aaron the truths of who he was. They formed a cacophonous sea of immutable voices raging and rumbling through the four corners of his psyche causing a horrible pounding in his chest. He felt like he'd been smashed into a million little pieces, all containing a fragment of a memory of his life that for some reason he couldn't recall. He imagined all those tiny little images of himself shattered on the bathroom floor, broken with no chance of repair, all screaming at him some unknown message, some unknown truth he was incapable of hearing.

"Aaron, are you done yet?" his brother Thomas called out. Aaron had spaced out for some time and wasn't sure how long he had held the toilet and sink hostage, but he gave himself one last look to see if there would be a reply before he vacated the bathroom.

Amanda had promised him a special meal and was renting a movie for them to watch together but Aaron struggled to get ready. His hands began to shake as he tried to put his socks on. He did his best to concentrate but a growing paranoia was interfering with what he wanted to happen, and the truth was that he was scared they might share a few moments of intimacy and something horrible might happen.

There were the vipers in his head that bit and hissed and slithered throughout his brain as he read the love note Amanda had given him at school the other day. What were they doing? It felt like something despicable and deeply sinful. He did his best to push down the panic. Everything was ok. But every step he took he could feel an invisible hand squeeze his heart, causing him to stop.

Aaron was determined to live a normal life. He wasn't ready or willing to let the vipers get the best of him. He walked over to his desk to a picture frame of him and Amanda together. He stared at the picture intently, willing his fake plastic smile to be true, wishing that the pain didn't exist. He told himself what a beautiful couple they made and what a bright future they had together, if he could only prove to Amanda his love for her by enduring through the pain.

He thought of the man from his dream, who showed Aaron the young man Aaron was meant to be, and he didn't want to let him down. Aaron never forgot the man and knew he was looking down on him somewhere, cheering him on as he made the hard choices and refused to relent to his internal turmoil.

"I won't let you down," Aaron said aloud as he made up his mind. He knew this was his destiny, so he ignored the pounding in his head and the trembling of his hands and put the picture down and headed for his bedroom door.

"Ok, Aaron. It's time to go." As Aaron opened the door he was hit with a tidal wave of fear and immediately fell to the floor, terrified of the man who was waiting for him on the other side.

Aaron curled up into a ball and began shaking violently mumbling, "Please no more, please no more, please no more." Aaron watched as the man's feet crossed the threshold of his bedroom and he fought the urge to scream. He could see the blade dangling from the man's hand and Aaron shook as if he were having a seizure.

"Please no more, please no more, please no more," Aaron kept mumbling, but the man's feet drew ever nearer, and his blade glistened in the moonlight as it approached Aaron's throat.

"The great feast is upon us, Aaron, and the coven is ready for your blood sacrifice." And as Aaron's body continued to tremble on his bedroom floor the stars in the sky all wept together, for they were helpless to protect Aaron from the great devourer who was not there.

Chapter 37

"Go ahead, Aaron. Just take a sip." Amanda raised the cup up to Aaron's lips but he stepped backwards out of her way. He wasn't interested in taking a drink, not even a sip, and there was nothing she could do to change his mind.

"Thanks, Amanda. I'm just not interested," Aaron responded.

"Oh, come on, Aaron. It will loosen you up. I promise it will help you relax and have a good time."

Aaron took another step back, doubling down on his decision. "I just don't want to drink it, ok?!" Aaron barked back with obvious irritation.

"Fine, then. I guess we can stand back here and watch everyone else have a fun time. Have it your way," Amanda conceded with her own look of frustration.

Aaron and Amanda stood far back from the rest of the party around the bonfire. Aaron just couldn't get himself to mingle in the crowd of his classmates. They were all drinking and at this point most were visibly drunk. Aaron watched as they all continued drinking and laughing and having a great time. David was in their midst and he looked like he was having the time of his life. Many had found a companion and a comfortable spot around the fire to share an intimate moment with and it made Aaron cringe. He desperately wanted to join David and his other classmates in the fun, but every time he took a step in their direction he was hit with a wave of fear and his brain went numb. He just couldn't get himself to put the cup to his lips and shake off the feeling that something horrible was about to happen.

Aaron told himself to take a deep breath to keep from passing out. Amanda stood next to him with a look of boredom on her face but her arm around his shoulder, watching him stare mindlessly at the fire in front of him. He knew he was supposed to be having fun and that these were supposed to be moments he would lack back on and cherish, but he desperately wanted to run away, far away and as fast as he could. Aaron stared at the fire doing his best to ignore all his classmates who were drinking and laughing and fondling one another and watched as the flames began to dance in front of him. The flames ebbed and flowed and bounced around the burning wood and seemed to have a life of their own. Aaron felt as if he were entering a trance when he felt Amanda's hand gently massage his crotch and he felt a bolt of lightning run through his body and watched the faces form in the fire.

Aaron watched, stunned, as he saw the beautiful woman in the red dress ushering Aaron into a room filled with a sea of naked men and women all humping each other. And he saw them all begin to dance and jump into the air in celebration. The images soon vanished and in their place formed a face Aaron was all too familiar with. It was his adoptive grandfather, and he was nodding at Aaron as if he knew something important and sinister were on the horizon. He took a puff from his pipe and Aaron's adoptive grandfather vanished along with his pipe smoke.

Aaron continued staring into the fire as Amanda continued to rub his crotch and the image of a child appeared in the flames. Aaron tuned out everything around him, including Amanda, and placed his sole attention on the shirtless little boy that was coming into full clarity. He was stumbling around as if he didn't know where he was going. His hands were out as if he were scared he might bump into something and he seemed lost. The boy looked vaguely familiar to Aaron which made his entire body tense up. He felt as if he were watching a movie he had seen before and wished he could skip the upcoming scene. But Aaron kept his eyes on the young boy and watched as someone removed the blindfold. As the blindfold fell into the flames Aaron saw the child's eyes light up with an enormity of fear, causing him to tremble and scream in the presence of some unspeakable evil. And as the boy continued to scream through the flames Aaron's whole world began to fade away.

Aaron opened his eyes and took a few seconds to get his bearings. He was now standing in a long hallway and everything was silent, so silent you could hear a pin drop. He looked all around to make sense of his new surroundings, to see if it were familiar at all, and while it seemed somewhat familiar it just wasn't a place he could believe he'd ever been to before. This place seemed almost as if it were a prison, for there were locked doors everywhere, steel doors with steel walls. There were no decorations; there was nothing ornate or pleasant about this place at all. This was not a happy place, not a kind place, and Aaron had a feeling he was about to find out just how unkind this place could be.

He took notice of himself and realized he was wearing a bright yellow costume of some kind. It was very strange, this costume, for he had never seen anything like it before. It was a giant yellow triangle that started at his knees and narrowed to his neck and he was wearing a yellow triangular hat. He was wearing a white shirt underneath and white stockings and little white shoes. What a strange contrast. Why would he be wearing such a bright and bizarre costume in this prison of a place? And that's when he felt the warmth of someone's hand grab his. He looked over to this unknown man and realized he only came up to his waist and gathered that he was no longer a young man but a child and he had been dressed to look like a piece of cheese. It was all so strange. There was no one giving him any sort of explanation for what was going on.

The man held Aaron's hand and ushered him down the steel hallway towards a door at the end of the hall. This was all very confusing, but the man wasn't planning on giving him any hints or explanations. So, as Aaron slowly approached the door he hoped for the best and prepared himself for the worst. And although he believed that he was prepared for the worst he was about to find out that there is no "worst," for man's ability to conjure up evil knows no ends, and some men dedicate all their attention and energy to stretching the outer limits of how much fear, pain, and suffering they can draw from a child.

They finally reached the door, and he was ushered in with no explanation, but taking in the contents of the room Aaron knew that no explanation would have helped, for this surpassed anything his mind could ever conjure up. There, lying in the middle of the floor, was the "thing" Aaron was brought for. Aaron wasn't quite sure who or what this was for he had never seen anything quite like it before, so he stood in the doorway, eyes wide open and mouth agape. There was a head, four limbs, and a torso completely covered in a tight dark blue latex material. Aaron assumed this was a human but had no idea of knowing for sure, and couldn't tell if it were male or female. A long tail was sewn into the backside and on his head were sewn large ears, and this "thing" very much looked like a giant mouse, and this mouse seemed to be tethered to the floor with a long collar on his neck.

What the hell was going on, and what was about to happen to him? Noticing the bright yellow cheese costume he was wearing he knew it couldn't be good. In fact, it would be far from good, the exact opposite of good, and even farther if possible. He stood paralyzed in the doorway, his whole body soaking in the confusion and the terror. He felt the malice exuding from this "thing" and he was soaking it up like a sponge, and he was so filled with it he couldn't move, but someone nudged Aaron into the abode of the thing that devours children.

He was now one step inside the thing's abode and could hear the door behind him slam shut and Aaron couldn't believe he was to be left alone with the sleeping terror. The giant mouse seemed to be resting soundly in the middle of the room, that is until he heard the slamming of the door, which caused the thing to open his eyes and set his gaze upon Aaron, his prize, his meal, his slave. Still incapable of moving Aaron was helpless to do anything but watch this thing open his eyes, give him a smirk, and slowly get to his feet. This thing stood there, staring at Aaron, as if he were soaking in the moment, savoring what was to come, but Aaron was so filled with terror he couldn't move or even understand what was happening.

The thing, which was chained to the floor, continued to smile at Aaron and time seemed to stand still. Slowly, the thing raised his right hand to his neck, grabbed his collar, and unshackled himself from the floor, and Aaron's whole body exploded with levels of fear he never knew were possible. And the thing slowly and delicately glided in Aaron's direction, still smiling at Aaron, and Aaron pressed his back against the door, praying he could find some way to get to the other side. But, alas, he was still stuck in this room of terror, locked in with this thing who was getting closer, closer, closer until he was a mere five feet away. And as the thing continued to encroach upon his meal his arms straightened out along with all his fingers to reveal tiny little sharp nails on each of his fingers. As it continued to glide towards Aaron he leaned towards him and opened his mouth and prodded Aaron. "You better run, little boy!"

Whatever was happening, it became clear to Aaron that this was some sort of game to the thing and whatever was to come the thing preferred to chase him down first and enjoy the hunt.

"You better run little boy!" the thing said again, but Aaron was still unable to move and closed his eyes. He was desperately wishing himself away but was jolted back to his situation by a jarring yell from the thing to get Aaron to move and Aaron was helpless not to run. And so the thing chased Aaron through this room, laughing, smiling, and gloating over the inevitable outcome. Aaron ran as fast as he could.

He ran, and ran, and ran, into a different room, up and down flights of stairs, until he finally found an open door which seemed to have a bright light exuding from the outside. The light was a sign of safety and security, his way out of this horrible situation. He was drawn towards the light which was becoming brighter and emanating reds, oranges, and yellows, indicating the outside world on the other side. But Aaron could hear the thing behind him, coming for him and laughing along the way. Aaron quickened his pace and along with the pull of the light, he felt down in his heart that he would make it out alive. Closer, closer, closer he ran to the door until he was a few feet away. He was going to make it out. He would be rid of this place and the terrible "thing" within the walls.

However, as he began to push the door open further, he noticed there was someone on the other side who was already opening the door. And as the door opened fully the light blinded Aaron and he ran into the doorframe and missed the exit. He quickly got back to his feet and where he was expecting to find freedom he found the deepest despair he could imagine. It was a man wearing a deep purple cloak with a crown on his head, emanating light from his eyes and letting out the most blood-curdling laugh, and he could feel the claws of the thing on each shoulder, and they were both laughing at Aaron, that he ever thought he had a chance other than to be completely consumed by the devourer. And they laughed at Aaron, louder, and louder, and louder and Aaron found himself smooshed in between the king and the thing who now had his hands around Aaron's neck.

The claws tightened further, suffocating Aaron, and the man leaned in closer to Aaron. "Remember me, Aaron?" he whispered.

Aaron was completely dazed by the insinuation, that they somehow knew each other, and he was helpless to watch as the man's mouth began to slowly open wider, and wider, and wider until lava began spilling out of his mouth and all over Aaron's body.

Suddenly, Aaron could feel a strong tug on his right bicep and heard Amanda's voice, "Are you ok, Aaron?"

Aaron was sitting up, realizing he had fallen over and lost consciousness at the party. He could see David in the distance chasing a girl around the campfire.

"Stop it, David!" the girl called out, chuckling along the way. David was smiling at her with droopy eyes and was closing in on her.

"I think I'd like to go home, Amanda," Aaron said before David finally reached his prize.

CHAPTER 38

"*Do you not know that the unrighteous shall not inherit the kingdom of God?*" Aaron read aloud with a worried look.

"*Neither fornicators,*" he stopped for a moment and bit down on his lip, "*nor thieves shall inherit the kingdom of God.*"

Aaron flipped through his Bible further until he found the passage he was looking for. "*The Son of Man will send out his angels, and they will weed out of his kingdom everything that causes sin and all who do evil. They will throw them into the blazing furnace, where there will be weeping and gnashing of teeth.*" Aaron put his Bible on the desk in his bedroom and let out a long sigh. He looked over at the painting on his bedside wall and could feel the pounding in his head begin to hit him and his feet went numb.

What was he going to do? He had plans later to see Amanda and David and some other friends, but he wasn't sure that was such a good idea. He thought back on his relationship with Amanda and the noises he heard in her basement and the buzzing static that filled his ears in fear. And he thought about the first time they kissed and all the other times he welcomed and initiated the intimacy and wondered if he was a fornicator who never knew God. Maybe he was cut off, forever and he was being punished for his sins. He thought about the vision of the man with the knife who came to his door ready to spill Aaron's blood and wondered if he were an angel sent by God to punish Aaron for his sins.

Aaron had to talk to someone, so he got up from his desk and walked out of his bedroom. Thomas was in the hallway. Thomas had also become a Christian and read his Bible pretty often and went to church. "Can I talk to you?"

"Of course. Let's go out back," Thomas replied, and they both marched down the stairs into the hallway and past the kitchen and out of the back door in the living room where their adoptive father was watching golf. The man never raised his head from the television to say hello nor did Thomas or Aaron acknowledge his presence, as they were both eager to be away from the man. They slid out into the back deck watching the sun slowly set and each took a seat.

"Ok. So, what's going on?"

"I was wondering if you knew what a fornicator was," Aaron asked.

"Good question. From my understanding it is someone who has sex when they aren't married," Thomas replied.

"Oh, that's it?" Aaron replied with a sigh of relief.

"Well, that's not it completely, because Jesus also said that anyone who looks at someone who isn't his wife and thinks about having sex with her is committing adultery, which is kind of like fornicating. It's one of the sins that gets talked about a lot in the Bible and seems to be a big problem."

"I see." Aaron fidgeted his hand wondering where to go from here. "But does God forgive sins?"

"Yeah, of course!" Thomas responded. "I think God likes to forgive sins, but he does ask people to stop sinning. So, it's a problem if someone keeps fornicating and doesn't stop. I think it means the person isn't really sorry about what they've done. Otherwise, I suppose they'd change."

"And I assume that the lake of fire is meant for people like that?" Aaron asked worriedly.

"I'm not a pastor, but I think you might be right. There is somewhere else where Jesus says, 'I never knew you; depart from me, you evildoers. So, if people keep doing evil then it's a problem," Thomas explained.

"I see," Aaron said, staring blankly out into the setting sun and watching the stars begin to dot the sky.

"Don't worry, Aaron! You're fine. Everything is going to be fine. Trust me. But I've got to run now. I'll see you later and let me know if you need to talk again." Thomas patted Aaron's shoulder and walked back into the house to grab his shoes.

Aaron stared up into the starry sky which had finally set, and he felt as if he were ruining everything and that his building anxiety and paranoia was God punishing him for his sins. He thought about the beautiful man from his dream when he was younger, the man with dark brown hair, tanned skin, and slender physique, and how kind he was to visit Aaron. He was so wonderful and made Aaron feel completely at ease. He seemed truly concerned about Aaron and showed him the young man he was always meant to be. He had reached out to Aaron to help him and Aaron had become a sinner after all. He must be so mad at him.

He didn't want it to be true, but he didn't know how else to make sense of all the pain he was in. But there would be no harm in going out with Amanda and his friends, so he grabbed his mother's car keys and headed out the door to pick up Amanda. When he arrived at her house she was waiting at the door and quickly ran out to the car.

"Hello handsome," she said to him with a smile.

"Hey," he responded with a sheepish smile while staring at the floor and feeling optimistic about the night. As he drove to the restaurant he did his best to pretend everything was ok, trying to drown out the pounding in his head and numbness in his face as Amanda talked about everything that had gone on this past week.

"Uh huh," he responded, and she would keep talking.

"Oh, wow," he went on as if he were paying attention. He could hear her talking but had no idea what she was saying.

"Gotcha," and he felt her hand rub his shoulder.

"No, Aaron. I asked if everything was alright," Amanda responded with a perplexed look on her face.

"No, Amanda everything isn't alright, and I am messing it all up!" he wanted to say, but instead he told her everything was fine, and he just blanked out for a minute.

"Well, don't blank out for too long, I've got some special plans for us tonight," she said with a smile as she caressed his inner thigh. Aaron's head began to explode in fear and paranoia wondering what was going to happen.

"That sounds great," Aaron said with a sheepish smile.

They finally arrived at the restaurant, and they noticed their friends sitting at the corner booth. They slowly made their way over, and he felt as if he were walking underwater. Everything seemed to slow down and all the sounds became muffled and everyone's faces became blurry. He did his best to concentrate on the corner booth and ignore the pounding in his chest and squirming in his head. Aaron took a seat next to Amanda and listened to the chatter of everyone around him: the smiles, the laughs, and the friendly banter. Aaron had his arm around Amanda and plastered a fake smile on his face and acted as if nothing was wrong.

"Aaron! There he is, the man of the hour!" David greeted Aaron and grabbed his hand in excitement. "That was an incredible play you made on Friday. Making it look so easy, too!"

Aaron had made a key tackle which kept their team in the game and started the big comeback victory.

"Uh huh," Aaron responded with a big smile.

"Seriously, Aaron, you did a great job! But don't forget that I saw you puking your gets out before the game! I'm glad your little tummy ache didn't stop you from playing," David joked with a big laugh.

"Oh wow," Aaron responded as he did his best to home in on David's face.

David gave Aaron a confused face, noticing that Aaron wasn't completely paying attention, "You ok, buddy?"

"Gotcha," Aaron responded to the garbled unintelligible words.

"Aaron, what the hell are you talking about," David replied, bringing Aaron back to the surface.

"Wait, what? Oh sorry, I must have spaced out there thinking about the game-winning catch. That was pretty amazing," Aaron said, rebounding from his underwater excursion.

"God, you're such a knucklehead, Aaron!" David yelled out, and Aaron laughed at the comment, doing his best to keep his head above water.

"Well, we're going to loosen you up, buddy. My parents are gone for the night and I've got some booze and I think we're going to get a little crazy," David informed Aaron while poking the girl sitting next to him. Everyone laughed so Aaron decided to laugh. And David kissed the girl sitting next to him, so Aaron kissed Amanda. And Aaron followed all the cues to keep the façade going, ignoring the pounding in his head and numbness in his face and doing everything he could to stay above water.

After everyone finished their meals they paid the bill and left to drive over to David's house. Amanda stared at Aaron in the car with eager eyes and Aaron gave her a wide smile, telling himself that nothing was going to happen and that everything would be ok. They held hands as they entered into David's house and were greeted by the sound of soft, rhythmic music and dimmed lights.

"Nothing is going to happen, tonight, Aaron," he forced himself to believe, thinking about the Bible verses he'd read earlier. Aaron and Amanda made their way to a couch in the living room and David brought them both cups filled with cheap liquor and it made Aaron's hands tremble. Amanda took a big sip and began moving to the rhythm of the music.

"Go on, Aaron. Take a sip," she told him. "I promise you it will make you feel better."

Aaron thought about it and brought the cup to his lips, but the far wall began smiling at him and changing colors and he instinctually dropped the cup to the ground.

"Fuck! Aaron, that's going to stain the carpet!" Amanda told him in a worried tone, but Aaron couldn't hear her because the beautiful man from his dream was shouting into his ear: "Neither fornicators nor drunkards shall inherit the kingdom of God."

Aaron was completely numb, and he found himself being led off the couch and down a hallway as the walls began to warp and change colors in sync with his heartbeat. He finally found himself lying on a big, soft, fluffy pillow and something inside him was telling him to run away as soon as possible and as far as he could. His head started pounding mercilessly and he was about to scream when he saw Amanda's face. She was lying next to him on the bed, and he realized he was alone with her in one of the bedrooms in David's house.

"Hello, handsome," she said to Aaron while she stroked his head. His heartrate began slowing down and the feeling in his face started coming back and he stared at Amanda realizing how beautiful she looked that night. He could see in her eyes that she cared about him deeply and told himself that everything was going to be ok. He thought of David and assumed he was probably off in some other bedroom doing the same thing with some other girl and gave himself permission to proceed. Aaron brought his face close to Amanda and kissed her passionately, and he caressed her body and brought her in close.

"Yes, Aaron. Yes," Amanda moaned, causing Aaron to pin her to the bed and proceed even further. He took his shirt off, and he ripped off Amanda's shirt as well, and as he lay on top of her indulging in the moment he heard the beautiful man speak to him again, "I never knew you; depart from me, you evildoers."

CHAPTER 39

Aaron saw the man peeking out through the closet, tapping on the closet door to get Aaron's attention. He was covered in red paint from head to toe and dripping with excitement. His eyes grew wider and wider in sweet anticipation and the largest smile adorned his face. Aaron was so very confused. Was he dreaming? Was this some strange nightmare? It didn't feel like a dream. He felt like he was very much awake. He could hear himself breathe and saw his chest rise and fall with the pattern of his breath. He could hear his brother Thomas sleeping above him on his bunk bed and the shuffling of sheets. And when he heard the tapping continue Aaron could feel the hairs on the back of his neck stand on end.

This couldn't be happening. This had to be some horribly strange dream. There had been too many uncomfortable incidents lately and Aaron could hardly bear it. First it was the woman at the dance, and then the thing at the campfire, and now there was someone in his closet tapping to get his attention. It was too much, and Aaron couldn't afford for any of this to be real. He just wanted to be normal. He wanted to spend time with friends, play sports, and enjoy what was left of his youth. He wanted to make the most of the carefree exuberance that comes with adolescence, so he forced himself to believe none of this was happening. No, there was no thing that had chased him, nor was there a masked woman from a strange world beckoning Aaron to come join him and there was certainly no one in his closet tapping to get his attention. He was just a normal teenage boy with normal teenage problems.

Aaron rolled over to face his bedroom wall, hoping the tapping would go away. He thought long and hard about his upcoming baseball game and what pitches he would throw, how he would hold the bat and how it would feel to hit a homerun. He focused all his energy on the upcoming game but still he heard the tapping.

"Pssst. Aaron, it's time to go!" Aaron refused to acknowledge this intruder who was beckoning him towards his closet. "Aaron, come on, it's time to go! It's me, Bobo! We're going to be late for the party!"

The tapping continued, and it appeared his brother Thomas was too deep in his slumber to notice.

"Aaron, come on, we're going to be late!" he prodded in a whisper. Aaron took a deep breath and finally turned over to face his open closet and there was the man covered in red paint crouched down in the corner of his closet as if he were attempting to sneak Aaron out of his bedroom in the middle of the night. He looked like a large blood stain on the wall coming to life and he flashed Aaron the largest grin and waved him closer towards the closet.

"We're going to be late, Aaron, come on!"

"Excuse me, do I know you?" Aaron asked.

The man in red paint chuckled. "Stop playing games, Aaron. It's me, Bobo! You know me, remember? We have to hurry. We're going to be late!"

"Late for what?" Aaron replied.

"Late for what? Why the party you silly! We can't be late for the party, Aaron. You're the guest of honor! Everyone is waiting for you!"

Aaron was both intrigued and alarmed, for no normal person would be covered in red paint from head to toe, but Aaron felt there was very little that was normal about the situation. And he had such a friendly demeanor that Aaron thought perhaps he might enjoy himself at this party.

Aaron slowly got his legs out of bed and sat up, rubbing his eyes to make sure he was seeing correctly. He scratched his head and yawned and focused his attention back towards his closet and Bobo was still there, waving and gesturing for Aaron to follow him through the closet.

"Come on, Aaron! I'm here to pick you up and it's time to go!" Aaron slowly walked towards Bobo who ushered him deep into his closet. At the back of the closet was a large hole that Bobo had crawled through to get to Aaron's room. It shimmered beautiful shades of red and had golden borders that Aaron found both enchanting and mystifying. Aaron was in awe of the spectacle and so he didn't fight when Bobo grabbed his hand and led him through this unknown portal. Aaron couldn't believe what was happening. It was the most absurd thing imaginable. But there they were, and Bobo was guiding Aaron down a deep, dark wormhole with glowing red walls. Aaron looked around at the walls and saw scenes from his childhood play out like a movie projector. He felt as if he were travelling back in time, or perhaps into another dimension and Bobo was beckoning Aaron further through the wormhole.

"You know, Aaron, we're going to play lots of games at the party, and there will be plenty of food for everyone. There will be dancing and storytelling, and laughter, and it will be the greatest night of your life. I promise! Come on, Aaron, keep up!"

Aaron did his best to keep up with Bobo who was beckoning him further down the wormhole to some unknown destination, for some unknown party where Aaron was the guest of honor.

"How do we know each other, Bobo?"

Bobo gave Aaron a large grin and told him that his adoptive grandfather introduced them. He told Aaron of all the times they played together, about his pet monkey and how much Aaron loved

Bobo's pet monkey. He told Aaron how they played hide and seek and tag and wrestled together.

It was absurd, for he didn't remember Bobo at all; he barely remembered his adoptive grandfather. He didn't remember ever playing with Bobo or his pet monkey. But, then again, how did Bobo know where he lived? Perhaps Bobo was a friend from his childhood after all. They descended further through the wormhole, which was growing ever darker as the descent continued.

"We're almost there, Aaron! Just a little further!" Bobo proclaimed with an eager childlike excitement. Aaron had a hard time keeping up with Bobo, who was practically sprinting down the pitch black wormhole .

"Ok, Aaron. We've finally arrived! Are you ready to party?" Bobo crawled through the end of the wormhole. "Come on, Aaron! It's your turn!"

Something felt off; something was wrong. Aaron didn't know what it was and was having a hard time putting his finger on it, but he could tell this party wasn't going to be all fun and games, and he no longer wanted to be the guest of honor. He wished he could crawl back up the wormhole into his bedroom and fall back to sleep. But the weight of the wormhole was directing Aaron towards the party and shutting behind him. Aaron fell through, landing face first onto the concrete floor. Aaron was immediately hit with strange but familiar smells and sensations and he became terrified when he heard all the screams in the background. He looked around the party, at all the guests and all the children and Aaron was hit with a deep and profound sense of revulsion and despair, completely overwhelmed with what he saw.

It was all too much, beyond absurd, beyond cruel, and completely macabre and he was so caught up in emotion he didn't notice the hand that grabbed him by the arm and ushered him towards some strange apparatus on the wall that looked as if it were meant to gut a deer or some other large animal. The screaming was too much for Aaron, it overwhelmed all the senses and so he didn't notice when they placed him on the apparatus, nor did he pay attention to the restraints that were fastened around his ankles and his wrists and his neck. All he could do was breathe in the toxic atmosphere, which was serenaded by blood curdling screams, and watch the party unfold.

The party guests departed from the other children. Each with a chalice in hand they formed a line facing a small wooden table with a figurine and burnt incense. One by one they kissed the figurine and splashed the contents of their chalice against the wall next to the table, creating a circle of smeared blood dripping to the floor. Aaron was secured on the apparatus and had nowhere to go. He was paralyzed in fear and helpless to do anything about it. And as the guests continued with the party he heard them begin to chant, "All hail the king! All the king! All hail the king!"

They all knelt down on the concrete in worship facing the table and tore off their clothes and began cutting themselves until they bled. "All hail the king! All hail the king! All hail the king!"

Aaron watched the madness ensue as these men and women bled for their king, showing their devotion until he made his appearance. And appear he did.

The circle of smeared blood began to slowly open as if it were giving birth. First there was one hand, and then another, and they each pushed off the concrete wall until he came spilling out into the room. And there he was, a great devil with bloodred eyes who stood ten feet tall. His hooves cackled against the concrete, and the keratin and bone of his horns scraped the ceiling as he made his way across the room towards Aaron. He was as black as night and bore a strange symbol on his forehead. He walked past his worshippers towards Aaron, glaring at him and hating him for ever being born. He came closer, and closer, and his mouth opened wide, spewing out blood and venom which rained down on his worshippers.

"All hail the king! All hail the king! All hail the king!" they chanted. The devil continued to inch closer and closer to Aaron, preparing to slaughter the great sacrifice presented to him. Aaron was so worried about the beast approaching him with his claws and protruding fangs that he almost failed to notice the lips that pressed into his ear. It was Bobo.

"I'm going to tell you a secret, Aaron. Sometimes I watch you sleep at night. I watch the air pass through your sweet little lips as you sleep peacefully, and I spank my monkey. I watch you sleep, and I choke my monkey. I choke my monkey so hard until it spits. And I'll let you in on another secret Aaron. Sometimes I get angry. So angry that I chop children into little pieces and fry them in a pan. I dip them into ketchup and eat them. And if you ever tell anyone about this party, I will burn your house down while you sleep! Do you hear me?!"

Aaron heard. He heard all too well and watched helplessly as the devil finally reached him, tearing him completely apart.

Aaron opened his eyes and sat up in his bed with such force that he hit his head on the top bunk his brother Thomas was sleeping on. He sprung out of bed in a panic and feverishly began looking through all of his things.

"Oh my God, oh my God, oh my God," Aaron kept mumbling as he saw the devil king from his nightmare everywhere in the room. He saw his reflection in the window and his symbol written on his books. The devil was clawing through the floorboards and banging from inside the walls. He was staring at Aaron from his closet and in each and every one of his photos of him and Amanda. He was in his sheets and sitting at his desk and Aaron scrambled out of his room to look for his mother. He ran down the steps where he saw the devil in the picture frames hanging on the walls and sprinted into the kitchen to find his mother smoking a cigarette. Aaron looked at his mother with wild, wide eyes and asked, "What day is it today?"

"I think it's October twenty-eighth. Why, what's wrong, honey?" his mother asked.

"I just need to borrow the car, Mom," Aaron told her as he looked through her purse.

"Why, where are you going?"

"Somewhere far from here," Aaron responded as he finally fished out her car keys and shot out the front door, escaping the devil in his bedroom, but he was unable to escape the devil in his mind.

CHAPTER 40

"Hey, Thomas, do you mind if I come with you?" Aaron asked.

"To where?"

"Can I come to church with you and your girlfriend tonight? I overheard you talking with Amy on the phone earlier today. I'm sorry to invite myself, I just feel a little lost" Aaron replied.

"Of course! I think it's been a while since you've gone to church anyways."

"Yeah, you're right. A few years. I think the church we used to go to shut down and I never bothered to find another one."

"Amy and I would love for you to tag along. You've seemed a little out of sorts, lately. I bet this will do you some good," Thomas said with a smile.

It wasn't too long afterwards that Thomas' girlfriend Amy showed up and they all piled into her Volkswagen Jetta and headed to church. Aaron sat in the backseat and felt his excitement grow as they pulled into the church parking lot. Aaron looked over at the building and all the nice, normal people headed in. They were all smiling and dressed well and holding hands with their children. One by one they entered through the front door and headed into the sanctuary.

As Aaron stepped out of Amy's car Thomas began talking about the church's pastor.

"I think you're really going to like him, Aaron. He just really seems to love and care about people. He actually is a celibate and has never married. He says he wants to devote his time fully to God and his congregants. I'm sure he'll talk to you if you're feeling lost. I bet he could help."

They headed through the front door. There was a man holding the door open who shook Aaron's hand and gave him a big smile. "I'm so glad you made it," he told Aaron.

Next, they stepped into the foyer and Thomas and Amy mingled with a few of their friends as Aaron looked around. He saw wooden crosses and paintings of the Christ Man and a long hallway leading to the children's nursery.

It felt safe. Aaron closed his eyes and the fear and anxiety melted away from him. Everyone began heading into the sanctuary and so Aaron followed suit, trailing Thomas and Amy. They found their seats in the middle and waited as the worship team took the stage and began playing beautiful music. The music touched Aaron's soul and warmed his heart and he felt like this was where he belonged. The music went on for some time and Aaron closed his eyes and felt his emotions come back to an equilibrium, and for a brief moment he felt like himself again.

The music eventually died down and everyone took their seats. And as the stage finally cleared a man walked onto the stage and stood behind the pulpit. It was the pastor, and he had a big smile on his face.

"Welcome, everyone," he said, greeting his congregants. Aaron gazed into the man's eyes. He had so much charisma and charm. It was clear that he loved humanity. Aaron had never met the man, but he already knew that he loved him and that he was sent by God to instruct Aaron on what he needed to do. Aaron listened intently as the pastor spoke and promised himself he wouldn't blow it.

"Alright, everyone. Would you please turn your Bibles to Hebrews chapter twelve verses one and two," the pastor directed his congregants and waited as the thumbs flipped through their Bibles.

"Therefore, since we are surrounded by such a great cloud of witnesses, let us throw off everything that hinders and the sin that so easily entangles. And let us run with perseverance the race marked out for us, fixing our eyes on Jesus, the pioneer and perfecter of faith."

As the pastor spoke the verses it was like a lightbulb turned on in Aaron's head and he knew exactly what he needed to do. He sat next to his brother Thomas and his girlfriend Amy and sucked in the pastor's message and felt it tickle down his throat and into his heart and he felt as if he were transforming.

Aaron leaned over to Thomas and whispered, "Do you think I can meet him?"

Thomas and Amy whispered to each other and Thomas gave him a smile and a thumbs up and Aaron smiled back as the pastor finished his sermon. The three of them waited in the foyer for the pastor to come out and greet his congregants and Aaron did his best to act normal and pretend he was listening to Thomas talk. But his eyes were steadfast on the sanctuary door, waiting for the pastor to come out, the beautiful man with a sparkle in his eye who understood the deep things of God. Finally, the pastor came strolling out and his congregants approached him, telling the man what an incredible sermon he had given.

"Your words really touched my soul, Pastor. Thank God for you!" an old lady said.

"Don't thank me, it is the spirit of God working through me, my darling, and I am his humble vessel. We are all the body of Christ and all have an important role to play," the pastor told the old lady while looking at Aaron as if he were waiting to talk to him and was grateful he came to church today.

"The pastor is actually really well known and has studied at Cambridge and Oxford and has several advanced degrees. It's pretty cool he's here, don't you think?" Thomas asked Aaron.

"Yeah, real cool," Aaron responded while staring at the pastor and watching him walk in his direction.

"Hello, you must be new here. I'm the pastor of the church and I wanted to make sure you knew that I saw you and am grateful you decided to worship with us today," the pastor told Aaron with a smile and slight English accent from his time at Cambridge and Oxford. He was a middle-aged man who had a muscular physique and a sweet-smelling aroma about him that put Aaron at ease.

Aaron was practically giddy as he responded, "Thank you, Pastor. Do you have a last name I should call you by, like Pastor Smith?"

The pastor chuckled. "No, my son. Please, just call me pastor. This church, this calling, it is who I am and all that I am and my only concern is ensuring that everyone I meet is convinced that they are deeply loved by God."

Aaron found the man's words to be deeply profound and he blushed. He had never before been around such a holy and well-spoken man, especially not one who had taken an interest in him. "Ok, well, Pastor, could I please ask you a question?"

The pastor stared at Aaron with loving eyes and with a sweet enthusiasm said, "Of course, son. That's why I'm here!"

"Well, I was thinking about the scripture from your sermon, about becoming so easily entangled. And I was wondering, do you think that we can get entangled with the wrong people who cause us to sin? Are there certain relationships that God doesn't want us to have and that they can hurt our relationship with God?"

"That's a great question, Aaron. And the answer is unfortunately yes. There are some people who promote sinful behavior and can lead us far from our Lord. Please, do be careful with whom you keep counsel, Aaron. There are always wolves in the sheep pen ready to devour and you must choose the right savior to guide you through this world. I'm hoping you will come back to my humble church again, and you are always welcome to talk if you have more questions."

Aaron looked at the pastor with a grateful heart and felt like a huge weight had been lifted off of his shoulders, that the pastor had given Aaron the answer he was looking for. "Thank you, Pastor. I really appreciate it," Aaron said as he walked out the door of the church and into Thomas' car.

Aaron smiled the whole way home and walked into his home feeling like a new man. He walked over to the kitchen counter and grabbed the telephone.

"Hi, Amanda. Can we talk?"

CHAPTER 41

"I'm sorry, Amanda." Aaron watched as Amanda began to whimper.

She stared down at her bed, not wanting to accept the moment. Aaron looked around her bedroom to see all the memories they had created together. She had several framed pictures of the two of them from special moment of their relationship, and Aaron soaked it all in, feeling horrible that things hadn't worked out. Tears began to spill onto her sheets, and she sniffled in an attempt to stay strong.

"I just don't know how to make you happy, Aaron," Amanda said in between sniffles. "But I'm trying, I've been trying all this time."

"I know you have. You're an incredible girl, an incredible person. I just need to focus on myself for a while."

"What else can I do to make you happy? Just tell me, and I'll do it."

"I know, Amanda. I just don't know what that is. Something is missing, and I think you know I've been unhappy for a while, and I need to figure it out."

"Yeah, sure. Ok, Aaron," Amanda responded in annoyance.

"I promise you, it isn't because of someone else. There is no one else. I just feel a bit lost and I don't think I'm ready for this," Aaron responded, tears now welling up in his own eyes. Amanda was a great girl, and she had tried everything to make Aaron happy, and it wasn't her fault. They both began to cry, and they embraced each other warmly.

"I'm sorry, Amanda. I really am. I never wanted to hurt you."

"I know, Aaron, but you did."

Amanda walked Aaron out of the bedroom and to the front door. He could see her parents in the kitchen acting as if they were busy, but they knew what was going on and Aaron was heartbroken that he would never see them again.

"Goodbye, Aaron."

"Goodbye, Amanda," Aaron replied with a mix of regret and excitement, and he drove off into the night carrying with him the weight and shame of breaking the heart of someone who truly cared for him.

Aaron arrived home and shared the news with Ruben and Thomas.

"It's finally over, guys."

"Good," replied Thomas. "I think you've lost your way a bit ever since you started seeing her."

"That's all about to change. Everything is going to be just fine, and I'll look back on this and be grateful for the time Amanda and I spent together and how much we tried to make it work. I think this whole experience has made me a stronger person," Aaron said.

"If you say so," Thomas and Rueben responded in unison. They seemed pleased with Aaron's decision. He wouldn't bother telling his parents. What was the point? The last few years had been difficult, but now he knew he could close his eyes and wake up in the morning a new man with a new spirit and a new hope. Aaron finished his dinner and headed up to his bedroom and spent some time reading his Bible and stared at the painting on his bedside wall. He felt calm, relaxed, and knew that this was all a part of a greater plan, a better plan that would help him understand this season of suffering. Aaron drifted off to sleep peacefully found himself walking down the stairway of his home and out the front door and he slid into the driver's seat of his mother's car. "Let's get out of here," he told himself with a smile and started the ignition. Aaron felt free and took a long, deep breath and exhaled all the fear and anxiety that had overtaken him the past few years. But it was all gone now, and he was looking forward to the peaceful days that lay ahead.

Aaron hit the pedal to the floor and drove as fast as he could, to get as far away from home as possible, and hopefully find himself in a much better place. He passed through all the streetlights and all the neighborhoods until he found himself staring peacefully at the patches of wildflowers and lilies of the countryside. He was driving a red convertible and could feel the cool breeze whip past his forehead as he took in the beautiful scenery. It reminded him of the warm breeze that had guided him towards Amanda when he first met her, and how odd it was that she never understood what he truly needed, that they never really clicked. Aaron kept driving and found himself in a beautiful meadow of tall grass and he could see the mountains in the distance. He felt completely at peace as he drove on a straight road leading towards a bright, white light. Aaron could feel the heat from the bright light all around him and soaked it in like a warm bath.

Aaron sped faster toward the bright white light, the smile on his face widening as he believed he was on his way to the very house of God and God was waiting for him, ready to wrap Aaron up in His arms. It was such a picturesque scene and Aaron was so grateful for the peace and bliss of the moment, a moment which had evaded him for several years. Finally, he was being rewarded for his good behavior and God's favor would fall on him once again. But as he got closer to the bright light he drove out past the meadow and through the countryside and he found himself back in his town. He drove past the neighborhoods and through the streetlights until he finally found himself back at his parents' home, staring at their houselights.

Aaron watched as flies surrounded the houselights, colliding into the light and falling to the ground dead. He was confused. Wasn't he supposed to be in the very arms of God, experiencing his favor and receiving his reward for breaking up with Amanda and choosing the hard path? But instead, he found himself right where he started.

What was going on? As he continued to contemplate his problem, watching the flies fall dead to the ground he could hear a slight chuckle behind him. And the chuckle turned into laughter and the laughter turned hysterical as the sound of someone falling over hit Aaron's ears. He decided to finally get out of the car and was both surprised and confused to see the creature rolling on the concrete, dying in laughter.

It was a strange creature, something that looked like a faun from one of his childhood books, and the faun was slapping his knee and kicking concrete as the hysteria in his laughter rose to a fever pitch. The faun barely knew Aaron was there, but he had the look on his face of someone who'd just pulled off an incredibly cruel joke and was savoring in the result and relishing in the pain he had caused.

"Wolves among sheep!" the faun cried out between laughing, tears forming in his eyes. "Wolves among sheep indeed!" The words triggered something in the back of Aaron's mind, and he dropped his head in sadness and fidgeted his feet as a nervous tick. The faun continued to yell out the words "Wolves among sheep!" and Aaron felt stupid for breaking up with Amanda, for he was now back at the place he was so desperate to leave behind.

CHAPTER 42

aron found himself driving frantically in the rain, desperate to find some answers. It had been a few weeks since he broke up with Amanda and he could still feel the pounding in his head and the numbing in his face and he was worried he might have made a mistake. He wasn't sure what God wanted from him, if this were all a test. Perhaps he should have never dated Amanda or perhaps he should have dated and persevered. He just wasn't sure. He called up the pastor and asked if he could talk through the situation. And, to Aaron's pleasant surprise, the pastor was eager to help and invited Aaron to stop by his house to discuss his dilemma.

The rain began pouring down and Aaron opened his eyes wide to make sure he didn't miss the address. He pulled into an apartment complex and homed in on each of the individual numbers until he found the one he was looking for. Aaron opened the car door and sprinted towards the apartment building, doing his best to avoid the rain. He finally made it to the entrance and run the bell to enter the complex.

"Hi, it's Aaron."

"Great, Aaron please come on it!" the pastor responded and Aaron heard the buzzing of the door unlocking. Aaron took a deep breath and did his best to wipe the rain off his face and clothes but he was soaking. He looked around at all the individual apartments, getting lost amongst all the levels and numbers. He kept walking to the end of the building until he finally found the number he was looking for.

Aaron stood in front of the door and took a deep breath, "Please, God. Help," he whispered as he began to knock on the door.

"Aaron! I'm so glad you made it!" The pastor ushered Aaron into his abode. "I've actually been waiting for you. When I saw you the other day at church, I could tell by the look in your eye that something was eating you up. Whatever it is you shouldn't have to bear it alone. I'm here for you."

"Thanks, Pastor. I just didn't know who else to turn to or who would care," Aaron replied.

"Well, I promise you that I care, Aaron. I care deeply. You are just the type of kid I've been looking for and I would love to help you find the path to God's love. Now, why don't we have a seat in the living room," the pastor told Aaron as he ushered him to an oversized couch.

"That really means a lot. I just feel so lost.".

"Well, I want to hear all about it. But first, let's get you dried up. You're soaking!" the pastor responded with a chuckle. He then got up off the couch and headed into another room. Aaron could hear him fumbling through a drawer and he came back out with a towel.

"Ok, here we go," and the pastor proceeded to wipe the rain off Aaron's face and dampened his shirt and pants with a towel. "I can't have you getting sick," he said with a chuckle as he sat next to Aaron on the couch.

Aaron looked at the pastor; he was so beautiful and strong and muscular. Surely this man could guide him through the mess of his life.

"Well, Pastor, I don't know where to start, but I just feel so sad and scared all the time. I had this girlfriend and I felt like she was becoming a distraction, and that God was punishing me for putting her first and doing things with her that we shouldn't do."

"What kind of things?" the pastor asked.

"Well, you know, the type of things kids shouldn't do," Aaron responded.

"You'll have to be more specific, Aaron. There are all sorts of things kids shouldn't do and I want to make sure we're talking about the same ones."

"Ok, well, first it was just kissing, but then we started touching each other. After a while we began talking our clothes off. We never had sex, but I just feel like it was stuff that I shouldn't be doing. And now I'm worried God is really mad at me because I am so scared all the time. I can't concentrate and I can't talk to people and I just want to stay curled up in my bed all the time."

"How did it feel?" the pastor asked.

"How did what make me feel?"

"The sexual promiscuity. Did it feel good?"

The question set Aaron slightly on edge, wondering where this was headed.

"Aaron, you're still soaking wet and I'm scared you're going to catch a cold. Here, why don't you take your shirt off and you can put the towel on your shoulders. I can go put your shirt in the dryer. Sound good?" the pastor asked, staring at Aaron's chest.

"Uhm, ok. Yeah sure," Aaron said as he lifted his shirt off and handed it to the pastor.

"Great, let me go throw it in the dryer quickly and I'll be right back!"

Aaron sat on the couch, his head pounding and brain going numb as he waited for the pastor to come back.

"Ok, I think that is much better. Now, where were we? Oh yes! I asked you how it felt to be sexually promiscuous. So, how did it feel?"

"Well, it felt wrong, like I was doing something that was really dirty and that really bad things were going to happen if I kept doing it. It felt like God was really mad at me for breaking his rules, like He thought I didn't care about everything He had done for me.

But I do care! I just feel lost and I feel confused and I'm not sure if it was all some horrible test that I failed."

"Aaron, I think you are being too hard on yourself," the pastor said with a smile. "I think you'd be surprised how much God cares for you, even when it doesn't feel like it. Life can be hard sometimes, but God wants us to enjoy our time here on earth and it's ok to indulge in pleasurable activities every once in a while," the pastor told Aaron as he gently stroked his shoulders and stared at his bare abdomen. "You keep telling me how guilty the sexual promiscuity made you feel in your head. But what I want to know is how did it feel in your body? Did it feel good?" the pastor asked, inching in closer and stroking Aaron's shoulders.

"Well, yeah. It did feel good," Aaron responded. He felt tense under the pastor's touch. Why was he asking that? The pastor was really staring at him.

"Good, Aaron. God created that, not the devil. Remember, God looked upon all that he had made and said that it was all very good, including your sexual desires." The pastor drew even closer to Aaron. "This may sound like a weird question, but it's going to help me understand how I can best help you, ok?" the pastor asked with a smile and dreamy look on his face.

"Uh, ok. Sure, Pastor. What do you want to know?"

The pastor moved even closer until they were only few inches away from each other. With his dreamy eyes he asked, "Did you cum?"

"What?!"

How was this going to help him know what to do with his life? His head started pounding and he felt the sudden urge to scream at the top of his lungs and run away.

"I asked you, 'did you cum?' It's ok, Aaron. It's perfectly normal to orgasm in the presence of something beautiful. It's something God intended for good," the pastor told him.

Aaron didn't know what to say, so he told him the truth, "Yes, I did."

The pastor gave Aaron a look of intense satisfaction, as if it was the answer he was hoping for and he began licking his lips.

"Aaron, I don't think you have any problems here. I think you are just being too hard on yourself. I think you don't see the full picture of God's love, and I would like to help you. Now, there is a photo album I have up in my bedroom that I keep at my bedside, and every time I feel a little sad, I look through the photo album and it reminds me that everything is going to be ok. Now, I think you should join me because you look like you need some cheering up. Will you join me?"

Aaron could hear the sirens going off in his head and he felt as if his heart were about to explode. The pastor was now practically sitting on Aaron's lap caressing his shoulders and thighs and Aaron was so confused he didn't know what to do.

"Actually, Pastor, I think I have to get going. This has been very helpful so I will think about everything you've taught me and I'm sure I'll feel better." Aaron eyed the front door.

"But your shirt isn't dry yet! Just wait a little while until it is dry. I really don't want you to get sick," the pastor pleaded with Aaron, but Aaron stood up from the couch and headed towards the door.

"You know what, Pastor, you can just keep it for now. I'm sure I'll be back some other time to get it."

"I'll hold you to that, Aaron! You're welcome to stop by any time!" the pastor said as Aaron jetted out of his front door and out of the apartment complex and back into the pouring rain. Aaron started up the car and drove back home, confused and unsure if he had done the right thing.

CHAPTER 43

"Alright, you turds, listen up! It wasn't great, but it wasn't horrible either. But either way, we've got our season opener on Friday so you all better be ready to bring the pain!" barked the coach.

"Hell yeah!" the kids responded after an exhausting day of practice.

"Alright then. Go hit the showers and don't fuck around too much tonight. I need you all to be ready to smash those motherfuckers into oblivion. You hear me?!"

"Kill them all!" cried out one player, and all the others responded with a raucous cheer, feeling excited and eager to start off the season with a big win. Aaron was chief among those players. His senior year of high school was about to begin, and he was ready to start a new chapter and put everything behind him. Amanda had a new boyfriend, but that didn't bother Aaron. He still didn't get along with his adoptive father but Aaron didn't mind that either. And he never understood what had happened while he dated

Amanda, all the voices he was hearing and images he was seeing and the intense anxiety and fear that followed along. But none of that mattered now, for Aaron was looking ahead. He was crafting up the perfect year, one in which everything would go right.

He desperately wanted to forget the last two years of his life and was committed to making the most out of his senior year. So, he joked around with his fellow teammates on the way to the locker room, acting as if he weren't on the verge of having a panic attack. He smiled and waved at David, acting as if they were still close friends who spent time together. He laughed at every joke that was told amongst his teammates and listened to what everyone was saying as if he were hanging on their every word. He did all this to maintain the posture of good kid with a bright future, and when he got to his car he slunked low into his seat and jetted out as fast as possible.

The truth was that Aaron was still very uncomfortable around people and preferred not to be alone with anyone. He did manage to make it to a few parties over the summertime, but he had it all planned out: when he would arrive, what he would say and what jokes he would tell. He knew who to spend time with and who to avoid and when someone brought out the liquor or the keg of beer it was always his cue to leave. So far things were going to plan, and he wouldn't let anything ruin it. So, when his head started pounding and his brain went numb on the ride home he told himself everything was just fine.

Aaron pulled up in his mother's car back home and walked in with a bag full of dirty laundry from football.

"How was practice, honey?" Aaron's mother asked.

"It was good, Mom. Thanks for asking."

"I hear you're supposed to have a good team this year," she replied.

"I think we'll do ok."

"They have a *great* team this year, and they're going to do more than ok. Right, Aaron?" Aaron's adoptive father chimed in. Things weren't horrible anymore, but then again Aaron did a good job of avoiding him. They only passed each other in the hallway every now and again. All Aaron's other brothers had left for college, so it was just him, Sally, his mother and adoptive father.

Much of the noise had died down and Aaron ate his dinner alone in peace, thinking how far he had come over the course of his life. There had been several ups and downs, in fact extreme highs and lows, and now Aaron had resolved to craft the happy ending to his adolescence that he was always looking for. He refused to let his youth slip through his fingertips without grasping at some of the carefree exuberance or childlike wonder and joy that would soon be lost forever. No, that wasn't the life Aaron wanted and so he stepped outside on the back deck of their house to have a quiet talk with God, pleading with Him to give Aaron a break and bring some beautiful memories his way.

Aaron took a seat and looked out into the starry sky. It was a warm night and Aaron felt completely in his element, as if all his experiences had brought him to this very moment. It was all so beautiful and it gave Aaron hope so he opened his mouth and began to speak.

"Dear God, I know it's been a weird couple of years. I know I haven't always been the best Christian, but I've tried my best. I've always done what I could to make you happy, to make you proud. I know I failed a lot, and I know I made some bad decisions when I was with Amanda. But I hope you can forgive me for that and see how sorry I am. I hope you can see how bad I feel and I hope you're not still mad at me. I'm hoping you can help me move on and not feel so scared all the time.

"I don't know why I feel so scared, but you know, and I know you can help me. I don't want to be the most popular kid or anything like that. I don't need to go to all the parties and make a ton of friends. But I would like to go to a few, and I would like to reconnect with some friends, and I would like to not feel so afraid all the time. I'm hoping you can please help me with that. Please, if you're not still mad at me for all my mistakes, help me to have a little fun and not feel like such a loser all the time. I promise to be a good Christian. I promise to make you proud and be the young man you always wanted me to be. I'll do my best to help other people and help my mom out around the house. I'll do my best to get along with my adoptive father and I'll be kind to everyone you bring into my life.

"I'm pretty scared even saying this out loud, and I can feel my hands trembling slightly. But I know you can take it all away, and I know you love me and that you will be with me this year. I know you want me to be happy and that you have incredible plans for me this year and I just want to thank you in advance for caring about me. Amen."

Aaron finished up his simple prayer and his mother peeked out of the screen door.

"Aaron. Honey, I need to talk to you."

CHAPTER 44

"Dearly beloved, we are gathered here today for mourning and celebration. We mourn the life of a man who abandoned his children and left them in the company of jackals and demons. We mourn that the man stood idly by while his children's innocence were ripped from their chests to never be returned. But we also celebrate for the man is no more. His last breath was taken from him and the great imposter will finally rot into the earth. We celebrate that his children are present to condemn him as he is buried into the ground."

"How could you?! How could you abandon these children and leave them in the company of jackals and demons?! And now the vultures are circling over you and the vipers are sharpening their fangs and preparing their poison for you. And you will rot forever alone in the barren ground and never enter the gates of paradise. Your days will forever be downcast and overladen with the burden of knowing that it was you who let loose the great wolf. It was you who gave him the keys to the sheep pen. It was your hands that were smeared with blood and your teeth that ripped through their flesh. You are the great wolf. You are the great betrayer and deceiver, and it will be the cries of your suffering children who will be the first to greet you on your descent into darkness!"

This was the eulogy that Aaron was expecting, but it was far from the eulogy that his birth father received. Aaron sat in the back row of the church two hours from his house and listened as the minister told the tale of the greatest man who never lived.

Aaron sat in the back row of the church two hours from his house and listened as the minister gave the eulogy.

"Dearly beloved, it is with the utmost sadness I stand before you to mourn the death of our great friend and brother in Christ. It was a shock to us all, for he was only forty-three, and none of us were prepared for it, least of all his wife and children. He was truly a great man, and we will mourn the loss of a key member of our community and the laughs that will no longer be shared and the good times that will no longer be had.

"It is easy to overestimate the impact of someone's smile, but Darold had such a beautiful smile and radiated such a carefree joy, such a comfortable demeanor that immediately put you at ease. It was a gift and a blessing. It was the joy of the Lord and the anointing of God that dwelled richly within him and we were fortunate to be blessed by him for the past thirty years.

"And while Darold will be greatly missed we must also celebrate a life well lived and the great reward that is awaiting him in the afterlife. He was a loving husband and committed father that stuck by his children through the good times and the bad. Darold and his wife raised their children in the fear and love of God and their marriage was a glowing example of how two people ought to love one another. And while Darold may now be gone his spirit is still with us. His smile is still with us and the great works of righteousness he fulfilled on this earth will carry his memory for all time."

"Blah blah blah blah. Blah, blah blah blah blah. Blah blah blah blah blah blah love. Blah blah blah hope. Blah blah blah blah blah peace everlasting. Blah blah blah blah kingdom. Blah blah blah blah blah reward. Blah blah blah blah blah blah blah, Amen."

It was all too much for Aaron, seeing all these strangers mourn for him, the great deceiver who left him and his brothers to rot in the care of their adoptive father. They were all broken up, the room was filled with sobbing and weeping and sniffling and people were shaking and holding each other and telling each other to stay strong. And one by one they came up in front of the church to tell stories of how incredible Darold was, what a great friend he was, what a great colleague he was, and how he would do anything to help a friend.

"When I was going through my divorce, Darold encouraged me to fight for my marriage, to put down the bottle and pick up the Bible. He stayed with me and prayed for God to help bring me and my wife together. And now, all these years later, my wife and I have Darold to thank for staying together," one man told and then burst into tears.

"He was such a great uncle. He always called me on my birthday, and he watched my baseball games whenever he was in town. He was so fun, he loved to have a good time and seemed to have a way to make everyone around him smile. He was always the life of the party and I'm going to miss him so much," another said through quivering lips.

"Darold and I worked together, and it didn't take long for us to become great friends. He had such an infectious laugh and made our job bearable. We would joke around in between sales and he always had me rolling. And he was so faithful to his family. He had a picture of his wife and children on his desk and always talked about them, about how proud he was of his children and how much he loved his wife. I was proud to call him a friend and I will carry his legacy with me for as long as I am alive."

The service finally ended, and Aaron and his brothers found their way into the foyer of the church where everyone was mingling.

"Thank you boys for coming. It really means a lot to me. And I know that Darold would have wanted it this way," Aaron's birth uncle told them. He had called Aaron's mother to share the news and she insisted that he and his brothers go pay respect to their father. Neither Aaron nor his brothers said anything; they just nodded in acknowledgment of his words.

"I need to say hi to someone really quick but I'll be back. Give me a minute," he said, leaving Aaron and his brothers to themselves. Aaron looked all around him and could feel his body being consumed with numbness. He tried not to make eye contact with anyone so he looked down as his shoes, but he could hear the whispers and feel all the eyes upon him.

"What are they doing here?"

"I don't know, should they even be here?"

"Should we ask them to leave?"

"I don't know, but I'm sure Darold had his reasons. No one is perfect."

"I know, it's just uncomfortable and this isn't how I wanted to remember Darold."

"Well, what do we do??

Aaron could hear footsteps coming their way but continued staring at his shoes, wishing in that moment that he never existed.

"Hi, you must be Darold's older children. I wonder if I can make a suggestion?"

CHAPTER 45

Several months passed since Aaron attended his birth father's funeral, and while he didn't want to admit it his senior year was turning out to be a disaster. He couldn't shake the thick numbness that covered his head, and he was always so sleepy as if his body were shutting down and refusing to cooperate. But Aaron had already committed to making the most out of his senior year and refused to acknowledge how humiliated he was from being ushered out of the church after the memorial service. He wouldn't think about the mind-numbing shame and embarrassment of having a father who never talked about him and being surrounded by everyone at the funeral wishing he didn't even exist.

Everything was fine. He ignored the severity of his condition and threw on a pair of pants and a shirt he grabbed from the floor and took his mother's car to school. He took deep breathes along the way in an effort to mitigate the pounding in his head and numbness in his face and arms. He did his best to concentrate on the road. Everything was going to be fine.

Aaron parked the car and walked towards the entrance and it reminded him of the day he and David had jumped off the school bus and started high school together. He thought about how great it was, how excited and eager he was to fit in and make friends. He remembered David being by his side and how David had grabbed his hand as they started their new journey unafraid. It was a beautiful moment, and Aaron did his best to focus on that memory and push through the fear and anxiety. He was walking under water; he could barely see or hear anyone. Everything has happening in slow motion and he couldn't tell if anyone were looking at him or talking to him. He walked through the high school doors and thought of David and what wonderful friends they were. And as Aaron focused so intently on that memory, he ran right into David who was walking and talking with a few of his friends.

"Woah, Aaron! Sorry I didn't see you there," David said, looking Aaron over with a look of worried embarrassment.

"That's ok. It's great to see you!"

"Are you ok? You don't look so good," David asked pointing at Aaron's outfit. "You look like you just crawled out of a dumpster," David cracked at Aaron as his two friends laughed in the background.

"Oh, yeah. I didn't notice," said Aaron as his eyes began blinking uncontrollably.

"Did someone piss their pants?" David asked, sniffing into the air.

"I don't think so," Aaron replied with a nervous chuckle, squirming as he realized that the family dog had urinated on his pants. He gave David a big smile and did his best to act normal ignoring the tingling in his hands. But David wasn't buying it.

"I hate to tell you this, Aaron, but you missed a huge spot on your face. You only shaved like half of your moustache off. You look a little crazy."

"Oh, I'm not crazy. I'm just a little distracted," Aaron responded, feeling his heart pounding through his chest. Aaron felt as if he were going to explode so he clenched his fists and bit down on his lip.

"Ok, well we've got to run. We spent the weekend at my parent's cabin, and we need to get to class early to do some studying."

"Oh, wow!" Aaron gasped. "That sounds fun! Why didn't you ask me?"

David gave Aaron an awkward look, trying to avoid the uncomfortable situation that Aaron had created.

"Yeah, next time for sure." David patted Aaron's shoulder and took off. Aaron's whole body went completely numb and he could feel something squirming in his brain. It was hissing and biting and bringing to Aaron's attention that something was wrong. Something was horribly wrong, and Aaron needed to address it. But Aaron kept moving forward, refusing to think about the last time he even hung out with David, refusing to acknowledge that it had been well over a year, and told himself it was just a few weeks ago. He thought about his first day of high school with David by his side and kept moving forward.

"David's still my friend. He's still my friend. He's still my friend," Aaron mumbled to himself, doing his best to maneuver through his school that was now completely underwater. He couldn't see anyone and all he could hear was a loud buzzing static sound, so Aaron failed to see his classmates pointing at him and whispering at him for being such a mess. He failed to see Amanda walking to class with her new boyfriend, shaking her head in pity as she passed him. Aaron missed it all, for he was trying so hard to remember what it felt like to clasp David's hand and he walked completely past his locker and straight into a wall. Aaron pretended it didn't happen. He smiled as he picked himself off the ground as if it were the most natural thing in the world. He found his locker and grabbed his books. Everything was fine. Everything was fine. David was still his friend. He was still his friend. Everything was just fine.

CHAPTER 46

Aaron sat at the back of the bus doing his best to keep his eyes from tearing up. He made sure to wear a clean outfit and to comb his hair, but the old sores around his mouth were weeping onto his crisp white shirt and creating little stains. He saw Amanda at the front of the bus with her new boyfriend and he saw David surrounded by friends and he told himself the walls weren't spinning and that he wasn't losing consciousness

Everything is ok, Aaron. Everything is just fine, he told himself.

"Are you sure? Why do I have the sudden urge to put my head through the window and slit my throat with its jagged edges?" he responded to himself.

"*Now, don't be dramatic. It's not that bad. This is your senior year party. This is supposed to be a fun time. In fact, it is going to be a great time and you will have a lot of fun with all our friends,*" he quipped back at himself.

"I've been to parties before, and they're not always fun. In fact, sometimes they can be horrible. Sometimes they can be downright terrifying and thinking about it makes me wants to scream!"

Aaron tried to stay calm, giving himself a pep talk. *Don't cause a scene, Aaron, and stop telling lies! We have a good life, and God has been good to us. We should be enjoying ourselves now and having fun.*

"I can't Aaron, I can't have fun. I can't fight the sudden urge to scream and run away where no one can find us. I've got to get out of here, Aaron. I just have to before something terrible happens. We can't stay here. Please don't make me go to this party!"

Aaron, we have to go to this party. We have to. We're not going to let high school slip through our fingers. We just won't. We're going to have fun like everyone else. We are going to make friends and laugh like everyone else. And you will just have to control yourself and enjoy the best years of our life. Now smile so everyone thinks we're having a good time!

"But I'm not having a good time! I can see them all staring at me and I'm scared they might hurt me. They might give me something to drink and do horrible things to me. Oh God, they're closing in on me, Aaron. They're getting closer and I can't handle it!"

Pull it together for fuck's sake! Why are you trying to ruin this for me? This is my last chance to say I had the time of my life in high school! This is it! So, get your shit together and smile, damnit!

Aaron forced an abnormally wide smile on his face, causing his sores to split open. His eyes blinked uncontrollably, and he pretended that all his classmates weren't staring at him as he mumbled to himself during the whole bus ride to the beach. The bus finally came to a stop and everyone began unpacking and heading out to celebrate. Aaron took his time as he was still fighting with himself about what to do. He was the last one on the bus. He took a deep breath and told himself it would be ok, that he was about to have a lot of fun. Aaron was standing by himself and looked around to see all the different cliques. He saw the joyful exuberance in their eyes and didn't want to accept that he was all alone and didn't belong to any of them.

"I told you this was a bad idea. Can we just get out of here?" he told himself.

But his other side fought back. *No, Aaron. We're not going to run away. We are going to have fun like everyone else.*

"But no one wants us here. No one is even talking to us. They all have already formed their groups and we don't belong to any of them."

That's not true! We do belong! They're just waiting for us to come say hello. That's all. David's just waiting for us to sit by him and hold his hand and talk about how fun it was when we started school together. That's all. It's all going to be just fine.

"I think I'm going to pass out. I'm definitely going to pass out, Aaron. I can't do this! I don't even want to talk to anyone! Why are you putting me through this?!"

Why are you being so damn difficult? Can we just have a good time for once?!

"No, we can't have a good time! They're all going to hurt us! Don't you understand? They're going to talk our clothes off and smack us with rubber hoses and laugh at us. They're going to put horrible things in us and record it on video. I can't go through that again!"

What the hell are you talking about? Shut up! Nothing ever happened to us you stupid fuck! Everything is normal! Nothing bad ever happened to us so just shut up! Just shut up! Just shut up!

Aaron walked the shore of the beach for hours, arguing with himself over what he was going to do as he stumbled into his classmates, barely aware of where he was going. He saw a group of classmates he knew and began walking in their direction but at the very last second he veered off, ditching the effort to socialize. He hid behind a tree and smacked himself in the head and wiped away his tears, telling himself to pull it together. This went on for the duration of the senior party until Aaron finally found himself slumped under a tree and staring at a group of classmates near the water.

It was David and he was in the midst everyone. They were all having a great time. They were laughing and shoving and hugging each other and telling all the great stories from the memories they had made over the past four years. They were high-fiving and telling jokes and throwing each other into the water. And there was Amanda among them with her new boyfriend and they both looked so happy, like they truly belonged together and that he was the boyfriend she always wanted and deserved. Aaron did his best to act like he didn't feel the dagger pierce through his heart.

Then he thought of the surprise birthday party that Amanda threw for him in his freshman year and all the smiling faces that were so excited to see him and eager to celebrate that Aaron was alive. He told himself that nothing had changed since then and that they were all still his friends who cared about him. He told himself that everything was fine and that he was having the time of his life. As he watched David clasping hands with one of his classmates, he fought the urge to run into the lake and swim out as far as possible and let the weight of his past carry him to the sandy bottom.

CHAPTER 47

"Hi! Do you need help unloading your bags?"

"Yeah, that'd be great!" Aaron responded to the college student who greeted him at his parents' car. It was the first day of college and Aaron was excited for all the changes that were to come. He hated to admit that he never did grasp the carefree exuberance of his youth he so desperately wanted. He hadn't soaked in the childlike wonder as he battled with himself for the rest of the school year and during the summer. He holed up in his bedroom all summer and told himself that college would be different. This was when everything would change, and his life could finally begin. As he stared at the friendly college student offering to help carry his bags, he knew it to be true.

Aaron looked at the campus around him and thought how enchanting it was. There were beautifully paved roads connecting the dormitories together and leading to the main campus. He stared at the different dormitories and various campuses and thought of all the great adventures that were to be had and the friends that were to be made along the way. Aaron walked past his dormitory and stared at the main campus. He smiled as he saw the sun glistening off its roof, giving it a golden majestic glimmer. It was an old, gnarly, rugged building with a bell tower at the top giving it a regal and sacred feel to it. He imagined all the wonderful things that happened in the main campus and all the lives that were changed from studying, learning, and growing within its walls. The place almost seemed magical. Aaron was excited to meet the wonderful young man he was soon to become.

Ok, Aaron. This is when it truly begins. He had spent the whole ride there practicing his lines. He knew everything he would say to his new classmates and what jokes he would tell. He'd prepared an outline of what he would share about himself and what he was hoping to study. It was all planned out, and nothing was going to stop him from finally having the best year of his life. He looked at all the students taking their things up to their new living quarters and thought of all the friends he would soon make and knew that this was where he belonged.

And as he followed the college student carrying his bags, he knew all his troubles had gone away.

"Alright, honey, if you need anything just give me a call," his mother told him.

"Sure thing, Mom. But I think I'll be ok."

"Good luck, Aaron," his adoptive father said, offering him his hand to shake farewell.

"Thanks, I appreciate it," Aaron responded, looking into his eyes. Aaron was eager for him to leave, eager for both of them to leave and never come back. They left Aaron's dorm room and for the first time he was all alone with himself in his new world.

He lay on his bed thinking about the freshman dance that was planned for the night and he told himself that this would be the best night of his life. It was now lunch time and Aaron was ready to head to the cafeteria and make new friends, but when he sat up he felt a horrible pounding in his head that caused him to lie back down. And then his face went numb, and he felt as if he were being restrained by a thick iron blanket.

No, no, no, not again! He did his best to push through the pain. But the pain was too much and he curled up in the fetal position in his bed, unable to move. They were going to hurt him. He couldn't let them hurt him. The terror in his chest began to build, and he started pounding his fists into his head. Stop it! Stop it! Stop it!

I'm scared, Aaron! Please don't make me go! he told himself, shaking violently on his bed.

This wasn't how he wanted to start this new chapter in his life, and yet he couldn't find the strength to get out of the fetal position, and he couldn't stop the tears from falling from his eyes, couldn't stop the madness from entering into his consciousness. He was now completely numb, tears soaking his pillowcase and still in the fetal position, but he was able to roll over to face his desk where his mother had left a family picture. Aaron stared intently at the beautiful family, each member brimming with a warm, gentle smile. He looked into each of their eyes and saw the joy radiating from them. He saw how happy he and his brothers were and he sensed their carefree exuberance. He imagined how many fun times they must have had together to have such smiles, and they must have had so many adventures together.

He sat up and smiled at the proof that nothing bad had ever happened to him in his life. And then he saw the smiling face of his incredible mother, who was competent, graceful, poised, and always put Aaron first. He could see in her eyes that she always showed up to his events, cheered him on in all his endeavors, and never let anyone hurt him. He chuckled as he realized he was mistaken all along, that he really was a part of a loving, nurturing family that made sure Aaron knew how incredible, how special and wonderful he really was, and how desperately the world needed him. He was surrounded by family and friends who loved him, who would die for him, and would be the support he needed to see all his dreams come true. Aaron put all the pieces together, and seared them into his consciousness, burned them into his psyche, and the illusion put a smile on his face. He wiped the tears from his eyes, stood up in bed, and thought about the incredible family he had, and with the utmost willful ignorance told himself, *Everything is going to be just fine*, and walked out of his dorm room and into his fantasy.

CHAPTER 48

The afternoon was turning into evening as Aaron walked down his dormitory hallway thinking about how wonderful his life was. He wiped the tears from his eyes and thought about the wonderful he had shared moments with his family, and his excitement began to build as he headed to the freshman dance that was taking place a few buildings away. He walked with confidence knowing how much everyone loved him and he waved at his new classmates as they passed by. His confidence began to build as he continued to lie to himself and allowed the lie to build within his psyche and restructure reality, all the while feeling as if he were slipping into a new world.

Aaron could feel his legs grow weak and the walls begin to warp as he stepped through the door and into paradise. He noticed the colors begin to change and he could feel the bright lights all around him tune out his surroundings. He kept walking, not quite sure where he was going, so he closed his eyes and waited for the light to subside. He closed his eyes and could feel his legs trembling, on the verge of falling over, but before he succumbed to the weakness in his knees the brightness died down. Aaron took a deep breath to face the world ahead of him. He slowly opened his eyes and drank in his surroundings. He was surprised to find himself in a hauntingly beautiful and familiar place. Had he been here before? Aaron wasn't quite sure, but for some reason, he felt like he was home.

He looked down and the streets seemed as if they were a soft, clear crystal, with the most beautiful stars he could possibly imagine visible underneath. To his left was a great mountain where dwarfs were feverishly digging for more gold, diamonds, and other precious metals. To his right was a sea of tranquility and he could see the heads of mermaids and mermen alike popping out of the water to welcome him back into his world. And Aaron could see brave adventurers in their ships who had returned from their travels to new and exotic lands, filled with wonder and excitement.

"Hello, Aaron! Good to see you again my dear boy! We always knew you'd come back!"

He looked behind him and he could see his brothers in a distant meadow enjoying the warm breeze of a late summer day.

They waved at him. "Hello, Aaron! Isn't this place the thing of nightmares?" to which Aaron didn't know how to respond or why his brothers were with him in this world. He looked above him, and the various planets, galaxies, and solar systems seemed so close to him that he could almost reach out, grab a star, and put it in his pocket.

And in the sky were great dragons, winged creatures, and all fantastical and wonderous things a boy could imagine. Aaron's heart was exploding with excitement and gratitude as he accepted what was happening to him and where he was.

Aaron continued walking on the path of soft, clear crystal towards a blinding light ahead, and he passed by various people wearing masks and adorned in the most beautiful outfits. They were all waving and smiling at Aaron as if they were expecting him and that this was where he belonged. Everything seemed so perfect, and he stood for a minute, closing his eyes, and soaking in the beautiful world he had been looking for all these years. This is where it would all begin, and so he smiled and let the tears streak down his face and felt the warm, gentle breeze carry him further down the path of soft, clear crystal to see what lay ahead.

As he continued to walk towards the blinding light his destination finally came into view: the golden castle. That was where he belonged; he wasn't quite sure if he'd ever been there before. In the distance, he could see the sun reflecting off the golden walls as if it were a glaring fireball, and just above the walls, the tips of the castle could be seen. There inside was his father, the king, waiting for him.

"I'm coming!" Aaron said out loud as he propelled himself further towards the castle before it disappeared.

The golden castle was growing ever closer and with each step strange and disturbing images flashed into his mind. There were bathtubs filled with cold water, and large thick plastic bags, and rooms that had no exit. They came and went in a flash of a moment so that Aaron could barely register what was happening, but the flashes continued. There were men in masks, and knives, and swords, and whips.

There were tall metal tables and there was blood, and there was the most horrifying red, yellow, and orange lights radiating from the eyes of some unknown man wearing a bedazzled crown. There were naked men, and filthy mattresses, chains, collars, and strange music. It was all so overwhelming for Aaron, but he kept running towards the castle and his destiny.

CHAPTER 49

Aaron walked through the entrance into the golden castle and found himself in the foyer, and the students casually strolled past him with smiles. It seemed they were so glad he was there! Aaron's face beamed with the brightest of smiles as he walked past the foyer and into a giant ballroom with marble floors, stone pillars, and the most exquisite ornaments! He couldn't believe how ornate, mysterious, and mystical it all appeared to be. He looked at everyone dancing and smiling at him, and he knew he was right the whole time: he just needed to push through a little longer and until it all finally came together.

Aaron strutted into the hall with the most charming and interesting version of himself he never knew existed, and it appeared the young men and women alike were drawn to him and he felt as if he belonged in their midst. He pushed through his angst and continued to lie to those around him about who he was, what he was, and how wonderful his life was and had always been and they all drank in the lie as if it were warm milk.

There was laughing and smiling and dancing (oh the dancing!) and Aaron felt as if this must be the greatest night of his life. He had finally found a place where he belonged, with people who wanted him and had great plans for him. It was all so beautiful and amazing, and Aaron began dancing and all his newly formed friends joined with him. He had found a way to transform his fake plastic smile into a genuine expression of joy and he knew he had found his home.

Across the room Aaron could see the most beautiful girl he had ever laid his eyes upon and knew this was going to be the greatest night of his life. She had beautiful blond hair with a tall, slender physique and she danced with such grace as if she naturally belonged in the room, and in any room. He was captivated by her beauty and the energy radiating from her. There was something very special about this young woman.

He was unable to stop staring at her, and they smiled at each other as if they had both been looking for each other their entire lives, and the beauty of the moment was bringing life to his soul. But before he could find the courage to take a step in her direction, he noticed a man standing at the back of the ballroom, leaning against a door, amused and casually watching Aaron finally come to life. He was the most beautiful man Aaron had ever laid eyes upon. He had dark brown hair, a tanned physique and looked very much like his birth father. He wore a shining crown with bedazzled jewels as if he were the king of this golden castle and he was smiling at Aaron as if he had always loved him and had been looking for him his whole life.

Aaron watched the king staring at him and then staring around the ballroom as if to say, "Can you believe it?! It's all real!" and Aaron gave him the biggest smile and didn't have to fake it at all. The man waved a finger at Aaron, beckoning him to come near, and Aaron almost exploded in joy as he made his way over to the king who always wanted him. As Aaron made his approach the king slipped through the door with a smile on his face. Aaron laughed at the game of cat and mouse and gladly followed suit.

Aaron swung the door open and he was immediately overwhelmed by the brightness of the room. Whatever was in the room was too much for Aaron to understand or take in and his eyes needed some adjusting to make sense of this beauty before him. He closed his eyes for a moment, and then another moment, for he thought it was all too good to be true. And as he opened his eyes, he found himself in the most majestic, opulent, and glorious hallway he could imagine and at the very end stood the king next to his throne. Aaron thought the room looked slightly familiar and laughed aloud as he soaked in the beauty of the moment, and the king gave Aaron the warmest smile as if to say, "It was all part of the plan." Aaron was overcome with emotion, so he sat against the wall and began to cry and let the love he had been longing for all these years soak into him.

But the king wasn't done. He ran towards another door and gestured for Aaron to follow along. Aaron laughed out loud and thought, *It gets better than this?!* He picked up his speed and briskly jogged to the end of the hall where the king was waiting for him on the other side of the door. Aaron made his way to the other room and looked around but wasn't sure what his surroundings were. It didn't make sense to him and it didn't have to, because he felt the king grab his hand and gestured Aaron to keep following him, and Aaron was so grateful for the time with his father the king whom he had been waiting for his whole life. And the king took off with a laugh beckoning Aaron to follow along. They passed into the guardroom, which housed the most beautiful coats of armor, made of gold, silver, bronze, and alabaster, and then through the kitchen where Aaron ran into the pots and pans, laughing along the way. The king kept Aaron in sight and told him to keep following him up the tower to see the beautiful view of his kingdom. There he could see the unicorns in the valley and the great adventurers setting sail in the harbor and imagined the day he would soon join them.

They strolled down the steps and made their way through to the bailey and into the royal chamber where the king grabbed a pillow from the bed and threw it at Aaron. Aaron grabbed the pillow with a smile and began jumping on the bad as his father watched with a contended smile on his face.

After their play they finally made it back through the ballroom and into a private backroom. Aaron was so grateful that his father the king had shown him his home, in preparation for Aaron to stay with him forever as the son he always wanted. This was it, this was the moment he had always been waiting for and would always remember for the rest of his life. Aaron looked around for the king in the private room but couldn't find him anywhere. The room was sparsely decorated without anything but a mirror and Aaron panicked, wondering where his father the king could have gone. He had been looking for him all these years and he had suddenly vanished. Aaron approached the mirror, expecting to gaze upon own reflection and was startled to find the reflection of his father the king instead.

Aaron was devastated, pleading to the king, "Please don't go. I need you."

The king looked back at Aaron with compassion in his eyes and tenderness in his heart as he slowly began to back away from the mirror.

"Goodbye, Aaron, I will miss you," he called out as he continued to back away from the mirror.

"I don't want this to end," Aaron whimpered, refusing to believe what was happening. He reached out his hand towards the mirror, hoping the king would change his mind. But the king kept moving away, and the further he backed away the deeper Aaron's heart sank until his father the king left the room entirely. And as the king shut the door behind him the walls begin shaking and changing colors in sync with the beat of Aaron's heart. And as the colors become brighter and more vibrant Aaron felt himself drift off into a new world.

Aaron touched down and was no longer in front of the mirror. He took in his surroundings and was both startled and puzzled. He was in a hospital room, near a hospital bed, and he knew immediately what was going on. It was the moment of his birth and Aaron felt the dread as his poor mother pushed out his defective and degenerate little body. Aaron saw the look on her face when she first laid eyes upon him. She knew, and he could see it on his mother's face. And then his father stood at the bedside staring at his infant son with a look of disgust and revulsion because he also knew. They both knew, Aaron's mother and father, that Aaron was inherently flawed and unwelcomed in this world. From the moment they laid eyes on him they knew he was a misfit, a reject, a degenerate and disgusting mistake. They both knew their son would never belong, never fit in, and he would never be loved, and the world would be forced to reject him every day of his life. Aaron watched as his father left the hospital room, never to return, never looking back, leaving Aaron's mother with the shame and embarrassment of raising Aaron all on her own.

Aaron watched as a venomous viper slithered into the room from the door whence his father had just left. The viper was jet black with dark green stripes upon its back and had two small horns upon its head and its fangs protruded out of its mouth. The viper was modest in stature but potent in venom and conviction and it crept its way into the void left by his father. The viper was free to hunt and infect and haunt the disgusting mistake nestled in between Aaron's mother's arms. Aaron watched as its belly slithered across the floor, onto the bed and up to his mother's back and nested atop her head like a crown. The viper nestled in his mother's hair, hissing into her ear, telling her what would happen next, but she acted as if she was completely unaware. Then Aaron watched as the viper slowly descended onto the baby, gliding down his head and wrapping itself around the child's neck, slightly suffocating him. The child began to cry, and his mother did nothing to stop the assault but watched indifferently as the viper squeezed tighter and tighter until the child's face began turning red. The viper finally reared its horned head up facing the child and stared directly into the child's eyes, watching the child squirm and cry, gasping for air.

Aaron's mother grabbed the remote control to the television and turned up the volume, ignoring her screaming child and drowning out his pain. The child was on the verge of dying, and just before his face turned pale the viper hissed violently and struck the child on his forehead, and again on his left cheek, and again on his right cheek, and finally darted up his nose, stretching out his nasal cavity and slithered its way completely inside the young child. The viper finally made his home inside the child and Aaron watched the child squirm in pain, crying out desperately for help, sobbing loudly for any help, any respite, any concern or attention, and Aaron's heart sank when he saw his mother turn up the television even louder. Aaron knew there must be something horribly wrong with that child, with him, to be treated in such a vile manner, and he heard a faint whisper tickle his ear, "This is who we are, Aaron."

"What's happening?" he asked himself out loud as the bright lights drowned out the scene and transported Aaron to a deserted beach. The beach was entirely empty, the sky overcast, the dirty blond sand disheveled from the rain trickling down from the sky. The beach was empty say for one lone individual sitting and looking upon the waves. Aaron watched the young man who sat curled up on the shore crying to himself. The young man was greatly distraught, suffering, and was inconsolable. He had the look of a man who had finally accepted a very difficult truth and must now act on that truth. Tears streaked down his eyes and he could see his lips whimper as he struggled to accept the truth of his life and how to proceed. Time continued to pass and with each moment the man's whimpering turned into weeping, and the weeping turned into sobbing until the man finally sprinted towards the water and began to swim as fast as he could. The man swam as fast and as hard as he could with a reckless abandonment that gave Aaron a pause as to what the man had planned. But he kept swimming further and further, deeper and deeper until he was past the point of no return.

He watched as the man slowed down, his feverish pace turning into a slight glide. He was, weakening, fighting against himself and his demons. He kept fighting until he could fight no more, and he began sinking. He sank further and further into the water, and Aaron watched as the man took his first deep breath and filled his lungs with the icy, frigid water. The man screamed in pain, screamed for help, but he was all alone and there was no one to save him. So, he sunk further and further until he reached the blackness of the bottom of the water. As the man's body turned cold Aaron was able to get a closer look at his face and Aaron realized he knew who this man was. It was him, and he was calling to himself, "Please, let me die, Aaron."

Aaron snapped out of his trance and found himself leaning close towards the men's bathroom mirror, staring at himself. He was crushed. His head started pounding and his body went numb as he stared into his own eyes and began to cry, finally accepting that there never was a king, and there would never be a king. He lay his head on the marble countertop completely distraught that he would never find the king nor be swept up in his arms to be loved like the son he always wanted. It all hit him at once like a ton of bricks, and he crumbled to the floor as he finally accepted the lie that had him barely holding on for all these years. He finally relented and allowed the walls to come crashing down on him, suffocating him under the weight of his own false hope, and as the great illusion was falling apart he condemned himself, crying, "Why'd you have to be so stupid, Aaron?!"

He continued crying on the floor when the door suddenly swung open and he quickly got to his feet and wiped his eyes as a few of his classmates walked in to use the restroom.

"Hey man!" one of the classmates called out, but Aaron kept his head down, staring at his shoes and bumped into the door on his way out.

"Stupid!" Aaron mumbled to himself as he finally exited the bathroom, unsure of what his plans were or what he would do now. But he found himself back in the ballroom with the rest of his classmates and as he watched them all having the time of their lives the room began to spin and he could no longer tell if he were at the freshman dance or some masquerade in an ornate ballroom. Everyone was wearing masks and dancing all around Aaron and encroaching upon him. They were closing in on him, closer and closer and closer and Aaron felt as if the whole world were laughing at him, jeering at him, and he knew deep down that he didn't belong after all.

Aaron took stock of the room, the contents, the people, and their jovial, carefree exuberance as if they had never known the shame of being alive. He thought about the moments of his birth and his inevitable death and concluded that he was different from the rest. He could feel the pain and fear swell up from his gut and into his throat and realized he wanted nothing more than to leave this world forever.

The feeling was all too much to take in, all at once, in a room full of strangers that he was beginning to believe very much disliked him and had sinister plans to hurt him in ways he couldn't even imagine. Maybe this was it, maybe this was his time to die. He remembered the lake that was in driving distance from the campus. Death had always been on the horizon; it had been planned for him so many years ago, and he would merely finish the job set in motion when he was a boy. And at that moment, he felt as if he were a boy again, alone in a dangerous world that hated him. He was ready to die.

As he stood there, he could feel the tears swell up in his eyes and so he jetted towards the door to leave before anyone could see. He walked quickly, staring at the floor so as not to make eye contact with anyone, but before he could make it to the door, he collided with someone: the utterly beautiful girl with blue eyes. She had found her way over to him.

Aaron quickly wiped the tears from his eyes and smiled at this beautiful girl. He was completely captivated by her beauty, her strength, and the human dignity she wore as if it were the most brilliant and beautiful diamond around her neck.

"Hi, I'm Susie. Sorry for running into you like this, but I saw you from across the room and was wondering if you wanted to dance."

Aaron was startled. What a moment to pick! "I actually saw you from across the room."

"Yeah, I saw you too and I've been looking for you for a while. Did you leave?" she asked Aaron.

"Yeah, I thought I was looking for someone and I guess I got lost."

"Oh, don't worry about it, I'm just glad you found your way back! Did you ever find the person you were looking for?" Susie asked.

"No, I didn't," Aaron said with a pause, "he didn't appear after all."

"I'm sorry to hear that, but maybe it is time to make some new friends!" Susie responded with hopeful expectation in her eyes.

Aaron smiled at her, staring into her beautiful blue eyes. He was beginning to accept the truth that something incredibly cruel, hateful, and almost unbelievable had happened to him at some point in his life and yet there was a God who was watching over him, who would refuse to let him live in denial any longer, refuse to let him deny his own strength, and he could sense Him and his eternal love through Susie's beautiful blue eyes.

"Susie, I'm actually not feeling very well. Do you mind if I lean on your shoulder for a little while?" Aaron asked, feeling on the verge of passing out.

"Not at all," Susie responded with a smile. "I'd like that. Lean on me as long as you want, I promise I'll hold you up," she said with a wink.

Aaron thanked Susie and drew close, leaning his head on her shoulder as they danced in complete purity. Aaron leaned on her for the rest of the night and danced through the pain, soaking in her strength and resolve. He finally gained enough strength to stand on his own and stared into her eyes.

"Thank you for coming over and finding me. You didn't have to do that."

"Actually, I did, because you are the only reason I'm still at the dance. I was waiting for you and just had to get at least one dance in. And I had so much fun with you, Aaron, and I don't think I can forget you. Whether you like it or not, I will always find you," she said with a jab. "Hey, would you walk me to my room? It's pretty dark outside."

Aaron grabbed her hand tightly as if he would never let go and they walked out of the golden castle forever.

EPILOGUE

aron stared at his reflection in his bathroom mirror, seeing the toll the last eighteen years had taken on him.

"Aaron, are you still in there?" Susie called out from the bedroom.

"Yeah, just give me a few more minutes," he replied, staring at the man he had become and wondering how so much time had slipped through his fingers.

"Ok, Aaron, but don't forget to take your medications. And before I forget, it's your mother's birthday tomorrow. I know it's tough but you should try and give her a call or even just send her a text message."

"You always do the right thing, don't you, Susie?"

"I do! So don't question me. And while you are wrapping up staring at your stunning features in the mirror I'd like to remind you that your son has only been waiting for you for like an hour!"

Aaron dropped his head to the countertop, appreciating the humor of the moment, "Ok, honey. I'm coming out." Aaron gave himself one final look and opened the bathroom door and walked into his bedroom giving Susie a slight wave that he was on his way to Scott's bedroom.

"Oh, and there's a book he picked out at the library that he's hoping you'll read to him."

"I think I can manage that," Aaron said with a smile as he shut the bedroom door behind him.

Aaron crossed the hallway and knocked on his son's door.

"Is that you, Dad?" he heard his son call out in excitement.

Aaron peeked his head through the bedroom door and stuck out his tongue at his son who giggled and stuck his tongue back out at Aaron and Aaron finally barged in with a loud clamor, announcing his excitement to be with his son.

Aaron wrestled his son to the ground and Scott laughed in his arms.

"Stop it, Daddy!" But it didn't take long for Scott to stick his tongue out, begging to be tickled again. "I love you, Daddy. You're my best friend."

"I love you too, Scott. You are the son I always wanted," Aaron responded with a smile. "Ok then, where's that book?"

"It's on the dresser."

Aaron picked himself off of the floor and walked over to the dresser to fetch the book Scott had picked out. "*The Golden Castle,*" he read aloud.

"That's it! Will you please read it for me, Daddy? I saw the castle on the cover and it just looked so cool!"

Aaron paused for a moment, feeling a silent trepidation growing in his heart. He swallowed hard and asked, "You're sure this is the book you want me to read?"

"Yes! Please, Daddy, please!" Scott pleaded.

"Well, alright then, Scott. Let's find out what the golden castle is all about," Aaron responded, feeling his fingers tingle slightly. "Ok, here we go," Aaron said as he turned to the first page.

"*Once upon a time, in a land far, far away, there was a great king who lived in a golden castle who ruled over a magical kingdom where everyone's wishes came true,*" Aaron began with a slight cringe. He continued on with the story about how incredible the king was and how he cared for his people. He read to Scott how the king commissioned ships to be built to explore foreign lands and how he built beautiful roads of precious stones and all the fantastical and wondrous creatures that roamed through his land and the great dragons that flew through the air.

"*And then one day, horrible goblins attacked his kingdom and raided his land and kidnapped a servant boy,*" Aaron read, feeling his heart beat through his chest. "*And the servant boy was taken back to their land where he was forced to feed them rotten fruit and vegetables and clean up after them and they made him sleep in a horrible dungeon. But word came to the king about the suffering of his poor servant boy and he sent a messenger to tell him that on the night of the next great goblin celebration someone would come for him and set him free,*" Aaron continued reading, gripping the book tight.

"Oh, I hope they can save him, Daddy!"

"Me too, Scott," Aaron replied, doing his best not to squirm. "*Finally, the night of the great goblin celebration came and while they were all gorging themselves on rotten fruit and drinking stale wine a faun snuck into their village and down into the dungeon and set the servant boy free. And they both snuck out into the night.*"

"Oh, wow! That's amazing!" Scott said aloud.

Aaron continued the story, "*And the faun led the servant boy by the hand back into the kingdom, but before they could celebrate his safe return, they heard the pounding of the goblins' footsteps from behind.*"

"Oh no!" Scott shouted.

Aaron's head began to pound as he continued reading, "*The servant boy became afraid that he might be captured again, but the faun grabbed him by the shoulders and told him to be brave, saying, 'It's all going to be ok. Remember, we are in the land where all your dreams come true.' And the servant boy smiled at the faun and he heard the goblins begin yelling, asking for help. And the servant boy and faun looked upon the goblins and laughed as they were stuck in a large pool of rotten fruits and vegetables. And the servant boy and the faun held hands and laughed as they found their way to the golden castle.*"

"Hooray!" yelled out Scott.

Aaron forced a smile on his face and continued, *"And the servant boy finally made it to the golden castle where the great king was waiting for him and he ran towards the servant boy and swept him up in his arms and told him how much he'd missed him and couldn't sleep until he was found. And the king showed the servant boy the entirety of his castle and told the servant boy he was welcome to come whenever he wanted.*

"And the king finally asked, 'How are you feeling?' and the servant boy told him he was scared about what had happened to him and that the goblins might come back. The king caressed the servant boy's face and sweetly told him the magic of his golden castle, that it had the power to take away all his fears and all he needed to do was believe. And the servant boy smiled, and the king swept him up in his arms again and told him he could stay with him in the castle, for he was the son he had always wanted."

"Wow, Daddy! Do you think a place like that actually exists?"

"Maybe, Scott." Aaron forced a smile and felt his skin crawl and head pound mercilessly.

Aaron tucked his son into bed, kissed him goodnight, and headed into his bedroom where he joined Susie in bed.

"How was your day, Aaron?" Susie asked, but Aaron didn't respond. He walked over to his bedside and sat up, staring out the window and at the starry sky and moonlight. "Did you hear me, honey?" Susie asked again.

"Sorry Susie, I'm just not feeling great right now," Aaron replied.

"Is everything ok?"

"No. But it will be."

Aaron turned off the lights and they both lay their heads on their pillows and Aaron stared at the ceiling which had clean, white paint on it with an old ceiling fan and Aaron listened to the blades turn gently, hoping they would rock him to sleep for the first time in weeks. Aaron yawned and closed his eyes and sunk into the bed when he heard a very light tapping. TAP, TAP, TAP. He looked over at Susie who was fast asleep. TAP, TAP, TAP. TAP, TAP, TAP. The tapping continued and forced Aaron to sit up in bed, wondering where the tapping came from. He forced himself out of bed and made his way over to the closet. He opened the closet door to find it empty of all but their clothes. Aaron shut the closet door and quietly opened the bedroom door and walked into the hallway, listening for any noises. He walked into the living room and noticed the television was still on and the volume was on low. Aaron found the remote control and turned off the television and went back to bed.

Aaron lay back in bed, grateful to have Susie, his comforter, and friend who had always stuck by his side. Thinking about her brought him peace so he closed his eyes to sleep, but before he drifted off in slumber, he heard a knocking. KNOCK, KNOCK, KNOCK! KNOCK, KNOCK, KNOCK! This set Aaron on edge and he shot right up in bed.

"Did you hear that Susie?" he asked, looking over at his wife who was sound asleep. He must be losing his mind. Aaron was getting a bit scared now, unsure what could be the cause of these unfamiliar sounds, for no one comes knocking at the door this late at night. Aaron took a deep breath and headed out of his bedroom door again. He walked down the hallway and into the living room and towards the front door. Aaron looked through the peephole and saw no one there. He opened the door: nothing. He headed through the living room towards the garage. He opened the door to the garage, turned the lights on, and saw Scott's bike leaning against the garage door, and there was a box of camping supplies that had spilled over. He picked up the camping supplies and put Scott's bike back in place.

Aaron turned all the lights back off and headed back to bed, hoping that sleep was close at hand. He found himself back by Susie's side and kissed her shoulder, smiling to himself and thinking how fortunate he was to have such a wonderful wife. He thought of the wonderful life they had created together, and how she had given him so much strength and stability, how she had given him such a lovely home. With her he felt they could take on anything. This brought a smile to Aaron's face and he closed his eyes once more, imagining he and Susie were on a beach. There she was, lying in an oversized beach chair staring into the beautiful ocean and Aaron walked toward her side. He was so grateful for this woman and everything she had done for him, and he was so grateful to spend the rest of his life with her.

He'd finally found his way to his beach chair and gone to lie down when he was startled by a loud pounding. BANG, BANG, BANG! BANG, BANG, BANG! Aaron was now standing on the bed, like a frightened animal waiting to be tortured, but Susie continued to rest peacefully as if nothing had happened at all.

BANG, BANG, BANG! BANG, BANG, BANG! Aaron felt like crying. He didn't know what was going on but felt like someone was trying to get his attention, calling out to him and only him. He thought of Scott and he thought of the king and he thought of the horrible pounding in his head and knew something horrible was about to happen. He wasn't sure what it would be, or who it would be, but it wasn't going away.

Aaron knew that he'd learned to accept many hard truths about himself over the years, but perhaps there were still more to acknowledge. Something was happening inside, and he knew he had to finally face the truth. So, he walked out to the living room and sat on the green couch in complete darkness.

BANG, BANG, BANG! BANG, BANG, BANG! Aaron listened intently to the pounding. It was coming from the basement, the last place he wanted to check. He hated basements. He wasn't sure why but figured that most people don't like basements either. But he really didn't want to go down there. Something deep inside him told him that something horrible was in that basement. Something disgusting, insidious, dreadful, and miserable. *Please, no.* Anywhere but the basement. Anywhere. He closed his eyes hoping that perhaps the banging would end and he could just go back to bed.

But the banging didn't go away. It grew louder. BANG, BANG, BANG! BANG, BANG, BANG! Something was frantically calling out to him from the basement and wouldn't relent until Aaron finally answered. BANG, BANG, BANG! Aaron's lips began to tremble, unsure of what he should do. However, he knew the banging wouldn't stop and that he couldn't run from the pounding forever. So, Aaron slowly stood up from the green couch and marched towards the basement stairs as if he were a dead man walking. He grabbed the side rail and gazed into the darkness below, listening to the relentless banging ahead. He slowly descended the staircase feeling an intense mix of emotions. It was all bubbling up from some unknown space for some unknown reason. With each step he took he could feel the pounding in his head intensify and the banging multiply in a declaration of some great and horrible truth that was about to reveal itself.

Aaron was practically delirious with the possibilities of what lay ahead and felt as if he were headed into a deep, dark dungeon where truly horrible atrocities occur. He touched down at the bottom of the staircase and turned the lights on and the banging finally stopped. He took stock of his basement and its contents: the couch, the television mounted on the wall, the table in the corner of the room. He looked into the laundry room and noticed the washer and dryer, their fake Christmas tree, and their bookshelf. Aaron walked out of the laundry room and back to the foot of the stairs when he realized there was something he had missed, something he was avoiding. It was in the corner of his peripheral, on the other side of the couch just past the treadmill. It was a mattress. There was an extra mattress not being used, just resting against the wall. Aaron hesitated to look at it for some unknown reason. But it was calling to him and he could feel the pounding in his head calling out to him, to face and accept the truth, as difficult as it may be.

His beautiful wife and children lay upstairs resting peacefully and all was well. He was safe, he was out of harm's way, and so it was time to wake up and see his life for what it truly was.

Aaron closed his eyes and gave in to the inner impulses and intuition that had guided him on this journey, and he could feel the carpet peel away and the cold concrete on his feet. He could smell musk and incense, nicotine and boiled sausage, mixed with horrible body odor. He was waking up. He couldn't dream any longer. It was time to stop running, to turn around, and finally see the truth. He slowly opened his eyes and awakened to see the concrete dungeon that he always knew existed. He could see the symbol on the floor and the table with the incense and figurines and the chalice. And he saw the apparatus on the wall that looked as if it were meant to gut a deer or some other large animal and he saw in the corner of his peripheral view a filthy mattress on the floor. No, this couldn't be happening. This couldn't be happening. He wouldn't let it happen!

This was it. This was always it and Aaron knew it and had buried it in some deep hole in the corner of his mind. And now he was forced to face it and he was nowhere near ready; he would never be ready. But there he was, and there Aaron was, and Aaron could feel his eyes on him and hear his chain rattling. Aaron knew that if he looked at him it would become real and so he paused with the greatest reluctancy to proceed. The tears began to stream down his face, knowing the magnitude of what was happening and that there was no other choice, no way out, and no one else to shoulder the burden. He thought of his sweet wife Susie who had given him the strength to make it this far. She was the embodiment of love and resolve and had convinced Aaron time and again that he was strong enough to face his past.

Aaron wiped the tears from his eyes and did his best to compose himself as he slowly shifted his gaze towards the mattress. His gaze finally fell upon the knocker who was standing on a filthy mattress and Aaron was hit with a deep and profound sense of revulsion and despair, completely overwhelmed with what he saw. The boy was completely naked with welts, scrapes, and smudges of red and white paint littered across his body. He had a swollen right eye, split lip, and a bloody nose. His knees were riddled with bruises and there were burn marks and a large laceration from his chest to his belly button. His hair was matted to his scalp and his knuckles were raw to the bone from a lifetime of pounding. And he wore a collar around his neck that was chained to a nearby pole. The boy gave Aaron a look of complete exhaustion as if he barely had any strength left to stand, and with the last of his energy he opened his mouth and cried out to Aaron, "Help."

Aaron keeled over in excruciating pain, sobbing uncontrollably like a wounded animal, pounding his fists into the concrete and banging his head until it bled. He remained alone with himself for the rest of the night, sobbing and refusing to be comforted.

ACKNOWLEDGMENT

I would like to acknowledge the immeasurable pain caused by child exploitation and all the lives lost and families torn apart. I would like to acknowledge the lies we tell ourselves and the lies our perpetrators forced upon us. I would like to acknowledge the incremental diminishing of our humanity as time passes by and the hopelessness that burrows itself into our hearts.

I would like to acknowledge the voices and faces that never go away, all the sleepless nights and the unwanted visitors that peak their heads into our bedrooms. I would like to acknowledge all the hands that have ever trembled and hearts that have pounded in the presence of the monsters who are no longer there. And I would like to acknowledge the little boy who will never stop crying out to be saved from a past that still haunts him. I would like to acknowledge the unknown hours of therapy and thousands of pills swallowed to keep death and self-harm at bay, and I would like to acknowledge the tears of loved ones who can't stand to see the unending suffering.

I would like to acknowledge the panic attacks, paranoia and the blurring of reality that still occurs occasionally when I leave the house. I would like to acknowledge all my perpetrators who find a way to infiltrate the mind and body of anyone who has ever sought to call me friend, and I would like to acknowledge the mental anguish of feeling alone in a sea of smiling faces. I would like to acknowledge all the work meetings, parties, get-togethers and various social occasions that I waited with clenched fists and quivering lips for the exploitation that had already happened all those years ago.

I would like to acknowledge the wounds that will never heal, the scars that will never go away and the carefree memories of childhood that have been shattered under the crushing weight of my exploitation. I would like to acknowledge all this, and the sea of unknown victims and survivors who are standing beside me, holding my hand and carrying me through the darkest moments of life. And I would like to acknowledge all my brothers and sisters holding me up who refuse to let go and let me die. This book would not be possible without you.